Retribution

Trading Terrorism on the Grand Union to a Final Full Stop

Bob Bennett

Clink
Street

Published by Clink Street Publishing 2021

Copyright © 2021

First edition.

ISBN:
???-?-??????-??-? - paperback
???-?-??????-??-? - ebook

Subdue by terror the enemies of liberty and you will be right, as founders of the Republic.

Maximilien Robespierre

1793

Terrorism is a terrible weapon but the suppressed poor have no other.

John-Paul Sartre

1972

Only in it fae the money!

Duncan 'Jock' McClean

1964

Retribution

This novel is an entirely fictional work. Whilst certain historical facts and events have been 'borrowed', a few liberties with the chronological context have been taken. The places and locations are real but the characters are personations of my imagination. Any similarity or resemblence to actual persons living or dead is purely coincidental.

Retribution is a novel in its own right although it is sequential to my first, Easier Than it Seems.

Bob Bennett

The Author

Born in Leicestershire just after WWII Bob trained as a classical musician and spent his working life as a professional performing musician, music teacher and most recently in London's West End as a full-time official of the Musicians' Union. He is now retired and lives on the beach in Suffolk.

Chapter One

It was 1972 – Monday morning 4th December. It was cold and wet. It was dark as is only to be expected at this time of year and Ben Blake stood on Platform 2 at Ipswich railway station having just arrived on the 05.34 local service, the so-called *Rattler*, on time for once. The branch line had been reprieved from closure which had been recommended in the infamous *Beeching Report* in 1963 but only after a hard-fought campaign by the East Suffolk Travellers' Association. The station clock said 06.12. Why, he pondered rhetorically, in the name of all that's righteous, should he be obliged to drag his sorry carcass from a warm bed at such an unearthly hour, more often than not with a hangover which varied on the severity scale? Invariably the mainline service to London was late or even cancelled. But he knew the answer to his own question. He needed to get to work. His position at the Royal Academy of Music had been hard earned and he didn't want to jeopardise it. Probably of greater importance from Ben's perspective was the need to earn a living to support the way of life he and his wife had chosen to live since leaving their native Leicestershire. The home he now shared with Tina was a quaintly named cottage, The Lobster Pot, located in the village of Orford just a short distance up the River Ore from the estuary with views towards the bird sanctuary on Havergate Island, Orford Ness Lighthouse and the North Sea beyond. It was proving expensive to maintain but worth every penny if only for the isolation and the air.

As he contemplated their lifestyle, Ben gazed into the station's dim lighting reflected in the puddles. He wondered whether they would have been better off staying in Burton Overy in his mother's cottage. 'Sweet Memories', the Roy Orbison song, drifted through his musings. Certainly the prospect of travelling to London was not one he relished, especially on a Monday. He hoped he would get a seat on the train. At least seated he would have an opportunity to sleep, perchance to dream. His reverie was interrupted by the station announcer, clearly a grade II glockenspiel player, he thought as she chimed the C major triad. Then, to the accompaniment of white noise came the distorted delivery of the all too familiar 'British Rail East Anglia Region apologises for the delay…' Even before the end of the announcement the crowded platform gave voice to their reaction. A C minor triad would have been more appropriate, Ben thought. The commuters' incantation was hardly reminiscent of 'The Chorus of The Hebrew Slaves', thought Ben. However, the lyrical sentiments, accompanied by colourful expletives based upon the lines of 'Oh, for goodness' sake, not again' somehow prompted a flashback to a recent production of *Nabucco* that he had seen at The Coliseum. He was reminded of music's power to articulate political sentiment in a far more vociferous manner than anything else he was aware of. Anyway, what to do? Not a lot of options. Late again, that's all.

Then, as in a vision, there she was. He caught sight of her over the tracks on Platform 3. She stood with her back to the weather but, even in the poor light, Ben could see she carried a briefcase in one hand and her kiosk coffee in the other. 'I bet it's cappuccino,' he thought. How did the Capuchin Franciscan Order take their coffee? When communing with himself, Ben always had difficulty staying focused! But there she was. Surely! He recalled the distinctive camel winter coat that used to hang in her wardrobe at Marsh Cottage, still looking as smart and expensive as the day she bought it. Was it really her? From what he could make out through the drizzle, the woman was certainly as attractive as he remembered but how could he be sure it was definitely her? How long was it since she left? Five years, six, seven? It was not the first time he had seen this woman but every time he'd attempted to get close enough he'd lost sight of her in the commuting crowds. He had to know. Was this his mother? He had a vague recollection of his dad once speaking of his mother having 'buggered off'. Why had she done it again? He had to know. Even as he stared, mentally urging the woman to turn and face him, the train she was waiting for drew to a stop at Platform 3 with a screech of brakes.

He who hesitates… in less than an instant, Ben set off at a charge like a wing-forward at the restart, pushing and shoving his way through the reluctant early morning masses of humanity and over the footbridge to the opposite platform. Without so much as a 'What the hell am I doing?' he got on to the waiting train, a Diesel Multiple Unit in the blue livery of BR East Anglian Railways. He spotted the woman almost at once and found a seat as close as he dared on the opposite side of the aisle. Why was he being so shy? The woman was intent on studying her magazine and didn't seem to notice him. The big hand of the clock on the platform ticked over to 6.18 and the train's engine revved, fit to bursting, and eventually pulled away to start its journey to who knows where – Ben didn't. The only thing he could be certain of at this time was that the train's steady acceleration was in the opposite direction to the London-bound track at Platform 2 where the slaves, more likely of a denomination other than Hebrew were still waiting.

Ben gazed through the window or so it appeared. There was nothing much to see in the still impenetrable gloom and anyway, he was actually staring at the reflection of the woman. 'Tickets please' jolted him back to reality and for the first time since his impulsive dash for the wrong train did he realise that his season ticket to London wouldn't get him very far in the wrong direction.

'I'm sorry,' he said to the conductor, 'I didn't have time to get one.'

'No problem sir. Where are you travelling to?' What a question! He had not got a clue. Having come this far he wasn't going to give up the opportunity to satisfy his curiosity now. If it was his mother, he'd finally get the answers to the questions which had haunted him for so many years. In a flash he came up with what he thought was a stroke of genius.

'A Ranger ticket please,' he replied.

'Ah, sorry sir, the Ranger ticket is not valid until after 8.45,' came the response, accompanied by a quizzical sideways look.

'Yes, of course, silly of me,' Ben mumbled mainly to himself. 'Where does the train terminate?' he enquired, as he felt himself beginning to get hot under the collar. In his peripheral vision he could see that the woman was now looking in his direction. 'Ely' came the reply.

'OK, a day return to Ely please.'

With his ticket transaction completed, Ben watched as the conductor examined the woman's season ticket. 'Aha,' he thought as he registered the fact that she made this journey on a regular basis. Still not knowing exactly what he would say. If it was his mother it would almost be like the first time he met her when she came to tea at his grandparents' house, shortly after his dad's funeral. How old had he been then – sixteen, seventeen?

Staring at the image reflected in the window he detected the first glimmer of a damp dawn. 'What am I doing?' he thought again . Try as he might, he could not justify 'lured onto the wrong train by a woman I thought I knew' as either an excusable or legitimate reason for not going to work, particularly with the Dean of Studies at the Academy. The Roy Orbison 60s hit was still echoing in his head. He thought he noticed her looking in his direction. 'She's bound to recognise me' he thought 'or maybe my moustache is too much of a disguise?' His pulse began to race.

'Next stop – Bury St Edmunds, Bury St Edmunds next stop.' The conductor's announcement could just be heard over the noise of the engine. Ben watched as the woman stood up and reached for her briefcase from the overhead rack. 'She's getting off. Shall I follow her?' he wrestled with his conscience. The train shuddered to a halt. An older woman with an oversized shopping bag struggled to lower the window in the door to allow her to reach out for the door lever. Ben was about to go to her assistance but his act of chivalry came second to a that of a boy in a school uniform. Ben looked back towards his mother if that was indeed who the woman was, but the woman wasn't getting off at all. She'd merely taken a book from her briefcase which she'd then replaced in the luggage rack. She sat down and as she did so, she looked in Ben's direction again.

After his dad had died from 'misadventure' Ben, who hadn't seen his mother since he was just a few months old moved in with her in a 'chocolate box' cottage in a picture-postcard village not too far from Leicester. She was worth a fortune having inherited a vast sum of money from various illegal activities that Ken, her husband and Ben's dad, had been involved with during and after WWII. And on top of that there had been the crate of gold bullion – Nazi gold – that had turned up, the sale of which realised over a quarter of a million pounds.

As the train approached Kennett, Ben became aware of someone sitting in the previously vacant seat behind him. He felt a tap on the shoulder.

'Have you still got the MGB?' Only one other person on this train could have known he owned an MGB. He turned around to face the person who'd taken the seat. It was his mother.

'Mum? Is it you?'

'Hello Ben – I'm not sure about the moustache!'

There was an uneasy silence as the train pulled into the station at Kennett. The first glimmers of dawn were just about visible through the clouds and it was still raining judging be the number of people with their umbrellas raised.

'Come and sit with me, would you Ben?' his mother invited. Ben moved into the aisle seat of the row behind him. She took his hand and squeezed it tightly.

'You cannot begin to imagine how much I've missed you,' she whispered.

'I'm sure' said Ben suspiciously. 'Be that as it may, you have got some serious explaining to do.'

'Yes, I know, and I will tell you everything but not here. Not now on the train.'

'OK, but where? When?'

'Why are you on this train? Where are you going now?' his mother asked.

'I was told you were working in London at the Royal Academy.'

'I am – I mean I do.' Ben sounded a little flustered. 'I'm on this train because you are. I have seen you in the past few weeks from across the tracks at Ipswich; well someone I thought I recognised as you. This morning I was determined to find out and I followed you onto this train.'

'Won't you be late for work?'

'I doubt I'll go today, now. It's more important that I spend some time with you, my mother. I'll telephone the Academy as soon as we get off the train.'

'We?' his mother queried. 'I have to get to work,' she insisted.

'Can't you call in sick or something? Don't you think it's really important that we catch up? There are seven years missing. Having missed so many years with my mother during my childhood, I'm not going allow the last seven to be written off just like that!' Ben was equally insistent.

'OK, I guess you're right' his mother conceded. 'I work in Ely and we'll get off there – it's the last stop for this train anyway. I know of a quiet restaurant near the cathedral where we can 'catch up' as you say. Have you had any breakfast?'

The train continued on its journey. With Newmarket in the distance Ben could see racehorses exercising on the gallops. The first hints of morning were beginning to manifest themselves and it appeared that the rain had stopped. Neither of them spoke. The countryside began to even out as they rode through the edges of Cambridgeshire and into the Fens. Beyond, the land was levelling to become completely flat and soon the majestically imposing sight of the West Tower of Ely Cathedral hove into view, but still neither of them spoke.

'Next and last stop, Ely – Ely last stop. All change please, all change,' came the announcement. Ben got out of his seat and collected his mum's briefcase from the overhead luggage-rack. She slid across the seats and stood in the aisle facing her son as she did up her coat. The train braked suddenly and as it lurched forward Ben bumped into his mother and she took her chance at this opportunity and wrapped her arms around him.

'You can give your mum a hug for a start!'

Chapter Two

It had been 1964 when Ben and his then girlfriend Tina celebrated their eighteenth birthdays with a very memorable party at his mother's cottage in Burton Overy to the south-east of Leicester. It had only been a few months prior to that occasion that he had 'found' his mother for the first time since he was only a few months old. She had been missing for most of Ben's first seventeen years. She was wealthy; very wealthy albeit with 'dirty' money the source of which Ben had never wholly got to the bottom of. And when she bought him a Steinway Boudoir Grand piano and a brand new MGB convertible sports car he hadn't really been too inclined to probe too deeply. But now, having been abandoned again for almost seven years during which time he and Tina had graduated from their respective higher education establishments and subsequently married, Ben was determined to learn the details of his mother's secrets.

They alighted from the train. The morning was now dank and miserable after the earlier rain. They walked quite briskly against the cold towards the city and Ben became aware that his mother had slipped her arm through his. He didn't mind. In fact he rather liked it. Neither of them had eaten breakfast so they went into the Almonry Restaurant & Tea Rooms. They both decided on toasted teacakes and coffee.

'After you left school and went away to music college,' Ben's mother began, 'I became very lonely. Apart from occasional visits to Frank's farm, the farm where I worked as a land-army girl during the war, or to see Albert and Mabel, your grandparents, I saw no one and I had no friends to talk to. My past life, when I, the irresponsible and impetuous Helen Blake ran away and joined the black-market trade on a narrowboat had begun to haunt me. I should have told you this at the time…'

'What?' Ben interrupted out of curiosity.

'Please Ben, don't interrupt. Let me confess everything now I've started. This is all very difficult for me.' She took a handkerchief from her bag.

'I know it was you who discovered your dad's body in the canal. I never told you before, but, but…' There was a lengthy pause as she hesitated before continuing; her voice trembling.

'I know how it got there.'

Despite his mother's request not to interrupt Ben couldn't help himself. He was deeply disturbed by this revelation.

'What do you mean, "I know how it got there"? Explain please!' No longer was the interruption out of curiosity. Ben's tone was accusatory. His mother continued.

'He was pushed. It was no accident. He was hit over the head with a winch handle, knocked unconscious and shoved from the boat into the lock.' Ben was visibly shocked. His mouth gaped open in disbelief.

'He was murdered.' There was a finality in the manner the three words were spoken.

'He was murdered,' she repeated as the silent tears began to run down her face. After a few moments, during which Ben tried to get his head around what he'd been told, his mother continued with more of the background.

'Before I upped and left you, your dad had left me, even before you were born. He, Ken, your dad, had been in league with a mate, Jock McClean, from his army days and the war. Together they had set up a very lucrative black-market business and made some shrewd illegal investments that would pay huge dividends after the war was over. From what I could make out at the time there was a mate of Jock's, Ron Nicholls, who occasionally did a bit of fetching and carrying who was trying to muscle in. It might even have been one of the reasons your dad left me. Anyway…' she interrupted herself. 'He left me, I left you with your grandparents and I must have been mad but I joined Jock in his racket.' Ben could hardly reconcile what he'd so far been told. His mum continued with her narrative.

'We'd mainly been at Foxton on the Grand Union canal, that is Jock and me, and I'd decided that I'd had enough of living on a narrowboat. For the best part of fifteen years I'd been dealing in illicit, illegal or stolen property and I'd finally realised that there was more to life, not to mention the lifestyle in general and Jock in particular. I'd had enough. More than enough! We were taking the boat to Kilby Wharf and from there I was intending to go back to my sister's, your Aunty Rosemary's,' she clarified. 'When we got to the lock at Newton, Ken, your dad was standing there almost as if he was expecting us. As the boat went into the lock, he stepped aboard. There was a confrontation between Jock and Ken. This led to a hateful argument and they were threatening each other… It was horrible. They started to fight with a ferocity which was frightening. I was screaming at them, trying to get between them, pleading with them to stop but Jock picked up the winch handle and swung it quite viciously two or three times connecting with Ken's head.'

'But,' Ben reminded his mother, 'the coroner's verdict was "death by misadventure".' Ben had always been disturbed by the inconclusive nature of the verdict.

'Yes, I know. And the fact that I was the only person who knew the truth was eating away at me. Being the only witness, I was becoming a mental and nervous wreck, forever looking over my shoulder, expecting an unwelcome visit from a murdering Scotsman who wanted to keep me quiet. It got to a state where I couldn't handle it any longer. My health was suffering, I couldn't concentrate, I just had to get it all off my chest. So, I went to the police and told them everything; the black market, the narrowboat, Jock, your dad, everything. Thing is, your dad was probably not the only one of Jock's victims to have been fished out of that lock. They pulled a corpse out fairly recently. Poor fellow had been shot in the head and it was generally reckoned that it was Ron Nicholls and that Jock had shot him.'

Ben could hardly believe what he was hearing. He tried to speak but no words came until he managed to choke out the obvious question,

'What happened?'

'I think the corpse in the lock was never pursued because the police couldn't find the one suspect they had. As for the rest, I was charged with handling stolen goods under the Larceny Act of 1916 and of withholding evidence in a suspicious death. The judge at Leicester Assizes said I was lucky not to be charged as an accessory to murder. I was sentenced to seven years at East Sutton Park Prison.'

'Where's that?'

'It's a women's prison somewhen near Maidstone in Kent.'

'Seven years? But that means...' Ben pondered while he did the calculation.

'Yes I know. I was released on licence after I'd served five years but I then had a year on probation.'

Ben was lost for words again.

'How long did Jock get? Life I hope!'

'Don't you remember?' his mum asked. 'We went to Foxton and saw Fred the lockkeeper, just before you left school, remember? He told us that Jock had disappeared into thin air.' Ben did remember and immediately sprang to his mother's defence.

'Well it hardly seems fair that you should have gone to prison when the murderer, perhaps even a double murderer has got away with it and the other guilty party in the black-market racket is no longer with us to be answerable.' He was most resentful.

'I wouldn't worry too much about that. If you recall, I've been more than generously compensated, financially speaking, and what's more,' she whispered conspiratorially, 'just between you and me, I've still got it all, invisibly laundered and secreted away in various accounts!'

Ben looked at his watch and remembered he should have telephoned the Academy. He excused himself and went to find a telephone kiosk. He returned ten minutes later. His mother had ordered a fresh pot of coffee.

'All OK?' she enquired.

'Yes thanks, all OK. I'll make up the time later this week.' He was now anxious to learn more of his mother's recent past.

'So, who else knows any of this? Does Frank know? Do my grandparents know? How come you work in Ely? Where are you living?" The questions were coming thick and fast. 'Why didn't you let me know?'

'Nobody knows. I haven't told anyone, well, only Frank my one true friend. He knows part of it. I just couldn't bring myself to tell my sister or you – the embarrassment in admitting any of this would have been harder to bear than being in prison. As far as anyone knows I no longer exist. I wanted a fresh start in a fresh place. I always knew that there would be only one person that I would share any of this with. You – my son Ben. I have a new identity now. I'm not Helen Blake any longer, I'm Hazel Black.'

Hazel continued to explain how she had taken a legal secretarial course whilst in prison and gained a level two diploma, and how with her new identity she had successfully applied for a position with a firm of solicitors in Ely; Meadows, Coleman & Pettegrew. She went on to describe how she was living in rented accommodation in Pin Mill, a village in Suffolk from where she drove to Ipswich every day to catch the train. She admitted that it was a long daily commute to Ely but her cottage, overlooking the River Orwell, afforded peace and tranquillity of a kind that she had never before experienced.

'I'm sure there'll be more you want to know in time, and I'll gladly answer all your questions. But now, I want to know about you. The last time I saw you was as you drove off to London to start your course at the Royal Academy of Music. So tell me, have you also taken on a new identity, what with the moustache? Tell me all about your last seven years. How was it?'

For the next hour Ben talked his mother through his college course and how he had returned to the Burton Overy cottage that first Christmas holiday only to discover no one at home.

'I was worried sick. I got in touch with everyone I could think of who might have had a clue as to where you were; Frank, Ernie, Aunty Rosemary, Kate and Stuart. I even went to see Fred at Foxton.' Ben proudly mentioned how he had achieved his Bachelor of Music degree and Associate Performer's Diploma in piano, but lamented the fact that, as a result of the accident at the lock when he was attempting to recover his father's body, he would never be quite good enough to earn a living as a professional pianist. However the Governors of the Royal Academy had offered him a position as music librarian. Ben went on to describe at some length how Tina had found a position with a prestigious gallery after she had obtained her fine art degree. He gave his mum chapter and verse on his wedding to Tina at St Cuthbert's Church in Great Glen, which had been followed by the reception at the Three Greyhounds. Jamie, his long-time best friend had been his best man, and Diane, now Jamie's fiancé, Tina's bridesmaid.

'It was a better party even than our eighteenth. There was just one thing missing.' His mother had been listening intently and knew full well what he was now alluding to.

'I know. I'm so very sorry.'

Ben related how it was as a result of Tina's mum dying that her dad, Dennis, had moved to live with his brother in Aldeburgh. The new Mrs Blake had wanted to be close to her father hence she and Ben had, coincidently, also moved to Suffolk.

'I was particularly keen on moving somewhere close to Snape Maltings Concert Hall, with its Benjamin Britten connection and the Aldeburgh Festival. We found a small place in a village called Orford. We love it there!' he exclaimed. 'Given the peace and quiet of the area it seems incongruous that we can see the buildings of the Atomic Weapons Research Establishment on the Ness. Thank goodness they're no longer used.'

'I know the area vaguely, I've been to Snape Maltings and heard the City of Birmingham Symphony Orchestra play the 'Sea Interludes' from *Peter Grimes* – so atmospheric.' Returning to other matters, she asked 'What about our cottage in Burton?'

'It's OK – I've let it and it's in the very good hands of ideal tenants. When I thought we'd lost you I heard that Kate and Stuart Cross had been forced to move from their house in Fleckney and were looking for somewhere. That left me and Tina free to move to Orford. I hope you don't mind?'

'Mind? After all that Kate and her dad Ernie did for me? Of course not!' Hazel reminded Ben how Frank's brother Ernie had let her live in one of his tied cottages after Ken left her when she was carrying Ben. Kate, Ernie's daughter, had helped the midwife with Ben's delivery, and she had subsequently married Stuart. It had been Kate and Stuart who had come upon the abandoned narrowboat *Emily Rose.* They chatted on for ages, reminiscing, with each offering their respective recollections of how mother and son had been reunited after Ken's funeral.

'Goodness, is that the time?' Helen was looking at the clock on the far wall of the café.

'I'd better pop into the office and speak to one of the partners face to face. I'm sure they won't mind. Why don't you go the cathedral? There's sometimes a lunchtime organ recital, you might be lucky. One of my bosses is a great organ fan and he tells me Arthur Wills, the cathedral organist, is brilliant. I'll come and find you there as soon as I can.' Ben paid the bill and they left the Almonry Restaurant & Tearooms together.

It had begun to rain again. Fortunately, the café was not too far from the Cathedral and as his mother had intimated, there was indeed an organ recital scheduled for that lunchtime. Ben joined a small queue of people waiting to go in through the Galilee porch. He was almost overwhelmed by the colossal building; its Romanesque yet Gothic style. 'What a stunning place,' he thought. The majestic feeling that Ben experienced upon entering was of monumental proportions; not unlike the building itself. Ben had time to walk around before the recital began. And as countless thousands before him, he was mightily impressed by the central octagonal tower surmounted by the lantern skylight. The length of the nave, he learned, was one of the longest in Britain. He took a chair facing the vast array of pipes of the magnificent example of what Mozart had called 'the king of instruments' and sat staring in awe. The events of the day thus far could not have been further from his mind right at that moment. He was lost in wonderment. When Arthur Wills launched into Bach's *Fantasia and Fugue in C minor* Ben experienced that incredible sensation that sends shivers down the spine. For all the world he was transported to another dimension and completely unaware that his mother had taken the seat next to him. Both mother and son were hypnotised by the might and power of the music; the unbelievable sonority as the sounds reverberated around the ethereal vaults of the Cathedral. Equally compelling were those moments of tranquillity; of beauty and delicacy. Perhaps above all it was the dazzling and masterful versatility of Arthur Wills and his unfaltering virtuosity.

With the recital over, it took Ben some considerable time to regain a state of mind approaching an ability for rational thought. The revelations of the day followed by such disarming yet captivating music had his mental faculties in disarray.

'What shall we do now?' enquired his mother.

'I need a drink,' responded Ben as he steered his mum towards the Minster Tavern.

After a couple of drinks and a very nicely presented plate of homemade and most excellent pastries, the couple continued with and revisited some of their earlier exchanges. The more he thought about it, the more Ben became incensed by the fact that his mother had acquired a criminal record for what amounted to nothing more than being in the wrong place at the wrong time. He felt certain that had it not been for the fact that she had witnessed a murder, and not just any murder but the murder of her estranged husband, his father, her conscience would not have been too troubled by the 'handling' and it is unlikely that she would have confessed to the police. She was fairly gung-ho about the vast amounts of cash and the proceeds from sales of Nazi gold when they were reunited back in 1964. What was more and if anything, Ben was guilty of having been living off the illegal earnings of the black-market and associated enterprises as much as she was. So, what to do? They both readily agreed that they would stay in regular contact with each other, having rejected the possibilities of house sharing in either of their homes. Reciprocal visits to each other on alternate weekends were mutually thought and agreed to be a good idea. They left the pub and walked to the station. It was no longer raining.

The density of the twilight had thickened to a deep purple which was gradually turning darker by the time the train arrived at Ipswich. They said their goodbyes and embraced in a manner befitting mother and son. It was drizzling again as Helen walked off to the carpark. Ben stood on Platform 1 waiting for his connection to Melton. He churned over and over what his mother had told him as he travelled back to Orford. He needed to talk everything over with his wife. He valued Tina's judgement in all things very highly. Surely matters could not be left where they were with his father's murderer at liberty.

Chapter Three

Ordinarily, although they left for London at different times in the mornings, Ben and Tina would aim to catch the train home together from Liverpool Street. She would leave the gallery in New Bond Street around 4.30 pm and he would leave the Academy in Marylebone Road at 4.00 pm allowing them time to comfortably make their regular rendezvous in the Great Eastern Hotel at 5.00 pm. If Ben was not there before Tina, she would know not to wait and make her way home independently. Almost home, he turned off the main road and into the lane leading to the Lobster Pot. As he approached the cottage the absence of Tina's Ford Escort in the drive indicated that she hadn't yet returned. Ben parked his MGB and went indoors. For all that it was cold outside, the cottage was warm. The wood-burner was still alight albeit in need of refuelling. He changed out of his suit into a pair of jeans and a sweatshirt and threw another couple of logs into the wood-burner. Rather than wait for his wife to get home and cook an evening meal he decided that he'd walk the few hundred yards to the Jolly Sailor, the local pub, have a few drinks whilst waiting for her to arrive then eat supper at the pub. He left a note to that effect.

By the time they left the pub and had walked home, their sitting room was cosy and the stove was glowing most satisfyingly. Ben had already told Tina that he had finally 'found' his mother and spent the day with her rather than going to the Academy. Tina was intrigued beyond measure to know more and not having had much of an opportunity to talk in the pub, they now sat together on the sofa whilst Ben related all the detail of what had happened to his mum, now Hazel, in the preceding eight years. Tina's intrigue metamorphosed into incredulity. In discussion they agreed that something had to be done to bring the murderer to justice, but what and how. The issues would require a great deal of thought and careful handling. They were also in agreement regarding keeping Hazel in the picture, well aware that mounting their own private vigilante investigation might be unlikely to get them very far. Tina took the initiative.

'Let's go and see your mum at the weekend and get ourselves organised.'

'Not exactly a plan, but at least a step in the right direction to making one,' Ben responded.

'Perhaps we could go on Friday evening and stay over? Does she have a spare room?'

Having forewarned his mum, Ben and Tina arrived at Pin Mill the following Friday evening 8th December. Hazel and Tina were mutually delighted to get together again, especially since they were now officially related albeit by marriage. The weekend was spent in relaxing, walks in the early winter Suffolk countryside along the banks of the River Orwell, two visits to the Butt and Oyster, where they sat and considered all the possibilities; all the options by which they might get somewhere close to the bottom of solving the mystery of McClean, the missing murderer. Quite understandably and not at all unreasonably, Hazel was somewhat reluctant to open the old wounds. After all, she had done time for her involvement with the crimes that Ben and Tina now wished to find the solution to. One thing that would be needed was time; a commodity that neither Ben nor Tina would normally have in abundance. However, Christmas was coming. There would be holidays. The Academy had already closed at the end of November and would not reopen until mid-January. Tina had less flexibility. The run-up to Christmas was a busy time at the gallery with wealthy clients looking to buy expensive pieces, prints and even originals as gifts. Hazel announced that she would hand in her notice.

She'd decided that the legal secretariat was not her calling any way and MCP her employers in Ely, who were fully conversant with her chequered background, would probably be relieved to let her go. Being a private investigator in a quasi-family-firm sounded like much more fun.

Chapter Four

It was on a December afternoon in 1964 that the narrowboat *Sheldrake* with Brummie boatman Pat Henderson on the helm stopped to offer *Emily Rose* a tow to Foxton. *Emily Rose* had, according to her owner, shredded her water-pump impeller and he was waiting by Taylor's lock Number 20 for delivery of a new one from a chandlery store in nearby Kibworth. Pat Henderson and Jock McClean, the owner of *Emily Rose* knew each other fairly well. They'd often got drunk together in the Foxton Locks Inn and Pat, on more than several occasions had bought black-market hand-rolling tobacco and Scotch whisky from Jock – so much cheaper than going to a genuine retail outlet. On this particular trip, *Sheldrake* was only running up to Foxton Bottom, Number 17, to drop off some bicycle parts then she would be heading straight back down, ultimately to Harris' yard where the Grand Union Leicester Line joined the River Wreake at Syston.

In truth there had been absolutely nothing wrong with *Emily Rose's* impeller. If anything at all had been faulty it was the boatman's nerve. For reasons he couldn't explain, irrational imaginings beyond his understanding, Jock was petrified by the Saddington Tunnel. Every time he'd been through the tunnel his pulse raced at an alarming rate and his heart pounded like a steam hammer out of control. He'd been moored on the bank just past Kibworth Number 18 for several days in the hope that a combination of sleep interpolated by bouts of binge-drinking would be sufficient remedy to overcome his Saddington paranoia. It was a demon he had to confront. It was on the last trip down to Kilby Wharf when the engine had cut out in the tunnel and he'd witnessed all manner of sensations that to Jock's disturbed mind might well have come from some fourth-dimensional cataclysm in space. He'd half expected to disappear into a black hole. Then, as if by an unseen hand, the engine had restarted and he had emerged into the daylight, a shivering, perspiring, psychotic loon. Was it all about to happen again?

Jock's worries on this occasion were compounded by the news that Pat had previously mentioned when he had offered the tow. Apparently, according to Pat, a corpse had been recovered from Number 25. Given the description of the bullet hole in the skull it could only have been the rotting remains of his former mate Ron Nicholls; the friend he had impulsively shot in the head and then 'buried' in the watery grave which was Newton Top Half Mile lock. Jock took some comfort from Pat not having mentioned anything about another body; that of Ken Blake; also one of Jock's victims disposed of in the same lock. Then in a flashback he recalled two other deceased victims that were probably set in concrete somewhere, given that he'd dumped he bodies into a wagon loaded with aggregate. He had to get away. He had to get to Foxton, leave the boat with Fred and flee the Country. Otherwise it would only be a matter of time before the police came looking for him. He could return to come looking for his share of the gold in the future when the heat had died down.

Wally Whitehead, on the helm of the *Nancy Blakemore* was just approaching the Smeeton Road bridge northbound just as *Emily Rose* tentatively drew into the Saddington Tunnel southbound. It was pitch dark. *Emily Rose*'s Russell Newbury engine gave a cough and died.

'Oh no!' cried Jock in a state of morbid dread. 'Nae again, please no!' he pleaded. But it was happening again. There was a rapid drop in temperature which took his breath away. Instantaneously there were totally blinding, kaleidoscopic, incandescent flashes of lividity accompanied by an ear-piercing oscillation of high frequencies accompanied by white-noise and an amplified scraping noise which sounded like over-long fingernails scratching at the inside of a coffin.

'Where am I?' Jock screamed, totally freaked out.

'Bloody 'ell Jock, look where yo're a-gooing will yo'. Strewth, watch out yo' daft Scotch bugger! Yo' pissed again?' yelled a voice Jock half recognised just as the bows of *Emily Rose* and *Nancy Blakemore* came together in a glancing collision, followed by the boats scraping down the seventy-two feet length of their respective sides with a terrifying screech. Blinded by the light and totally enervated, Jock initially staggered as a result of the jarring jolt of the collision. Then, having seemingly lost his sense of spatial awareness he passed out and tumbled headlong into the open hold of *Nancy Blakemore*. At the exact same moment, the Russell Newbury on *Emily Rose* fired into life and propelled her gently towards the light at the end of the tunnel and ultimately into the reeds and on to the mud at the edge of the canal just beyond the south portal.

'Jock, yo' silly bastard! What're yo' playin' at? C'mon, wake up, wake up.' Wally had manoeuvred *Nancy Blakemore* into the shallow water at the edge of the canal bank. He had jumped into the hold which was empty apart from the lifeless form of Jock McClean. Despite Wally's insistence that he should 'wake up' Jock remained comatose. Wally went back to the cabin and returned to the hold with a blanket, cushion and a large tot of whisky. He raised Jock's head onto the cushion and covered him with a blanket. He was about to waft the scotch under Jock's nose when he remembered that he'd read somewhere that hot, sweet tea should be administered to casualties in a state of shock. He downed the tot himself and went back to the cabin again and put the kettle on. By the time he'd made the tea and returned once more to the hold, Jock's eyes were wide open, staring as if confronted by an apparition, his face as white as a sheet. His penetrating stare was symptomatic of a state of terror and most unnerving. Wally was unsure of what to do for the best.

"Jock, Jock are yo' OK mate? Speak to me Jock, it's me, Wally. Oh my gawd!"

Jock turned his head slightly and tried to speak but no words came. Wally proffered the mug of tea and Jock took a sip. A few seconds passed and he came round.

"Och Wally thank God it's yoursel', but have ye nothing better? Och man, ah've just had wan near-death experience and ye expect ma tae drink tea? Get ma a bloody dram!"

Wally was visibly relieved and rushed off to the cabin and returned with two glasses and the best part of a full bottle of Glenfiddich.

"Yo' 'ad a near-death experience? What the bloody 'ell do yo' think I've 'ad? Damn near shat mesel'!'

After they had both knocked back several good measures, Jock eased himself up with Wally's assistance and they both made it into the cabin and finished off the bottle. Jock slumped back on the bed, comatose again but this time for an altogether different reason. *Nancy Blakemore* moved down the fifty yards or so and made fast in the moorings by Fleckney Bridge. Wally opened a tin of condensed chicken and vegetable soup added water and put it on the stove to heat up. When the soup was ready he managed to persuade Jock to have a little after which he tucked him up in the bed and walked off down the track to the Old Crown in Fleckney village. After the way his trip had gone coming through the Saddington Tunnel, and with his last remaining bottle drained, Wally needed another couple of stiff ones.

The morning after Jock's 'near death' experience he awoke feeling stiff and sore and with an aching head. He rolled and lit a cigarette and thought about his next move. He was sure the police couldn't be far behind him, ignorant of the fact that the investigating officer six years earlier, Detective Chief Inspector Mosely had consigned the mystery of 'the body in the lock' to the 'cold cases' archive. Jock desperately needed to get away. While his bank account was still very healthy, he regretted leaving the stash of cash on the narrowboat. There was no way he would attempt to retrieve it now anyway. He was thinking that it had also been a mistake to leave the revolver on the boat as well. It was a murder weapon as indeed was the winch handle. Wherever the *Emily Rose* had ended up, the police would have crawled all over her by now and going back to the boat would be tantamount to handing himself in.

'Why and where had it all gone wrong?' he asked himself as he stood urinating into the canal. 'Where shall ah gae? What shall ah dae? What dae ah want to dae?'

'Who're yo' talkin' to?' Wally Whitehead had been roused by Jock's incoherent mumblings to himself which, when coupled with the need to relieve himself, had been sufficient to get him up and about.

'Och man, sorry Wally. I didnae mean tae wake ye. Look, I cannae thank ye enough fae saving ma life, but I've got tae get awa'.'

'Where're yo' a-goin' then?' Wally was at the stern, himself taking a leak into the canal.

'I dinnae ken yet but I'll let ye know when ah get there.' And so saying, he checked the inside pocket of his jacket and reassured that his wallet was there he stepped from the *Nancy Blakemore* and moving gingerly, made his way across the Fleckney bridge and up the track towards Kibworth and the railway station.

Jock and Wally had been mates for several years. In fact, Wally was the boatman who had given Jock some practical and 'other' advice on boat handling the first time they had almost collided on Jock's maiden voyage. He was a true salt-of-the-earth pal. He'd become a good customer as well as a reliable friend and Jock knew that he could trust Wally Whitehead to say nothing about this encounter. Jock was mightily stiff and sore from his tumble into *Nancy Blakemore's* hold. 'If only she'd been carrying straw,' Jock thought as he staggered off rubbing his backside.

Chapter Five

When he arrived at the station his examination of the timetable revealed he had two options; Leicester or Market Harborough. The next train to arrive was bound for Leicester, thus the choice was made for him. There was sufficient time to get a cup of coffee, a pack of cigarettes and a local newspaper before the train was due. 'Can ye believe it – five-bob fur a bloody packet ay fags.' Since his black-market stock had all gone Jock still had trouble reconciling the retail price of things. He'd been used to paying nothing for anything for so long. Thinking ahead, he'd decided to make his way to the new East Midlands Airport and fly to somewhere – anywhere! Where exactly, would be determined by whatever flights were available. Jock had had reason to go there on many occasions when it was RAF Castle Donnington. The RAF had opened this station during WWII as an operational training unit for Bomber Command. It also handled a good deal of freight traffic and cargo planes were a regular feature landing and taking off from one of the three runways. When the base was busy there was always an alternative for Jock's purposes, at the albeit smaller field at nearby RAF Wymeswold. Back in 1944 and '45 during the first few years of their enterprise, and with the collusion of various dishonest quartermasters and other nefarious personnel, the dubious partnership which was the Jock McClean and Ken Blake import, export and marketing business had tons of goods flown into Castle Donnington. Military transports would be requisitioned in completely 'legitimate' guises but with spurious documentation and manifests. Jock often dispatched his mate Ron Nicholls, in his dark green Morris 10cwt van the twenty-five miles or so to Donnington to collect crates, cases, cartons, boxes and bags from one of the outbuildings on the airfield. It was a real inconvenience to the partners when the RAF decommissioned the station in 1946 – coincidentally the year that Ken Blake's son Ben was born.

Upon his arrival at Leicester's London Road station, he bought a single ticket to Derby. He had considered risking travelling without one but when he thought about it, the last thing he wanted would be a confrontation with a ticket inspector or some other 'official'. He must maintain a low profile and keep below the radar. From Derby he took the bus to the new civilian airport. He didn't recognise it at all. Since the RAF had moved out and the site had been redeveloped the transformation had been radical to say the least. He entered the departures concourse and studied the destination indicator board. He found a seat and stared at the names of places to which he could disappear. Only then did it occur to him that his choices were limited as he didn't have a passport. He did have his National Identity Card with him though. So, Belfast it would have to be. There was an evening flight scheduled – Aer Lingus. He found the ticket desk and paid cash for a ticket. He had three hours or so before he needed to check in so he found WH Smiths to look for a guidebook which might give him a clue as to what he might expect to find in Belfast. He then found the cafeteria. He hadn't eaten anything substantial for days. He chose a steak and kidney pie with chips and carrots. As he ate, he flicked through his copy of *Belfast: A History and Guide* and was encouraged by his interpretation of what he could make out, reading between the lines. Jock had always had that entrepreneurial nous and it looked like there could well be a situation developing throughout Northern Ireland, not just Belfast, that he could manipulate to his advantage.

Chapter Six

Since 1921 and partition, the Ulster Unionists had dominated politics and the Catholic minority had been marginalised by the Protestants' 66% majority. The situation was further exacerbated by local government boundaries favouring Unionist candidates even in predominantly Catholic areas like Londonderry. It seemed to Jock that there was a bias favouring Protestants in almost every factor of daily life throughout Northern Ireland. Police harassment, exclusion and many forms of discrimination resulted in the Catholic community's highly charged state of alienation. Jock could sense that the Province would likely be engulfed in turmoil before too long. Jock liked turmoil. As WWII had proved, there was money to be made from turmoil.

Northern Ireland had been left relatively prosperous by World War Two and the boom in heavy industry has continued he read. Jock was becoming engrossed in his reading and his pie and chips had long since gone cold. *A new Prime Minister took office in 1963 after twenty years of Ulster Unionist domination. Former army officer Terence O'Neill, has promised to introduce many initiatives which he hopes will improve the economy once social and political issues have been addressed.* The more he read, the more he could see potential for the improvement in the fortunes of Jock McClean. *Staunch Unionist, the Reverend Ian Paisley maintains that O'Neill's policies will represent serious threats to the Republic's constitution which should still cover the whole island of Ireland. Catholic hopes will be raised and strike fear into the Unionists. The situation is already simmering and could easily boil over into violence.* Jock was not averse to violence. It often provided exactly the cover he needed for his brand of profiteering as had been apparent during the war. The situation, Jock believed, was tailor-made for his sort of enterprising skills. He couldn't wait to get there and make some friends; friends of the right sort, obviously.

After Jock's flight had touched down at Aldergrove Airport he cleared through what formalities there were fairly quickly and found a taxi. He asked the driver if he could take him to a modestly priced bed and breakfast style boarding-house in central Belfast, a place where he could stay for twelve months or so. The taxi driver was happy to oblige and attempted to engage Jock in conversation. Jock merely grunted an occasional grunt in response to the driver's friendly chat but being a garrulous Irishman, he merely carried on talking anyway. Eventually he pulled up outside a slightly seedy looking terraced establishment on Donegall Road not far from the city centre. The driver knocked on the front door which was answered by a middle-aged woman he presumed to be the landlady. Jock immediately suspected that there was an 'arrangement' between the two of them. He paid the driver and so did the woman. Jock was then invited inside by the landlady who proceeded to introduce herself.

'Good evening sir, I'm Mrs O'Rourke, the proprietor. If you'd care to follow me, I'll show you the room.' She led Jock up a flight of stairs, with a well-worn, almost threadbare carpet. The wallpaper had probably been quite pleasing when it was first hung. She showed Jock into the room she had available and turned on the light, the unshaded bulb of which hung from a central ceiling rose. In the dim glow of its 40 watts Jock cast his eyes around the sparsely furnished room. There was a double bed, a chest of drawers and a wardrobe. Beside the bed there was a small cabinet upon which stood a table-lamp. The curtains would have benefitted from dry-cleaning, and the net curtains were yellowed and full of holes. But at least the room was at the front of the house and had a view of sorts which looked out across the street. Mrs O'Rourke announced her terms and after some negotiation Jock agreed that they and the room would be acceptable. He reached into his pocket and took out a roll of banknotes and peeled off sufficient to cover six months' rent in advance. By such a gesture he instantly became a highly favoured tenant and Mrs O'Rourke's demeanour became much friendlier. She recited the house rules and announced that she was a widowed lady. Jock estimated that she was of about the same age as himself and he could tell that she had been a very attractive woman just a few years ago. He offered his hand.

'Ah'm Duncan McClean but ye may call ma Jock. Most people do. Ah'm please tae make yer acquaintance.' Mrs O'Rourke shook his hand and momentarily mesmerised by his suavity despite his somewhat unkempt appearance, probably held it just a little longer than she should have done. She blushed. She noticed he had no luggage to speak of.

'Your suitcase will be following on then Jock?'

'Ah'm afraid it wullnae. Stupid aye, but ma mind was preoccupied an' I forgot the bloody thing – och excuse ma language – and ah left it on the train in England. I'll need tae buy some new stuff in the morning'.

'Ah well, there are plenty of gentlemen's outfitters will suit you fine I'm sure, sir. Now, can I get you anything after your long journey?' Jock realised he was hungry and he readily accepted Mrs O'Rourke's offer of an ample portion of a traditional Irish stew with suet dumplings. After he had eaten, he went straight to bed and soon fell asleep whilst reading his Belfast history guide.

The following morning after he had devoured the gargantuan fried breakfast Mrs O'Rourke had prepared especially for him, Jock ventured forth to buy some clothes and other essential requisites. By the time he was equipped with whatever he needed for the immediate future it was almost lunchtime. He returned to his lodgings to deposit his purchases in his room. He could hear Mrs O'Rourke singing to herself in the kitchen.

"Ah'm sorry tae trouble ye Mrs O'Rourke, but…"

"It's no trouble at all, at all, and call me Margaret, or Maggie if you'd prefer. Now what is it you're after Jock?" Jock hesitated. It had been a long time since… his mind fleetingly wandered back to the last time he'd shared a bed with a woman. Eventually he blurted out, 'Could ye recommend a local hostelry?'

'Ah, a pub is it you're after? I thought it might have been something else.' Was Maggie O'Rourke reading Jock's mind? 'Ah well, but then you have the look of a man who likes a tipple or two – as indeed I do myself!' she confessed. 'Go to the right and it's a short walk, no more than five minutes. Just on the right is Bradbury Place now, off Donegall Road. You can't miss it at all. The pub's called Lavery's and it's the oldest family run pub in the city and one of the best and friendliest in Belfast to be sure.'

Sartorially elegant in his new clothes Jock found Lavery's without any difficulty and it certainly appeared to have the potential for making some local acquaintances and acquiring the 'lie of the land' so to speak. After all, Jock was on a mission to make up for his share of what his erstwhile partner, since deceased, had appropriated. He approached the bar and drew a few stares from the early lunchtime drinkers. He ordered a glass of Old Bushmills Irish whiskey and invited the barman to 'have one yersel'.' The invitation was accepted and, as he had anticipated, the ice was broken and Jock introduced himself. He was confident that in time the small-talk would lead to more meaningful and productive conversations. He turned to face the locals and raised his glass in a friendly salute which most of them returned. He was in!

After another couple of shots Jock left Lavery's and went in search of the public library. It didn't take him long to find the oldest library in Belfast – the Linen Hall Library in Donegall Square. He enquired of the librarian where he might find information on recent local history. He was, or so he lied, particularly interested in the relationship between the

Republicans and the Loyalists, as part of his research for a degree from the recently established Open University – he convinced the librarian, a pretty and bubbly redhead young enough to have been his daughter. Jock had certainly not lost his ability to turn on the charm, especially with the ladies, who, more often than not would find him most beguiling. The librarian showed him to a reading room and suggested that he should sit at a desk. He did as bidden and she disappeared briefly and returned after a few minutes bearing a pile of books and other reference material.

'I'm sure you'll find something to further your research amongst these.'

There were more volumes than he would ever even flick through never mind read. He selected an edition of *The Constitution of the Free State of Ireland* and a work by Eamonn De Valera also on the constitution and pushed the others to one side. Realising it would give some credence to his 'studying' pretence as well as being useful for his own purposes, he determined to make a few notes. He left the books on the desk and sought out the librarian. With a smile that would melt a maiden's heart, he made a request for writing paper and a pencil as he'd foolishly come without. She gushed and obliged without hesitation. She appeared anxious to help this debonair Scotsman with his studies and accompanied Jock back to his desk in the reading room. He was about to light a cigarette until he noticed the admonishing glare from the librarian.

'Ah'm sorry, I wis forgettin' ma sel' there,' said Jock. She giggled and resumed twinkling.

'No need to apologise. Now, if I'm to be helping you, you may call me Ciara. I'm Ciara Doyle, one of the librarians and very pleased to make your acquaintance Mr....?' She curtsied.

'McClean, although everyone has always called me Jock.' They shook hands and Ciara began selecting from the various texts suggesting which would be the most informative. For all that Jock was enjoying Ciara's company and the attention she was paying him, he really wanted to come to terms with how he might profit from the sectarian unrest he'd previously read about in the book he'd bought at East Midlands Airport. This was clearly a line of enquiry which he considered had great potential as a money-making scam and he didn't particularly want to share it with the lovely Miss Doyle. So, in the most respectful manner he could muster he dispensed with her assistance.

'Ciara ma dear, I really dae appreciate yer help, but ah'm sure there must be other things ye should be doing an' I've no wish tae keep ye from yer work.'

'Well yes, I am quite busy and it's Emma's day off. If you're sure? I'm only over at the desk, if you need me I'll happily come running.'

Jock needed her alright but his need was not of the sort that Ciara was referring to. But then he was hopeful that Maggie O'Rourke might satisfy that particular requirement. Forcing himself to concentrate on the reason he was in the library, he began to read and make some notes from the Irish Constitution.

The Partition or division of Ireland in 1920 was only intended to be temporary; a means to facilitating Home Rule until reunification became possible when the sides were reconciled. The Anglo-Irish Treaty established the Irish Free State, which was in effect a self-governing British territory but this upset the Nationalists in the south who wanted nothing at all to do British rule. This led to a civil war between the Republicans and the IRA who opposed the Treaty on the one side, and the Nationalists who supported it, on the other and who emerged victorious. In 1922 the government of Northern Ireland dissolved its association with Dublin shortly after the Irish Free State was established and Partition became permanent.

Jock was really getting into the history and his interest was now well and truly ignited.

The radical Republicans did not accept the existence of Northern Ireland. They considered Partition an illegal act forced on Ireland by an imperial power. They insisted that the only answer was a Republic that encompassed the entire island of Ireland. Catholics and Nationalists were in the minority and there were great concerns about them forced to live under a Unionist government in Northern Ireland.

Jock was beginning to get an idea of where this was leading. He himself was a lapsed Catholic and Celtic supporter and he was already feeling a sense of allegiance to those he believed were the underdogs. His sympathies lay with the Nationalists; the Republicans. As he sat musing over what he had discovered so far, Jock reveries were interrupted by Ciara.

'It's 5.30 Jock and we're about to close, so we are. I'm afraid you'll have to come back tomorrow. If you will, we can leave the books and papers on the desk here.'

'Ah, right ye are lassie. I'll be back in the morning… if ye're done fur the day, would ye join ma fur a wee drink?' Ciara fell for his charms.

'Did you have somewhere in mind?'

'Aye, near my lodgings, a fine pub called Lavery's.'

'Oh no, I can't be going there.' She was quite adamant.

'Why ever nae?' Jock clearly didn't understand.

'Lavery's is favoured by the Loyalists. I'd have thought you might have understood the way Belfast is segregated from your research this afternoon.'

'Aye, ay course. I didnae realise you were Catholic. So, do ye ken a pub where we'd be welcome then, for ah'm masel' a Catholic. It's a pair a Catholics that we are.' Ciara's smile radiated her attraction to him and Jock's mind wandered off trying to remember when he had last seen such a perfect set of beautifully white teeth. Probably Helen's. Ciara's infectious giggle brought him back to the present.

'For sure, the best Republican pub in my opinion is in Springfield Road, the Blackstaff Bar…' Before she could finish her sentence Jock had taken her arm and was heading towards the door.

'The Blackstaff Bar it is then.' Ciara locked the library door and off they went.

Ciara insisted on crossing Donegall Square to the east side to show Jock the Titanic Memorial. Jock would have preferred to have gone directly to the pub, but he made a pretence of being interested. Ciara's grandfather had been a shipbuilder at the Harland and Wolff yard in East Belfast and she was so proud of his part in this most famous shipbuilding company; the company which had built the legendary *Titanic*. As part of his research Ciara thought it important that Jock should be informed of how rioting and unrest, driven by politics and religion at the time of Partition had led to unemployment of almost 20%. This had given rise to tensions, the culmination of which had been a march on the shipyard by Protestants which had forced thousands of Catholics out of their jobs. Jock now understood the reason for the detour past the memorial. They chatted easily as they made their way westwards towards the Falls Road and Jock soon learnt that nowadays the segregation had less of a basis on religion. It wasn't so much a case of theological beliefs but the opposing ideology of Nationalist Catholics' principles with those of the Unionist Protestants'. The two groups conscientiously avoided each other. They lived in separate suburbs, used different shops and even read different newspapers. It was, so Ciara informed Jock, that despite their separated existences, government and business had come to be dominated by Unionists very much to the detriment of the Catholics.

They attracted a lot of attention as they entered the pub, but then a pretty young girl accompanied by a man almost old enough to be her father but so obviously not her father, would always attract attention. Jock thought this was probably not such a good idea given that he would need to maintain a low profile if his 'business interests' went the way he was hoping.

'Evening Ciara.' It was the barman. So, she was known in this Republican stronghold.

'Ah good evening Michael,' she responded with a wink.

'Who's your friend?' Michael enquired as he looked the stranger up and down suspiciously. Ciara made the introductions.

'Don't get fretting now Michael, it's OK he's one of us!' With that, there was relief in Michael's expression.

'Welcome it is then Jock. What'll you be having – it's on the house.'

After an evening of drinking, talking politics and flirting, Jock offered to walk Ciara home.

'Ah now then,' she giggled, 'you already did. I've been teasing you.' Now she was laughing out loudly, as was the man behind the bar and most of the rest of the pub's customers.

'I live here. Michael's my daddy.' Jock felt a proper chump and didn't know what to say for once. He took Ciara's hand and kissed it. Michael was watching as Jock made to leave.

'You're welcome here Jock. I believe we can probably help each other.'

Chapter Seven

On the long walk back to Donegall Road Jock was thinking about what Michael Doyle had said, "I believe we can help each other." What did he mean? Maybe he would find out more following another day of reading and another visit to the Blackstaff Bar.

It was late and Jock let himself in as quietly as he could. Maggie O'Rourke was in her sitting room but heard the front door open and close.

'Is it yourself Jock?'

'Aye, sorry tae disturb ye.'

'Won't you come on in for a while?' Jock accepted the invitation and went into the private sitting room which was far more comfortably furnished than his room. Maggie was sitting watching a late news programme on the television. The news anchor was reporting on the formation of the Northern Ireland Civil Rights Association which was to be a non-sectarian organisation to tackle the perceived bias of the Unionist majority government against the Nationalist minority.

'I don't suppose any of this bothers you Jock.' Maggie was sure.

'Ah, but ye're wrong there Maggie. It's why ah'm here.' He was about to continue, the drink having dissolved any inhibitions, but stopped short when the sudden realisation hit him – if Maggie drinks in Lavery's she'll likely be a Loyalist. Now, here was a dilemma. How would he find out without declaring his own hand? Maggie turned the TV off.

'Will you be joining me in some cocoa?' she asked.

'Aye, please. That'd be greet.'

She went to the kitchen and returned a few moments later with two steaming mugs of cocoa.

'So, Jock, is this your first visit to Belfast?'

'Aye it is that.'

'And how do you find it?' Jock instantly perceived an opening through which he might ascertain Maggie's political persuasion.

'Ah like it fine enough. It seems tae have so much more going for it than the area of Glasgow where I hail from.' She took the bait.

'Where would that be then?'

'Paisley,' he lied.

'I'll thank you not to mention that bloody name in this house!' Bingo! The mere mention of the Loyalist politician's name had incensed his landlady.

'But ah got the impression that ye like a drink at Lavery's. Is that nae a pub for Unionists?'

'It is, but I keep myself to myself. I don't go there very often and the only reason I do is because it's the bloody nearest.' She laughed. 'You won't hear me singing "God Save the bloody Queen".' Jock stood up and drained his mug.

'Ah'm pleased tae hear it – nae the anthem – I mean…'

'I know well what you mean Jock. I think we're going to get along just fine, you and me. Now, what time do you want your breakfast?'

They said their goodnights and Jock went upstairs satisfied that the friends he'd made so far were the right sort. He slept soundly.

Over the next few weeks Jock became familiar with the locality which became equally familiar with his face. His days followed a regular routine; library until midday, Lavery's at lunchtime, a snooze in the afternoon and the evening in the Blackstaff Bar. Michael Doyle, the landlord at the Blackstaff was always keen to know of any Loyalist snippets of information that Jock might have picked up during his lunchtime sessions. The two of them became firm friends and Jock felt sure that when his 'business' was up and running, Michael would prove himself an extremely useful ally.

During the next few weeks the situation was developing nicely from Jock's perspective. The Civil Rights Association organised a march to protest against housing in Londonderry. The government at Stormont banned the march but it went ahead anyway ending in violence when the Royal Ulster Constabulary baton charged the marching protesters injuring around one hundred of them. The whole thing was captured on camera and broadcast on television. The prime minister, Terence O'Neill defended the reforms he was proposing and made a speech which was greeted with much enthusiasm by the Nationalists.

What kind of Ulster do you want? he had asked. *A happy and respected province or a place continually torn apart by riots and demonstrations, regarded by the rest of Britain as a political outcast?* The Peoples' Democracy movement were galvanised into organising another march, this time from Belfast to Londonderry. The marchers were attacked by a Loyalist mob with sticks and stones as members of the Royal Ulster Constabulary stood by and watched. Day by day there was outrage upon outrage and both factions in the sectarian 'Troubles,' as they were becoming referred to, were escalating and exacerbating the civil unrest.

One evening whilst enjoying a drink and the company of his newly found friends in the Blackstaff, Michael called Jock over. He took a bottle of whiskey and two glasses from the bar then lead the way into a private back room. They sat and after a few moments of small-talk Michael began to speak in hushed, conspiratorial tones.

'You'll forgive me now, but I've been doing some checking up on you. We can't be too careful about who we mix with and especially people we're not sure about.' Jock was about to protest…

'No, you listen now; hear me out. I'm now happy that you're one of us and I get the impression that you want to help. Am I right?' Before Jock could answer Michael continued.

'I'm told you ran a very successful operation let's call it, and after the war you had some dealings with guns and armaments that you'd been "appropriating" let's say, from the British Army."

'Who told ye this?' Jock was on the offensive.

'Now, now, don't you be getting excited now. We, that is to say the Provisional Irish Republican Army, have our contacts and I'm reliably informed by my brother Gerry that you were helping him out and the local Kilburn Battalion in their particular "operation" on the London docks during the fifties.' Gerry had indeed been Jock's best customer for the illegal weaponry and explosives he had acquired during WWII. Jock was now putting two and two together.

'Well ah'll be… so Gerry Doyle is your brother?'

'Indeed he is so'

'Is he here in Belfast?'

'Some of the time. Let's say he is our 'commercial traveller,' our peripatetic agent. Now, are you with us?' Jock agreed that he was and with an extremely generous measure of Bushmills, he was thus inducted into the Provisional IRA.

Chapter Eight

Over the next several years, with Jock having decided to extend his stay indefinitely, his relationship with his landlady, Maggie O'Rourke, had become friendly. They had begun to 'step out' together with fairly regular visits to that monument of art deco design that is Belfast's Strand Cinema. After seeing *You Only Live Twice* Maggie was convinced that Jock's Scots dialect had become influenced by Sean Connery and she let him know just how sexy she found it. Rather than deny any such influence Jock's accent, perhaps subconsciously, took on more of the delicately modulated tones of Scottish gentility as distinct from the guttural grating of the Glaswegian Gorbals. Secretly, the movie's title also had some significance for Jock. Whenever he thought back to what he still regarded as a near-death experience, his life now in Belfast was suiting him down to the ground and he was living for a second time. They went to see *The Dirty Dozen*. For all that he was no Lee Marvin he could relate his membership of the Provisionals to being one of the twelve unwashed.

Visits to the cinema were favourite nights out which were usually rounded off with a couple of drinks at the Blackstaff before heading back to Donegall Road and a cup of cocoa in Maggie's sitting room. After one such an evening, when they'd been to a screening of *Cool Hand Luke*, Jock finished his cocoa and gave Maggie a goodnight kiss before going up to his room.

'Why, Jock, thank you. I didn't know you cared, but I was hoping.' She kissed him back. He hadn't been in bed very long before there was a soft tap on his door.

'Jock – are you asleep – may I come in?' Jock had been in that trancelike transitional state somewhere between awake and asleep and before he could respond to her request, Maggie had indeed come in, not just to his room but into his bed as well. It wasn't long before Jock was wide awake. Neither was it long before the initial fumbling became an easy familiarisation of each other's naked bodies which the participants were enjoying in equal measure.

Maggie was up early and in the kitchen cooking breakfast when Jock came downstairs. The radio was playing 'Give Peace a Chance' by the Plastic Ono Band immediately after which, somewhat ironically, there was a newsflash. *We are getting reports of serious rioting in the Bogside area of Derry between Nationalists and the RUC. The riots started when the RUC, backed by Loyalists entered the Nationalist Bogside in armoured cars using water cannon, CS gas and firearms tried to break up an Apprentice Boys march.* In something of a panic Jock apologised.

'Ah'm sorry Maggie, but ah dinnae hev time fer any breakfast. Ah must go and see Michael straight away.' He was gone before Maggie could protest. He ran all the way towards the Falls Road and panting hard from the exertion of the run he hammered on the locked door of the Blackstaff. It was Ciara who unlocked and opened it.

'Ah, Jock, you've heard the news then.' It was a statement. 'Come in, come in.' Ciara ushered Jock into the bar which was already packed with Nationalist supporters, many of whom he recognised as regulars at the pub. Michael had been addressing the Blackstaff Republicans and they were now about to meet up with other Nationalist groups to protest against the Unionist action in Derry. No longer a confused rabble, but an organised and galvanised body of men, many in the paramilitary uniform of the Provisional IRA, they formed an orderly line awaiting their turn to be issued with a weapon which Michael was handing up from a secret arsenal in the cellar. Jock took his place at the end of the line and was given a Webley revolver and a handful of ammunition as Michael emerged from the cellar. The last of the group filed out of the door to meet up with others of the same persuasion in the Falls Road. Ciara handed Jock a knitted balaclava.

'Here, put this on. You don't want to be getting yourself recognised now.' Jock agreed and complied with the order and he and Michael left together to join the others. Ciara locked and bolted the door behind them.

It had been intended to be a peaceful protest. The weapons were 'just in case'. But confrontation was inevitable. Violence flared up when Loyalists began attacking Nationalist districts. Scores of houses, shops and businesses were set alight, most of them owned by Catholics. There was complete mayhem. Rioting factions – a mass of humanity intent on maiming each other. This was the opportunity Jock had been waiting for and wearing his balaclava to preserve his anonymity he maximised on his chances to loot and pillage wherever and whatever he could find that would have a saleable value. He may have been a lapsed Catholic but first and foremost he was Jock McClean, a Scot looking after himself. He had little if any interest in fighting for the Republican cause *per se*. As hundreds of people fled from their burning homes Jock was readily able to steal a van, a fairly new Ford Transit. A decent mode of transport had been the single most important item impeding his Northern Ireland business so far. His luck was in when he witnessed the owner of a liquor store dragged from his shop and beaten. The store had been about to take delivery of a large order of beers, wines, spirits and cigarettes when the delivery-van driver was also given a vicious beating. As he lay injured and bleeding beside his vehicle a dark pool of blood was spreading across the tarmac from the back of his head. When the riot moved on down the street Jock merely stepped over the severely injured driver and, showing no compassion he made to get into the van when someone saw fit to challenge him. The challenger was wearing the uniform of the RUC. 'Fair game,' thought Jock.

He withdrew his Webley from the waistband of his camouflage trousers and without flinching and devoid of any feeling, shot the policeman dead before driving off in the opposite direction to the fighting, with the liquor store order intact. The riots continued for three days with sporadic gunfire and petrol-bombings overnight. Jock was able to maintain his low profile throughout, snatching an hour's sleep now and again. He found a suitable location where the Transit and contents were locked and hidden out of harm's way. When he finally returned to Donegall Road, Maggie was anxiously waiting for him. The moment Jock got into the house she all but threw herself at him and gripped him in a tight embrace.

'Oh dear Jock, I was so worried about you.' She kissed him, passionately.

On television the newsreader reported that thousands of families, mainly Catholics had been forced to flee and refugee centres had been established over the border in the Republic. There had been rioting on a similar scale in other Nationalist districts and the action was regarded by many as Europe's biggest organised sectarian persecution since the second world war. One of those shot dead in the rioting was a British soldier, on leave, trying to defend his home. Soon after that the deployment of the British Army on the streets of Northern Ireland was augmented.

Over the next months the fighting continued. An Orange Order march in the Springfield Road, very close to the Blackstaff Bar provoked intense rioting. The violence lasted for days and the British Army made extensive use of CS gas. There were heavy casualties on both sides. More Orange Order parades took place with marches through Catholic areas which many considered to be deliberately confrontational and intentionally provocative. There were gun battles between Republicans and Loyalists with fatalities sustained amongst both Protestants and Catholics. Much of the IRA's weaponry dated back to the Second World War and was unsuitable for this kind of guerrilla warfare and no match against the Army. However, supplies of guns and ammunition were now being received from sympathisers in America. The Armalite AR18 was the weapon of choice and millions of dollars-worth were smuggled from the States by Irish crew members on board *Queen Elizabeth II*. The guns were then collected and they found their way to Belfast and IRA cells elsewhere though a sympathetic warehouse in Southampton. Jock with his newly acquired van were deployed by Michael and Jock became the collection and distribution agent for the illegally imported armaments. It was hazardous if not downright dangerous but, more importantly for Jock, it was lucrative. Here was another opportunity for him to appropriate a few guns including Heckler & Koch rifles which he then sold to the highest bidder irrespective of their allegiance. Several shipments didn't make it to Northern Ireland at all. They were crated and by a 'special arrangement' between Jock and a certain ex-Northern Irish patriot, Billy Kelly, secreted away in the warehouse, labelled 'to be collected by D McClean Enterprises'.

When the British Army mounted one particular raid on the Falls district the initial riot between soldiers and residents developed into a gun battle between the military and the IRA. The Army imposed a curfew of the area and raided many homes again under cover of CS gas. Yet another opportunity for Jock and when the UK Home Secretary, Reginald Maudling, declared war on the IRA, Jock acquired by fair though more often foul means enough items of khaki that one might have believed he had been recruited into the British Army. But enlisted he certainly was not. He'd been there in 1941 and decided it wasn't for him. Jock was simply pursuing his own self-serving motives. Even then, when it suited him, he could swap his gas mask for his balaclava and switch sides. Jock was on no one's side but his own.

It didn't take many months for Jock to amass a small fortune. He was selling guns and ammunition to both Unionist and

Nationalist civilians who were prepared to arm themselves at any cost for their own self-protection, and who could blame them? He was stealing all manner of supplies from the British Army and the Royal Ulster Constabulary base in Springfield Road and there was a great demand from residents in mainly Catholic areas and not just of Belfast. Jock was making home-deliveries in Derry and Armagh, Crossmaglen and Dungannon too.

Away from the fighting Jock was at all times keeping up the pretence of being neutral. He was always welcome in the Blackstaff and equally so in Lavery's. He and Maggie didn't get to the cinema very much in these times but they did occasionally make a night of it in Lavery's when the coast was clear given that it was closest to their Donegall Road home. They always left before the National Anthem at closing time. To the Belfast population in general, Jock was a visitor, a Scotsman undertaking research for an Open University degree, but caught up in the 'Troubles'. However, the situation was escalating and Jock was sufficiently astute to recognise that his luck couldn't hold out indefinitely. The time would come sooner rather than later now when he would need to distance himself from the British Army, the IRA and Northern Ireland altogether. He could then cash-in and get on with life.

When a bomb was thrown into the Army and RUC's base in Springfield Road an Army sergeant was killed and several RUC officers were wounded along with two other soldiers and around two dozen civilians. This action precipitated the introduction of internment and it wasn't long before armed forces were arresting people in their hundreds suspected of being involved with the IRA. Most were Catholics. Civil war had well and truly broken out and was now a way of life for some and death for others. This was Jock's cue and he needed no prompting. He had been devising a plan which would involve driving to Rosslare where he would board a Sealink Ferry to Fishguard. He knew this route very well having travelled it on many occasions when he was gun running between Southampton and Northern Ireland. More importantly the authorities at both ports were familiar with the affable Scotsman with the pencil-line moustache in his white Transit van with the distinctive JAZ numberplate. The registration number had almost landed Jock in trouble on one previous trip; the AZ clearly identifying the vehicle as registered in Belfast. Thankfully, on that occasion, and despite the tightened security arrangements at border crossings, the Garda didn't want to see his registration papers or inspect his insurance certificate. Even if they had they would have been hard pushed to do so as neither existed. They were only interested in the contents of the van, which, being on the way to Southampton, was empty. 'Wis they stupid or just Irish?' Jock had thought at the time. Rather than risk another close call though he would need to find some English registration plates or a different vehicle.

'A minor problem,' he thought, 'these Irishmen couldnae smell shite in their own moustaches.' His confidence and self-belief were riding high and it was time he put his escape plan into action. But there was to be a complication.

Chapter Nine

Jock had been in Northern Ireland now for almost eight years. The television was on in the sitting room of the Donegall Road terraced house. The newsreader had just announced that twenty-six unarmed civilians had been shot by the Army during an anti-internment demonstration in Derry. Of the twenty-six, thirteen had been killed outright and one fatally wounded. Also reported was a bomb exploded by the Ulster Volunteer Force in McGurk's Bar, a Catholic owned pub in Belfast. Fifteen Catholic civilians had been killed, including two children, with 17 others wounded. This had been the highest death toll in a single incident thus far. This was most definitely it; time to go.

'Maggie, ah'm nae prepared tae stay in Northern Ireland any longer. This shooting is way oot ay order and they'll be looking fae me soon, ah jes' know it.'

Maggie's reaction was initially one of bewilderment but then she became distraught. Jock tried to comfort her. She smelled strongly of Pears soap and disappointment.

'Where will you go, what will you do?' She became very agitated and began to cry whilst pounding Jock's chest with her clenched fists. Through her tears she managed to accuse Jock in the most vociferous tones, totally uncharacteristically.

'You know, don't you? You bastard! You bloody-well know, and you're going to bugger off and leave me in the lurch!' Attempting to defend himself against the physical abuse which was now losing its impact in direct proportion with the increase in the sobbing, wailing and verbal abuse he spoke softly hoping to calm the situation.

'Know whit pet? Whit is it ah'm supposed tae ken?'

'Don't you "pet" me you bastard. I'm pregnant,' she blurted. 'I'm having your bloody baby! The sobbing continued. In all honesty, for once, Jock didn't know. This announcement was a bigger body blow than any of the physical punches he'd received a few seconds earlier. He considered his response as his expression took on a look of disbelief like a bull realising he'd just been stung by a wasp.

'Ah promise I didnae' know. Ah'll nae insult ye by asking if you're certain, but if ye' are, and the bairn is rightly mine, ah'll stand by ye. In fact…' he paused, swallowed and took a deep breath before continuing… 'Ah'll be proud tae be the child's father, an' if ye'll hev me…' Maggie threw herself into his open arms and they held each other in a long embrace and the histrionics were instantly quelled. Stephen Spielberg could not have directed a more moving scene. After a while Jock tenderly kissed her and whispered,

'We cannae stay here in Belfast. It's nae safe. Nae fer ye an' the bairn, nae fer ma sel' – fer us. Wull ye nae come wi' me tae England at least until these troubles are over?' He was expecting to encounter all manner of opposition but there was none. Maggie sat quietly as Jock ran through the detail of the escape plan.

Jock only had one change of clothes and it didn't take him long to pack a bag. Maggie, on the other hand couldn't decide what she would take with her. Should she take a winter coat? How about her wellington boots? Will I need my Sunday clothes? Jock was getting just a little irritated and decided to go and fill the Transit with diesel and say goodbye to Ciara whilst Maggie was making her final selections from her extensive wardrobe.

At the library Ciara, no longer the sweet, innocent and bubbly young woman he'd met all those years ago, was initially less than pleased to see him.

'Well now, 'tis yourself to be sure.' The greeting was tinged with sarcasm. 'We haven't seen you in a while – thought the

Proddies had got you.' Jock chose not to respond to what was clearly intended as a reproach.

'How are ye Ciara, and how's Michael?'

'As if you care! We're both fine and dandy and lucky to be so too! When the petrol bomb was thrown through the pub window last week we managed to escape but Finn McCann, you know Finn, was badly burned. Stupid sod wouldn't leave until he'd finished his pint.' Jock could barely believe what he was hearing.

'And the pub? Is it…?'

'It'll be a while before we can open again – if we ever do.' Jock was genuinely shocked and concerned. He was also feeling ever so slightly guilty.

'Ah'm very sorry tae hear this, Ciara.' He swiftly moved on to the excuse he'd prepared.

'Ah've called in tae say goodbye. Ah'm moving awa'.'

'Whatever for? We need every man we can get.'

'Ah ken but ah've been spotted. Ah wis in Lavery's spying fer Michael two days ago and a couple squaddies fra the Royal Highland Fusiliers recognised me fra when ah raided the RUC stores in Springfield Road.' Jock had always been a convincing liar and Ciara was credulous.

'Oh no!'

'Ah managed tae conceal ma sel' in Bradbury Place and watched 'em go haring awa' up Donegall Road. But they'll come looking. They'll be back, after me, and nae jes the two ay 'em either! So, ah'm awa' back to Scotland,' he lied. 'Ah wish ye, yer father and the cause well.' He leant over the counter, kissed her on the cheek and left. Ciara stood and watched him go, her fingers touching the cheek he had just kissed. She attempted a smile but the result was more of a sardonic sneer as she spoke only to herself. 'The cause? 'Tis a bloody cause alright. There's no justice. Without justice our courage is weak!'

When Jock returned to Donegall Road, Maggie's packing was finished at least, but there were two very large and heavy suitcases in the hall. He loaded them into the van. He went back into the house to urge Maggie to get a move on, but, remembering her condition, decided she'd be better left to prepare herself in her own time. Eventually, she joined him in the Transit and they began their 200-mile drive to Rosslare. It took about forty minutes to reach the border crossing and as he drove down the so called 'Concession Road' in Castleblayney to the security checkpoint at Dundalk, Jock's stomach was churning. He was experiencing sensations not unlike those he had had all those years ago in the Saddington Tunnel; sensations he'd rather not be reminded of.

As Jock knew only too well the increase in violence in Northern Ireland had resulted in both British and Northern Irish authorities attempting to prevent republican fighters from crossing the border. The British Army had all but transformed the border crossings into militarised checkpoints, blocking off roads and carrying out personnel checks. Prior to these 'checkpoints' it was fairly easy for men and women with subversive or malicious intent, with or without weapons or explosives, to cross the border in either direction. The border crossings had now become specific targets where the Republicans could attack the British Army and the RUC patrols. Jock's brain was buzzing with rhetorical questions to himself. 'Will the Army recognise me? Will they recognise the Northern Irish number plate? Will the RUC know the van is stolen? Will they want to see an insurance certificate? What do I tell them? What chance would I have trying to outrun them?' He immediately ruled his last thought out of the question. He did take some comfort from the knowledge he'd recently read somewhere that, in a four-month period during 1971, over 200,000 vehicles had been searched in Northern Ireland and only about ten had contained wanted men, guns or explosives been found. The odds were on his side.

'Are you feeling OK Jock?' Maggie was staring at him quite intently, worried by the erratic way he was now driving and concerned that he seemed to be shivering in spite of the sweat which was running down his face. Jock's response came in the form of an instruction.

'Dinnae fret Maggie. Leave all the talking tae me. Ye jes sit there and smile at 'em.'

An RUC officer clutching a semi-automatic machine-gun across his chest stepped into the road and directed Jock into a layby. The position was heavily fortified with sandbag defences and corrugated iron sheeting. Jock complied with the direction and wound down the window.

'Passports!' the officer demanded. Jock passed him his National Identity Card and Maggie's passport. The officer examined them.

'What's the purpose of your journey?'

Jock had preprepared an answer. 'Ma partner here, well ye can see she's in the family way and what wi' the "Troubles" in Belfast, and complications wi' the bairn, I'm taking her tae Dublin tae see an obstetrician.' The officer peered in through the open window and Jock could smell the stale tobacco and whiskey on his breath. If he'd have had any, Jock knew he could have bribed this guard with a bottle of whiskey. He looked suspiciously at Maggie, who, having heard Jock's story, was now playing the part, clutching her abdomen and giving a little groan every now and then.

'What's in the back?' demanded the officer.

'Jes' our things, clothes and stuff,' Jock answered truthfully, for once.

'Open them up!' Jock got out of the van and subtly checked the Webley in his waistband as he walked around to the back doors which he opened. He reached in and pulled his own small bag towards him, unzipped it and pushed it in the direction of the RUC man. He had a cursory rummage but found nothing incriminating. Jock then heaved one of Maggie's cases towards him, unsnapped the catches only to reveal an assortment of women's clothing, accessories and accoutrements. The officer nodded. He didn't bother with the second case. Jock rezipped his bag and closed Maggie's case and the back doors. He walked around to the driver's door and the officer returned the ID documents.

'OK,' he said, and almost with a smile, 'go safely, and I hope it all goes well with the lady and good luck with the bairn.' Jock needed no second invitation and after he'd gently pulled away and into Eire he put his foot down only to stop after a mile or so in order to relieve himself, light a cigarette and stop shaking.

Chapter Ten

After ten minutes or so, Jock had calmed down sufficiently to continue the journey to Rosslare. He estimated that the trip would take around three hours provided there were no more hold-ups. It was mid-afternoon when they arrived. Jock parked the van in the carpark at the harbour. Maggie, who was in desperate need of a toilet wandered off to find the facilities whilst Jock went to book the tickets. Maggie returned to the van with two portions of fish and chips and two bottles of Guinness which they consumed whilst waiting to load onto the Sealink Ferry *Invicta* for the evening crossing to Pembroke Dock in South Wales.

Never having travelled on a ferry before, Maggie was quite excited albeit somewhat apprehensive at the same time.

Apart from a few lorries there were not many other vehicles and Jock was beckoned on board with the only formality being an inspection of the boarding passes, his ID card and Maggie's passport. Having parked the van on the vehicle deck, they made their way to the passenger lounge and found a couple of seats by a window. It was not too long before both of them were asleep; Jock with his arm around Maggie's shoulder; she with her head resting on his chest. Some five hours later they were awoken by the general hustle and bustle of passengers preparing to disembark. They too made ready and returned to the Transit on the vehicle deck. Jock again was experiencing butterflies in his stomach knowing that they had to run the gauntlet of immigration and customs formalities. In the event, both were nothing more than a formality, not even a raised eyebrow.

'Perhaps they don't like working at night?' observed Maggie a little naively. Jock just smiled. He wound down his window and asked the only customs officer on duty if he could recommend a hotel close by. He directed them to the Old Cross Saws Inn. Jock's eyes lit up when they arrived there.

'Perfect, jes' ma kindae place!' he exclaimed and they went into the bar.

'Sorry, we're just closed,' the rather flamboyant landlord announced in his best male-voice-choir singsong tenor. Jock's smile turned to a frown in an instant. He turned to Maggie but before he could say anything, she did.

'We were hoping for a room; bed and breakfast?' pleaded Maggie.

'Ah well, in that case boyos you've just become residents. Welcome! My name's Bryn Morgan and I like to play the organ. What you 'avin'?' Jock's frown turned to a forced grin and back to a frown. 'Stupid Druid,' he uttered in a stage whisper.

'A pint ay heavy… sorry bitter, och and a large dram, Scotch nae your Irish rubbish if ye please. How about you Maggie?'

'I'm thinking for sure I should stick to soft drinks in my condition.'

'Up the duff is it then?' the landlord enquired with a few wholly inappropriate gestures. Maggie clearly didn't take very kindly to the personal nature of the question nor the familiarity with which it was posed.

'That'll be none of your business. Guinness please!'

'Sorry if I caused offence. None intended I'm sure.' The landlord was genuinely apologetic and he began pouring the drinks.

'So, an Irishwoman and a Scotsman walked into a bar run by a Welshman… sounds like the start of a joke.' At this, Bryn Morgan fell about laughing. His two guests couldn't understand what was so funny.

It had been the first night in a long time that their sleep hadn't been disturbed by the sound of gunfire or rioting. Mrs Morgan served them with a hearty but distinctly unhealthy fried breakfast and after Jock had settled the bill with a stolen credit-card they were soon back on the road and heading east. Jock failed to notice the white Ford Cortina, with the distinctive 'go-faster' stripes down the sides that had tucked into the east-bound traffic behind him. The stripes certainly distinguished this car from other white Fords.

'Where exactly is it that we're going?' Maggie asked.

'Well, ah'm picking up a crate from Williams' Shipping warehouse in Southampton and then we're heading up north tae the Midlands where ah used tae work before I came to Belfast and met you.' Jock had turned on his Sean Connery voice. He was enjoying Maggie's company on the trip but somewhere in the recesses of his mind there was a worry; a worry that was deeply troubling him. Was she really expecting him to marry her? Had she not realised that he was merely using her? He may have fathered the child but did she really expect him, Duncan McClean of all people, to be the child's father, a family man? This particular problem would require some very delicate handling and the more he thought about it, the more his mood became devoid of optimism and consumed by depression. This was an altogether unnecessary complication he could well do without. Then there was the matter of the American. He'd met Tom Wenzl a couple of years earlier on a Southampton run. Tom, Jock had discovered, was into the same racket as himself – the illegal arms trade. Since that initial meeting, they had been corresponding and putting together a plan which, although extremely risky if not downright suicidal, would be mutually beneficial. Today was destined to see phase one of the plan implemented. The pregnant woman was certainly not a part of the plan.

Chapter Eleven

Parts of the road in South Wales had recently been upgraded to motorway standard and the driving was easy. They pulled into a service station near Swansea for diesel and a toilet break. Jock failed to spot the white Ford Cortina at the pump behind him. The Transit continued past Bridgend, Cardiff and Newport before crossing the Bristol Channel into England. It wasn't until they were on the A36 that Jock began to suspect that they were being tailed. Maggie noticed he was constantly staring into his wing mirrors, first one and then the other; speeding up and slowing down.

'Whatever is it Jock?' she asked, clearly aware that something was bothering him.

'Ah may be wrong but ah think we're being followed. Ah've hud a white Ford Cortina behind us fur several miles the noo.'

'Ah come on now, who'd want to be following us?' Little did she know just how many people might want to be following Jock McClean. Without warning or signal he made an abrupt turn off the direct A36 route on to the A350, just south of Warminster. The Cortina followed. Jock pulled into a lay-by as they crossed Brimsdown Hill. The Cortina sped past.

'There you are, you silly old fool, you're getting paranoid.' Where had he heard that before? Jock admitted that maybe he was being overly cautious but he was relieved to see a totally clear road behind him now. By the time they had cleared Shaftesbury both Maggie and Jock were feeling a bit peckish and they stopped at an old coaching inn in Blandford Forum; the Greyhound.

'Well the noo! There's a bloody coincidence if ever there wis!'

'What're you going on about now?'

'Ah, it's a lang story involving another pub wi' the same name. Bloody dog, bin dogging ma fur years. Maybe it's an omen? Och dinnae bother yersel' wi' it.'

Back on the A350 the white Ford Cortina which Jock thought he'd shaken off was behind him again but he didn't notice it until the junction with the A31 near Wimborne Minster.

'Damn an' blast it!' he cursed, and with a reckless regard for traffic he stopped; no signal, no warning. The Cortina had two options – run into the back of the Transit or swerve to overtake it. The Cortina chose the latter and it wasn't until it had disappeared into the congestion ahead that Jock made a violent U-turn and doubled back onto the A350 almost hitting an oncoming motorcyclist in the process.

'Whit the feck! Who are these guys? It couldnae be the polis surely? I cannae believe that. The polis would have pulled me by now surely?' Maggie didn't have a clue what Jock was ranting on about.

'I'll be thanking you for moderating your language if you don't mind!' Jock apologised. Several miles ahead, the Cortina had stopped at a telephone kiosk near Ringwood. The driver was on the phone.

'The bastard managed to lose me. I've been with him since Pembroke but he got the better of me a few miles back. Still, I reckon you were right – to be sure he's going to Southampton, no doubt about it. What do you want me to do brother?'

Jock had joined the A35 near Poole. He was now driving cautiously, not only from not wishing to attract unwanted attention from any police patrols, but the brake pedal was feeling spongy and the brakes were not as responsive as they should be. Jock mentioned this slight problem to Maggie, then immediately wished he hadn't.

'I'm not surprised! You've been driving like a lunatic. I'm only surprised that we haven't had an accident,' she chided. They were now travelling east towards Southampton. As the Transit approached Totton at the head of Southampton Water they could make out the majestic lines of the *QEII*. Jock would collect his crate from the warehouse the following day. They pulled onto the forecourt of the Braemar Lodge; a traditional yet comfortable looking guest house. Jock was quite satisfied with the recommendation that had been made to him by an American some months earlier on a previous trip to Southampton. Judging by the framed photographs in reception, the proprietors had clearly been on holiday in the Scottish village and borrowed its name for their bed and breakfast establishment. Jock and Maggie checked in for one night under the names of Mr & Mrs O'Rourke. Maggie was tired and the moment after they were shown into their room she'd kicked off her shoes, lay on the bed and was fast asleep, all within a matter of minutes. Jock was still slightly perturbed by the white Cortina that had plagued the day's journey. Still not entirely sure who it could have been following him, the fluidity of his thinking process was clotted by the skeletons in the closet of his distant past.

'It mustae been the polis. Who else could it ae been?' He'd barely given his most recent past any consideration at all until a flimsy element of doubt crossed his mind. 'Surely nae someone from the IRA?

'It's as well we'll be getting a different van. The feckin' Transit's clapped out. Ah hope the transport the American's bringing will be summat whit'll blend in. A van whit merges in wi' the traffic is what we need,' but Maggie was asleep and knew nothing of any American. He went down to the lounge where he browsed through a copy of the *Southern Daily Echo* and smoked a roll-up.

'Will you and Mrs O'Rourke be joining us for dinner?' It was the receptionist who disturbed Jock's reverie.

'Och, ah dinnae think so thank ye.' He looked at his pocket-watch. 'He should be here the noo,' he thought to himself. Intentionally leaving his tobacco pouch on the occasional table, he went outside as if to stretch his legs with a walk around the carpark area of the Braemar Lodge. There was a black van parked next to the Transit. It hadn't been there when they arrived. He had a good look around it. A Ford, but an American Ford. An Econoline E20 with New York State registration plates. The tinted windows were as black as the gleaming paintwork. Was this the van? The receptionist had followed him outside.

'This guest has just arrived' she said pointing at the van. 'An American I think, maybe he came on the *QEII* or perhaps he's waiting to board tomorrow, who knows? Quite a van isn't it? Impressive looking.' Then remembering why she'd come outside, 'Oh sorry, Mr O'Rourke, I brought your tobacco pouch out, you left it in the lounge'.

'Ye're very kind, Thank ye.' The receptionist smiled sweetly and returned to her post. Jock opened his tobacco pouch. The book of *QEII* matches was there. This was the signal. He looked again at the American Ford. Impressive looking? Yes! Was this the van? Quite a van indeed! He'd expected something similar but not quite as ostentatious as this. He tried the door. It wasn't locked.

'Och, feck me man, bloody left-hand-drive!' He hadn't anticipated that. Poor planning, but then how hard could it be. He was a driver, a professional driver. He walked around to the left side knowing that when he tried the door it too would be unlocked. He got in and, impressed with the leather upholstery and general level of comfort, he pulled down the sun-visor. There were the keys. Yes, this was definitely the van. He sat there for a while going over the plan in his mind. Jock wondered if the Yank's foresight, in his blissful ignorance, had developed cataracts of stupidity. It certainly seemed that way to Jock. His newly found partner in crime had most certainly taken leave of his better judgement. When they were initially putting their plan together had it not been the Yank who had made the eminently sensible suggestion regarding the need for inconspicuousness? There again, maybe this model was as common in America as the Transit was in the UK. But here it was. It would have to do. Quintessential to the strategy was that Jock would 'steal' the American's van and its contents. This ruse would not cast any doubts on the American's integrity. Any suspicion would be diverted away from the American. Michael Doyle would never know that this consignment of guns, ammunition and explosives intended for the IRA had become the interest of an alternative organisation for which it was now destined as a result of a heist meticulously planned by Jock and Tom Wenzl, the American..

Jock crept back into his room in the Braemar Lodge, collected his bag and the Transit keys. Without a word to Maggie who had now made herself comfortable actually in the bed where she was absolutely sound asleep and out for the count he crept out again. He left the keys behind the visor on the driver's side of the Transit and removed the IRA issue Webley pistol from the glovebox. Should he leave Wenzl the American a note about the brakes, suggest that he steals another car? No, he couldn't be bothered. It was not in Jock's nature to have any concern for others, even if one of those others was supposed to be his partner If Wenzl didn't like the Transit he could make his own alternative arrangements. He located the driver's door and climbed into the Econoline.. He released the handbrake and allowed the van to coast down the gentle slope before joining the road and starting the engine. The mighty 5.0 litre V8 engine roared into life. Jock roared with laughter. It might not have been as inconspicuous as he would have hoped for but at least here was a van with some grunt he thought to himself. Hell of a difference to the Transit. He drove off into the night. The plan was coming together. Phase one was up and running.

Chapter Twelve

There was just the briefest of moments when Jock felt just a slight twinge of guilt about leaving Maggie totally in the lurch. She was carrying his baby after all. But Jock wasn't the sort of character to dwell on such matters. Oh no, she'd merely been a means to his end, a 'home comfort' and housekeeper whilst he took advantage of her good nature and hospitality. Driving carefully, as he became familiar with the left-hand-drive controls of this latest vehicle, he smiled in the knowledge that whoever had been following the Transit would no longer be tailing him. What was more it seemed that he'd successfully and painlessly ditched his female encumbrance. The woman would only have complicated matters. OK, she was pregnant. So what? He just wasn't ready for fatherhood, if indeed he ever would be. He could now see his way clear to cashing in on the arms deal. The arsenal accumulated over the last few months should be crated and waiting for him to collect from the Williams' Shipping Company warehouse on the Town Quay at Hythe. Jock was also considering himself to be something of a philanthropist, a pacifist even. By depriving the IRA of these weapons, he, Jock McClean was doing his bit for peace in Northern Ireland. This particular shipment would not be exacerbating the 'Troubles'. It didn't seem to matter to Jock that the guns would now be delivered to a different terrorist organisation. But then Jock wasn't particularly politically enlightened when it came to international terrorism, dissident groups, or any other groups of aggressors. Who knows, who cares? Certainly not D McClean esquire. As far as Jock was concerned the sale of his crated arsenal together with the most recent contribution from the

United States and already in the van would see him financially comfortable for several years to come. The American individual, if indeed he was an American, and Jock had his doubts; the man with whom he had become a co-conspirator was most certainly politically predisposed. This guy's moral fibre was cut from the same cloth as Jock's. He sounded like an American but in an affected sort of way which had Jock wondering whether or not he was genuine. Why had he banged on about the significance of 16 September 1970? So, who were or what was the so-called Black September Organisation anyway? Another feckin rock band? Jock wasn't bothered. Blue November or Pink February, who cares? Not Jock. Genuine Yank or not, in Jock's line of work one had to take risks. He had finally been convinced however that there was a ready market for what they had to offer; a potential customer who would outbid any other, especially if they pooled their resources. Jock was easily persuaded given the prospect of a greater return and he readily agreed to bide his time. That time was now. It had arrived. The game was on and that's what it was to Jock – a game.

He arrived at the Williams' Shipping warehouse without incident and parked. He may have been a driver but he was never a member of the Observer Corps. Again, he didn't notice the white Ford Cortina with the 'go faster' stripes parked in the shadows just a short distance ahead of the warehouse and the Econoline. He entered the warehouse by the loading-bay doors.

'How do Jock. You're a day early. I wasn't expecting you until the 6th.' Jock was pleased to hear the familiar greeting from Billy Kelly the warehouseman with whom he had previously dealt on several occasions to such an extent that a special 'working relationship' had been formed. On Jock's previous visit his new partner had become privy to the storage arrangement as well. It hadn't occurred to Jock that being a day early could have caused a problem. 'What if Billy had Tuesdays off and some other bloke was on duty?' Jock wondered to himself. Still, he didn't. Here he was and all was well.

'Gude evening yersel' Billy. How's it hangin'? Aye, slight change ay plan. Sorry ah didnae gi' ye warnin'. Ye hev a crate fur me?' Billy found the paperwork which they'd forged between them on the occasion of Jock's last visit and he disappeared into the nether regions of the warehouse. He returned to the loading bay after a few moments driving a forklift truck carrying a very large and heavy custom-built wooden crate. Jock meanwhile had reversed the Econoline into the loading bay and opened the van's doors to receive the consignment.

'Where's your Transit Jock? This one's bigger than usual. It'll be a bit awkward getting this in there.' It was a larger crate than Jock had been anticipating.

'The Transit? – ah it's a lang story. I dinnae ken whether this is the Yank's idea of a joke. Still ah couldnae get anything else at short notice and this is part loaded already. It'll be OK wance ah get this other stuff oot the way.' Not having previously looked in the rear of the black van, Jock was unaware that so much room would be taken by what it was carrying. There were two very large wicker baskets of the type one might find in a laundry or a theatrical costume department. Jock took a cursory look inside. Brand new frocks lay on top of the contents. He didn't bother to dig too deeply he knew what was concealed beneath.

'A pity the bloody Yank didnae load this beast ay a bus a bit better,' he said to no one in particular. Billy did eventually manage to squeeze the crate into the van which sighed as it sank down on its springs. Jock handed him an envelope which he pocketed; the negotiated 'consideration'.

'Cheers Jocky boy, stay lucky and see you in a month or so?'

'Aye, maybe. Up the Irish!' he quipped as he went to get in the wrong side of van again.

Jock pulled away from the Town Quay still oblivious to the Cortina even though he drove right passed it. He did notice the white Ford Transit with the distinctive JAZ registration plate and spongy brakes. But then he'd been looking for it. Exactly in accordance with the plan the second vehicle had now arrived on the quay. The driver was a fellow in a 'Giants' baseball cap below which his ears protruded like the handles on some pretentious silver-plated sporting trophy. In the passenger seat sat a pregnant woman. She certainly did not feature in the plan. The white van attempted to tuck in behind the black van but the Cortina managed to squeeze in between them. And so, in loose order the three vehicles headed north looking to connect with the A34.

Chapter Thirteen

Gerry Doyle was attempting to maintain a discreet distance behind the Econoline and in doing so his concentration was fully focused on the vehicle he was following rather than on the one which was following him. The American Ford pulled into a late-night service station in Winchester. Gerry held back. The Transit drove passed both the Cortina and the garage. The JAZ number plate hit him in the eyes like a laser beam. 'Now what?' he wondered. 'What the blazes is happening here?' He got out of the car and stood in the middle of the road and watched as the Transit pulled into the kerb some 200 yards ahead. It was obvious they were waiting for the Econoline to move again as well.

The lights in the service station went out, and Gerry watched the cashier set the alarm, lock up the shop and the pumps. The Econoline did not move for the next four hours. It seemed that Jock was taking a nap. Gerry decided to go and have a word with the occupants of the Transit hoping to discover what their interest was. 'Maybe it's just a decoy,' he thought. 'On the other hand it might be a gang of 'Proddies' looking to intercept an IRA shipment.' Given this latter thought he decided against having a word.

At about 4 am the unwitting convoy moved off. It had begun to rain, quite steadily. In the Econoline Jock was feeling refreshed although a bit miffed at having only received £2 change from a £10 note for the tankful of petrol. He'd previously had no idea of the correlation between fuel consumption and engine capacity but he was now beginning to understand just how 'thirsty' the 5.0 litre V8 engine was. He made a mental note to reconsider using the big Ford in favour of something more economical if any form of road transport would be needed for the final stage of the plan. But then, if the plan went 'as planned' that wouldn't be his problem. That would be down to the rock band or whoever the purchaser was. So, the Econoline was something of a misnomer, Jock was pushing it hard unperturbed by the excessive fuel consumption. The speedometer needle was hovering around the 80 mph mark and such a speed was easily attainable. He tried to avoid looking at the fuel gauge visibly moving from 'F' towards 'E'. In the Cortina, Gerry was feeling very sleepy and bleary-eyed after having driven all day and then having kept Jock under surveillance for the last four hours. In the Transit the American in the baseball cap was struggling with the controls of the right-hand-drive confusing the switches for windscreen-wipers, main-beam headlights and indicators. The noise of the badly worn wipers on the windscreen was hypnotically irritating. The rain was getting worse and visibility was poor at best. Proceeding north on the A34 towards Oxford, Jock became aware of the vehicle maintaining the pace behind him but he couldn't make out what it was. With the accelerator flat to the floor he was making almost 90 mph despite the heavy load. The Transit was now a long way back at such a distance that Jock wondered whether he could lose the American altogether and execute the plan on his own. That other vehicle, right behind him was becoming a worry though, doing the same speed and far too close especially with the heavy rain persisting. There was next to no other traffic.

Hammering south on the A34 having collected its load of ammonium nitrate fertiliser from the marshalling yard at Didcot Railway Station was a Seddon Atkinson 'Leader'. A monster of an articulated curtain-sided truck with a brake-horsepower of 240 doing around 60 mph on the comparatively straight section of the A34 across the Berkshire Downs.

The Transit had fallen well off the pace and Gerry decided to make his move. He eased the Cortina even further forward, dangerously close behind the Econoline and, flashing his lights between dipped and main-beam, he 'tailgated' the American Ford and started to nudge its rear bumper. Jock was not best pleased to say the least.

'Ah'll nae be doin wi' any ay this! Feck off ye bastard!' Without warning he wrenched the steering wheel viciously to the right and the rear end of the van swung to the left as it almost spun out of control and tipped over. Jock corrected the skid and as the suspension groaned he successfully negotiated the turn onto a minor road towards the small village of East Ilsley. The driver of the Atkinson was leaning on lorry's klaxon and screaming at the Econoline as it made its suicidal manoeuvre directly across his path. Goodness only knows what the driver was thinking of. God only knows how the van made it.

The Cortina didn't.

The collision was horrendous; indescribably horrific. With a combined impact of something in excess of 120 miles-per-hour the Atkinson violently slammed into the Cortina and all but totally crushed it into a twisted, mangled wreckage as it forced what was left of the car some 100 yards south, crossing both carriageways in the process, before finally tossing what now resembled a heap of scrap metal into the air, the lorry itself bursting into flames as it overturned. The resulting inferno and conflagration were intense and suddenly the volatile cargo went off like a bomb, the explosion sending a fireball into the air followed by a mushroom cloud of smoke. Burning debris like shrapnel was flung far and wide and littered the road for yards in all directions.

As the Transit came through Beedon, the occupants could clearly see the flames and smoke up ahead. Maggie clasped her hand to her mouth and gasped,

'Oh no, is it Jock? – please God no – not Jock,' she implored. The American was seemingly devoid of even the slightest exposition of emotion, shock or horror.

'Nope, ma'am. 'Tain't my ve-hi-cal.' Was the extent of the American's drawl. Maggie screamed and screamed. She became hysterical and continued to scream until the sounds just wouldn't come any more. Then as the realisation of just what was happening hit him, the American put the full force of his right leg on the brake pedal – nothing. He pumped the pedal – nothing. Panic! He yanked on the handbrake. The rear wheels locked but the Transit's momentum was such that it barely slowed down as it ploughed into the burning wreckage which was strewn all over the road. Then came a second explosion. The American was deafened by the power of the blast. All he could hear were Maggie's silent screams and a tinnitus-like ringing in his ears. White noise. White heat, the intensity of which, generated by the burning ammonium nitrate was so fierce the Transit caught light. The American managed to crash the gearbox into reverse and, foot hard down, back away from where they would surely have been burned alive. The Transit's tyres had exploded and were now burning. He leaped out of the cab. and ran around to the passenger side. He wrenched open the door. Maggie could feel his hands grasping her arms. He was shouting at her – silently. He hauled Maggie out and onto the verge. She made no sound. The attitude of her expression was identical to that of the character on the bridge in Edvard Munch's famous painting.

The American staggered off some distance into the field and vomited. He noticed a piece of smouldering wreckage, a door panel perhaps. There were other Cortina parts which had become detached in the collision and thrown clear of the melting tarmacadam. He dropped to his knees, clearly distressed and in shock. After minutes had passed he regained an awareness of the hell he had just experienced and looked back towards the carnage. 'Bloody Scotsman,' he cursed. 'He knew that van was a crock of shit!' On his hands and knees he returned to where Maggie was lying on the verge, not moving, perfectly still. He stroked her forehead, awkwardly, believing it might comfort her.

'I reckon that there piece of wreckage is from the ve-hi-cal we were tailing.' Maggie appeared not to have heard. He suggested to her again, 'I do declare it's the front of the ve-hi-cal we was following; a white one with distinctive "go faster" stripes. I guess we'll just have to sit here until the highway-patrol and fire-trucks arrive. Yessiree, that bastard's getting clean away with my ve-hi-cal. This ain't at all what we got planned.'

He was still speaking to Maggie but hadn't noticed she had stopped breathing.

Jock, the bastard, was indeed getting clean away. He didn't even stop to look back at the fatal accident his dangerous driving had caused. But, from the rear-view mirror, he knew what had happened. Had he known that it was his old acquaintance Gerry Doyle, with whom he had often had dealings in the past who had been killed, he might have felt some sympathy – but not for long.

The road through East Ilsley eventually came back upon the A34 to the north of the crash site. At the road junction Jock looked to the left where the glow from the burning ammonium could still be seen. 'Wan doon!' he thought. He turned right and continued on his way towards Oxford, humming Elton John's 'Rocket Man' to himself, unaware that it was actually two down.

Chapter Fourteen

When the emergency services arrived at the crash scene the ambulance personnel confirmed that both Maggie and her unborn baby were dead. The American was mortified. He was sobbing uncontrollably and resisted the attempts made by the ambulance crew to examine him. After a moment or two in which the American regained a little of his shattered composure one of the policemen approached him. The choking stench of burning rubber and ammonia hung in the air.

'Did you see what happened here?' he enquired. The American choked back his sobs, removed his baseball cap and dried his eyes.

'A car was following a panel-van – an Econoline E20 – black. Mine! Stolen from the Braemar Lodge guest house in Southampton yesterday. This 'ere ve-hi-cal' he pointed to the partly burned out wreck of the Transit, 'is his – or was his; the thief's. We were following the car.' A second policeman had been inspecting what was left of the Transit.

'This is the one,' the second policeman confirmed to his colleague.

'What do yo' all mean? asked the American.

'This van was reported stolen in Belfast.' It was all getting a little confusing for the American.

'Not by me, it wasn't!' he stated with indignation.

'Did you witness the accident?' the constable asked again.

'No sir,' said the American. 'Now can we get after my ve-hi-cal?'

'We'll get to your stolen car....'

'Econoline E20' interrupted the American.

'We'll get to your stolen Econoline E20 all in good time sir.'

After almost two hours since leaving Winchester the night sky was just beginning to lighten. The fire was all but extinguished by the fire brigade, steam and smoke dissipating into the early morning mist. One side of the road had been cleared sufficiently to allow the morning traffic northbound and southbound to pass alternately, as directed by a policeman on point duty.

Another police car had arrived and a uniformed sergeant was consulting with his colleagues and making notes.

'Now then, Mr…?'

'Wenzl – W-e-n-z-l'. The American spelt his surname in the belief that all members of the British police force were stupid. 'Tom Wenzl.'

'You say you didn't steal the Transit.'

'Not from Belfast but technically I guess I did, yes sir. I took it from the Braemar Lodge in Southampton to chase the bastard that stole my Econoline. This unfortunate young woman, bless her soul, asked if she could ride with me. Seems she knew it was the guy who had the Transit who took my ve-hi-cal and she knew where he was going too.' They all looked over to where the ambulance crew were moving Maggie's corpse onto a stretcher and into the ambulance. With due reverence everyone stood with heads bowed.

'Tell me again, how did you know where he was headed?'

'Maggie told me.'

'Maggie?' The American made a gesture towards the ambulance and crossed himself.

'The late Mrs O'Rourke,' Wenzl offered in a tone which rang somewhere between sarcasm and disgust. 'She told me quite a lot about herself and the guy she thought was her partner. She was under the impression they were going to be married before their baby was born.'

'Go on,' the sergeant encouraged him. Tom had taken serious umbrage at Jock disappearing without him. That was not in the script. Still, he was emboldened by what he considered to be a masterstroke; telling the police the truth. This would surely place him above any suspicion.

'Seems our thief was a member of the IRA and into gun-running.' Stayed in Mrs O'Rourke's guest-house in Belfast whilst he was fighting with the IRA.'

'Did she give you a name?'

'Duncan McClean, though everyone called him Jock on account of him being scotch an' all.'

'And what about the man driving the car that was involved in the accident – we'll not be getting much out of him, poor chap. What do you know about him?'

'Nothing! Maggie said he had followed them all the way from Pembroke, I think she said. They'd stayed in a pub in Pembroke after getting off the Ferry from Dublin two days ago. They were on their way to Southampton to collect a consignment of guns from IRA sympathisers in America. The car was a white Ford Cortina, like yours, except it had sort a distinctive "go faster" stripes. I reckon one of its doors is over there in the field.'

'Take a look will you Nick,' the sergeant asked his constable, then continued.

'So Mr Wenzl, What's your connection with the IRA?'

'I'm not connected to the bloody IRA in any way. I'm a commercial traveller in ladies' fashion garments.' The sergeant and the other constable had great difficulty suppressing a snigger.

'I see,' said the detective, though it was clear that he didn't. 'Anyway, sounds like a rum chap, this McClean character.'

'You're telling me!' Tom Wenzl stated quite emphatically. 'Now, what about my ve-hi-cal and all the stock I was carrying?'

'I'm just going to call it in on the radio. It's most important we find this Scotsman and whatever weapons he's got. And to do that we'll have to trace and apprehend your ve-hi-cal,' he mimicked. 'Now, I'll need you to come to Oxford Police Station and make a full statement. It's obvious there's more to this accident than meets the eye. I'm guessing you have no means of getting to wherever you were travelling.' 'Guessing?'

thought Wenzl. 'Bloody obvious I'd have thought – dumb bastard limey cop!'

'I can give you a lift to Oxford and if you're up to it you may as well come straight to the station and make your statement.'

'Yeah, OK let's do that. Does your station do breakfast?'

So, on Friday 8th December in Oxford, at St Aldate's police station Tom Wenzl, a most unlikely commercial traveller in ladies' fashionwear from America was drinking a mug of tasteless brown lukewarm water purporting to be coffee whilst being interviewed by Detective Sergeant Doug Armstrong. Acknowledging that Wenzl must have had a very traumatic experience, Armstrong wasn't too hard on him. When the DS was satisfied that Wenzl was nothing more than an innocent victim he asked him to make a statement. Wenzl hesitatingly dictated whilst the DS took down the dictation directly on his typewriter.

My name is Thomas Wenzl. I live in Buffalo, Erie County, New York State. I am employed as a traveller in ladies' fashion by Oscar de la Renta. I arrived in the UK at Southampton on the QEII on Friday 8th December 1972 driving my black Ford Econoline E20 registration number 2239-TL New York, delivering new top end fashion lines to the Oscar de la Renta boutiques in the UK.

I checked into the Braemar Lodge guest house in Southampton on arrival and parked my vehicle in the yard. When I returned to collect some belongings from the vehicle it had gone. I went to reception to call the police and met a lady in distress. I said to her 'My vehicle's been stolen.' She said she suspected it was her partner who had stolen it and she knew where he was going. She asked to come with me so we took the Transit van that had been left in the yard and went to the Williams' Shipping Warehouse where I saw my vehicle being loaded with

*a crate. A Ford Cortina car followed it when it left and
me and the woman followed the car.*

*The woman told me she was Margaret O'Rourke from
Belfast who had escaped from the 'Troubles' with Jock her
partner, real name, Duncan McClean who was a member
of the IRA. She was pregnant with his baby. When
McClean stopped for gasoline I was going to confront him
but Mrs O'Rourke told me he could be violent and that he
had a gun so I decided to continue to follow. The Cortina
was also following. We couldn't keep up their speed but
when we were some way south of Didcot we saw fire and
smoke. It was clear to me that there had been a collision.
As I approached the burning wreckage of a truck and
another vehicle, the brakes on the Transit failed and we
could not stop before running into the flames. The heat
was scorching and the Transit caught light. I backed
away and pulled Mrs O'Rourke out of the van onto the
verge. I think she may have been unconscious. I threw
up in the field at the side of the road and noticed a piece
of wreckage which had come from the Ford Cortina.
I couldn't see either the driver of the truck or the car and
my Econoline was clearly long gone. By the time the police
and the ambulance arrived Mrs O'Rourke was dead.
This is a truthful and accurate statement to the best of my
knowledge and belief.*

Signed T Wenzl

DS Armstrong read out Wenzl's statement and accepting what
was typed as truthful and accurate Wenzl added his signature.
The DS then informed him he was free to go but that he should
leave his contact details with the front desk sergeant, in the
event that the police should need further assistance with their
enquiries. Mr Wenzl was quite forthcoming and announced
that by some bizarre coincidence it had always been his plan to

stay at the Chesterton Hotel in Bicester – which he pronounced as 'By-cester'.

'I have already made my reservation at the Chesterton, you see Oscar de la Renta has a boutique in By-cester. I hope they'll not be too disappointed that their new stock has been stolen,' he elaborated.

'When we have news of your van we'll be in touch.' DS Armstrong hoped his parting comment would be at least consoling if not encouraging but realistically he knew there would be little chance of recovering it.

He sat and reread the statement. Duncan McClean. Why did this name ring a distant bell? He picked up the phone and dialled the Thames Valley Police headquarters in Kidlington.

'DS Armstrong for DI Cartwright please.' The detective inspector was newly promoted and recently transferred to Thames from the Leicestershire Force.

'This is Cartwright.'

'Sorry to bother you guv but we've got an incident here and I was wondering if the name Duncan McClean might mean anything to you?' The response was instant.

'Jock! Gotcha, you elusive bastard!' Cartwright was almost bedside himself with excitement.

Chapter Fifteen

DI Cartwright had been a detective constable based in Leicester back in 1964. He had been extensively involved in the aborted so-called 'body in the lock' case. His guvnor, DI Mosely, had been too idle to pursue it and had convinced his superior DCI Rees to consign the unsolved murder to a cold cases file as there was little chance of it ever being solved. Mosely had been holding Cartwright's promotion back despite the running around and covering he did for his boss. Many in the force considered the DI to be biding his time as he approached his retirement. When Mosely finally did retire Cartwright was immediately promoted which often gave him cause to smile when he recalled Mosely's words, *You'll never make DS!* Well, not only had he made DS he was now a DI himself and very well regarded at Thames Valley – motto *Sit Pax in Valle Thamesis.*

'Doug, this is brilliant news if it's the same McClean as we failed to get back in the day. Has he been referred to as Jock at all? Fill me in with the details.'

Armstrong related all that was known thus far and offered to fax over a copy of Wenzl's statement.

'Well, it certainly sounds like our Jock. It has all his hallmarks. I'll get an arrest warrant issued and a BOLO.'

'BOLO guvnor?'

'Sorry, an Americanism – be on the lookout for,' Cartwright explained.

'Must we?' Armstrong would have preferred an English all-points bulletin.

Meanwhile, in Belfast, Michael Doyle was serving some of his regulars in the firebombed Blackstaff Bar. Although some of the windows were still boarded up and the stench of burnt fixtures still lingered, the pub had been cleaned up to sufficient an extent to allow it to reopen. Ciara had the afternoon off from the library and was busy in the kitchen preparing sandwiches for the meeting due to take place in the bar that evening. Since the previous summer the Provisional IRA had not launched any major offensive, fearful now of not only the RUC and the British Army, but also the recently formed UDA; the Ulster Defence Association, sometimes known as the Ulster Freedom Fighters, the UFF. The declared aim of this particular organisation was to defend Ulster Protestants in Loyalist areas. Certainly, that December, five Catholic civilians had been shot dead in a gun attack in Londonderry and the UDA was believed to have been responsible.

Michael was worried. He was pretty sure that Jock McClean who he had been convinced was an ally and staunch supporter of the Nationalist cause, was now ripping him off. On too many occasions when Jock had driven to Southampton to collect shipments of arms from American Irish Republican supporters, the delivery was short of what he'd been led to expect through the Harrison Network, his contact in New York. Michael suspected that guns and ammunition were being appropriated by the Scotsman for his own profiteering enterprises. He was known to have sold guns to Gerry, Michael's brother during the early 60s when Gerry was putting an IRA cell together in London. So, he had instructed Gerry to tail Jock and report in at least once a day. There had been no telephone call for two days.

Meanwhile, back in Kidlington, DI Cartwright was pulling out all the stops. This time, McClean would be apprehended. His team of detectives had been instructed in no uncertain terms that the arrest of Duncan McClean was now the top priority. The Chief Constable had also given an assurance that uniformed officers would be available as and when required. What's more, thanks to Tom Wenzl's statement, McClean was now known to be a member of the IRA. There was much speculation in the corridors of the constabulary as to what manner of weapons were in the crate which had been collected from the docks in the stolen American Ford Econoline. Cartwright was confident. The Thames Valley Police had a force of almost 3000 men and women which, when added to the manpower available from colleagues from other forces, would surely be enough to ensure that this nasty little man was brought to justice. And, if he was smuggling firearms for the IRA, Cartwright would not hesitate to call in Thames' Counter Terrorism Unit. The DI decided that he should go public with his BOLO and it was arranged that he should put out a press statement and make an appeal to the public on television.

Having given his statement to DS Armstrong, it was arranged for a constable to drive Tom Wenzl to Bicester where he checked into the Chesterton Hotel later in the morning of Friday 8th December. Having gone for over 24 hours without sleep he went straight to bed once he'd taken a leisurely bath. It was well into the late afternoon when he woke and already dark. He thanked his lucky stars that he'd had the good sense and foresight to keep his suitcase with him when he checked into and out of the Braemar Lodge; lucky too that he'd rescued it from the burning Transit and not just from the clean clothes perspective. Concealed within the case were some highly sensitive documents. He took a shower and dressed in some fresh clothes. After dinner he had a stroll around the town centre and, should anyone have been following him, meandered fairly aimlessly passed the Oscar de la Renta boutique before returning to the hotel bar and eventually turning in for the night. He lay in bed wondering how on earth the original plan was still on track, if indeed it was, given the various 'curveballs' which had been lobbed at him. The IRA thought he was 'on side'. Of this he was sure. The police now knew for certain that Jock was an IRA member. He had said as much in his statement. The

IRA probably had their suspicions as far as Jock's loyalty was concerned. But how likely was it that they suspected that Jock or indeed he and Jock were embroiled in a conspiracy against the Nationalist's interests? The 'stolen' van ruse had worked well so far but Tom would now need to be extremely diligent if he was to successfully pull off his role as a double agent. He lay in bed worrying over the events which might unfold over the next few days before he eventually drifted off into a fitful sleep. The following morning at breakfast, Wenzl decided he'd give himself the weekend off before executing his part in any task assigned by Michael Doyle or Duncan McClean or anyone else. The situation would hopefully remain quiet at least until Monday.

Chapter Sixteen

DI Cartwright picked up the phone and spoke to one of his detective constables, recently promoted from the uniformed ranks.

'Find me Helen Blake and bring her in for questioning.'

'Where do I start?'

'Use your bloody initiative man!' The case was beginning to irritate the DI. After a pause, he harkened back to those very words being delivered by Mosely straight out his manual of 'how not to treat your subordinates', and he rang the DC again. 'I'm sorry Ray, I didn't mean to be short with you. I think you might get a lead from her probation officer. She did a seven stretch in East Sutton Park. Got out after five. She used to be somewhere in Leicestershire – place called…' he checked his file, '… Burton Overy, but she could have moved.' Ray Davies' promotion had been well-deserved. He was a bright lad and Cartwright was confident he would do well. He hoped his outburst hadn't stifled his DC's enthusiasm or commitment.

'OK guv, will do. Give me a couple of days – oh and don't beat yourself up. I can see how this case is turning into a real nightmare and giving you grief.' Maybe not the sort of familiarity a DI might have expected from a new DC but he was absolutely right. It was turning into a nightmare. Cartwright was now pinning his hopes on Helen Blake's confession to Mosely eight years earlier as his best source of a lead on McClean.

It had been late in 1969 when Helen Blake was released from East Sutton Park Prison and the draconian seven-year sentence she had received. Release had been conditional upon her reporting to a probation officer once a month throughout 1970. The probation officer assigned to Helen was herself a probationer but in a different context. Marion Fisher, a recent graduate had only been appointed to the probation service a month before being given this assignment, Helen Blake being considered a suitable 'safe' case for a debutante probation officer.

Ray Davis followed his guvnor's advice and having traced Ms Fisher, he'd made an appointment to meet her. Following their meeting, DC Davis was able to report to DI Cartwright that Helen Blake had been a model prisoner whilst inside, and since her release. She had studied to become a legal secretary and got a job with a firm in Ely. The DC referred to his notes.

'Apparently, according to Ms Fisher, Helen Blake ticked all the boxes on the Home Office questionnaire guv. She didn't do drugs, she had never been tempted to commit another crime, she hadn't mixed with any known criminals, and she had a permanent address in that village you mentioned, er... Burton somewhere...'

'Overy,' interjected Cartwright.

'Yeah, that's the place, where she lived alone since her son had moved away. Anyway she completed all the terms of her licence and Helen Blake's now a free woman. I've checked the address in that Burton place guv but she's no longer there. There's a young couple there now, a Stuart and Kate Cross. They rent the cottage from Ben Blake, Helen's son. Now get this!' The DC was relishing the prospect of the next piece of information he was about to impart.

'It was Stuart Cross who tipped off your old guvnor about that narrowboat, the *Emily Rose* where the Luger was found.'

'Yes, I remember, I was there!' Cartwright didn't really need reminding. 'But still, it's a bit of a coincidence as you say – and like old Mosely, I'm beginning to dislike coincidences almost as much as he did. Do we know where she is now?'

'Afraid not. I rang the firm of solicitors she was working for in Ely, Meadows, Coleman and Pettegrew,' the DC said, referring to his notes again, 'but they'd never heard of Helen Blake. They did have a woman of a similar age, Hazel Black who just upped and quit earlier this month without leaving a forwarding address – do you reckon our Helen might have changed her name?'

'I should say there's a fair chance. Well done Ray. You'll make a detective yet. What's your next move?'

'Ah well guv that's just it. I was hoping you might point me in the right direction on that one.' Cartwright scratched his head.

'Did you actually speak to Stuart Cross? Surely he'd know where his landlord is, and surely Ben Blake would know where his mother is?'

'The Crosses weren't at home when I called there. I got the information about the son being their landlord from the barmaid at the pub in the next village – a real looker with a lovely pair of…'

'… never mind that. Keep your mind on the job! Which pub was this?' They both laughed.

'OK I suggest you get yourself back to Burton Overy at a time when Mr or Mrs Cross is likely to be at home. Might be worth talking to your barmaid again she might know where we can find Ben Blake.'

'Righto guv – will do.' The DC relished the prospect of another visit to see 'his' barmaid.

Chapter Seventeen

On the morning of Monday 11th December, in a field beside the A34 about a mile north of the village of Stanmore, it was barely daylight when farmer Jim Baldwin was out with his Border Collies. The dogs had disappeared into a patch of rough grass and started barking. Baldwin followed the dogs to where there lay the body of a man. Jim Baldwin knelt beside the body and placed his ear close the man's face. He was breathing – just. Jim ran into the road and without a thought for his own safety he stood in the carriageway and frantically waved down an approaching car whilst the collies sat like sentinels at either end of the body. The driver of the car pulled over, and irately got out and demanded to know 'what the blazes' Jim thought he was doing.

'There's a body.' Jim was still panting from the exertion of the frantic waving. 'Please, can you stop at the first telephone box and call the police and an ambulance. A man's body – badly injured – I don't think he'll last much longer without emergency treatment. I think he may have been a casualty in an accident – looks as if he's been here some time. He's in a real mess.' The car driver was immediately calmed down and he clearly understood the sense of emergency and was anxious to help. He jumped back into his car and sped off northbound. About three miles up the road he stopped at a telephone kiosk by the junction with the A4185 at Chilton. He dialled 999. Some ten yards or so further on from the body and closer to the road was a badly damaged piece of wreckage which to Jim looked like it had been a car door panel; a white one with 'go faster' stripes.

Jim Baldwin and his dogs remained with the body hoping that it wouldn't be too long before an ambulance turned up. The man's clothing which was torn was also soaking. He was thoroughly wet through. Jim removed his own coat and covered the man as best he could. The position in which his legs were lying suggested that at least one of them was broken. His breathing was very shallow. Jim felt for a pulse. He discovered one but it was extremely weak. He heard a siren in the distance and went and stood by the side of road. A white Ford Granada, with flashing blue lights pulled up. Two policemen got out and Jim led them to the body.

'If this bloke is a casualty from last Friday's accident he's got to be one of the luckiest men alive.' One of the policemen made this statement in a matter-of-fact manner. 'I was on duty that night and me and my mate were first on the scene. You've never seen anything like it...' Before he could continue with his description for Jim's benefit, the approaching ambulance's siren could be heard. The second policemen went to the road to halt any traffic and give directions to the ambulance. Two ambulance personnel and a doctor examined the unconscious form and very quickly assessed the casualty's condition as 'critical – touch and go'. The body was immobilised and eased onto a stretcher. A mask supplying oxygen was placed over the nose and mouth of the victim who was then carried on the stretcher and loaded into the ambulance. The doctor walking beside the stretcher carried the gas cylinder. The ambulance departed with siren blaring and lights flashing closely followed by the Granada, but not before the door panel had been loaded into the boot of the car. Jim and the dogs went home.

The Registrar in the intensive care unit of the John Radcliffe Hospital in Oxford was speaking to the policemen.

'It's a miracle he survived. The extent of his injuries as far as we have been able to assess so far includes a comminuted fracture of the right femur, a femoral neck fracture of the left leg, there is internal bleeding due to trauma – we're not sure whether it's from the spleen or the liver yet, and he's in the advanced stages of hypothermia. There may be more. All in all, he's in pretty poor shape.'

'What're his chances doc?' asked one of the policemen, showing serious concern.

'It's too soon to tell but given that he's lasted out in the open for three nights, he's obviously strong, I'd put the odds at slightly better than 50:50.'

'Do we know who he is; any identification?'

'Yes. He had his passport in his jacket pocket but not much else apart from a letter from an address in Belfast, a sum of money, cigarettes and lighter, oh, and you'll be more interested in this, a 9mm Browning handgun.' It's all bagged up for you to take away.'

The policemen left and went directly to St Aldate's police station and the office of DS Armstrong. The bag containing the casualty's belongings was placed on his desk and after a preliminary examination of which, Armstrong telephoned DI Cartwright at Kidlington headquarters.

It didn't take very long for the DI to work out that the crime he was investigating had just become a whole lot more complicated. He began sketching out a composite table-cum-flow diagram on a whiteboard as a visual aid to what was known and what was suspected. All the time he was mindful of something that one of his lecturers had once said at Hendon Police College – *Anyone can solve a crime – proving it requires a special talent!* At the top of the board, in red felt pen he wrote 'Duncan McClean aka Jock – wanted for murder.' From there various threads lead to 'IRA connection,' 'Gerald Doyle,' 'Michael Doyle' 'stolen US van,' 'crate of weapons,' 'Maggie O'Rourke,' 'Tom Wenzl'. Cartwright had sent for the original files on 'the-body-in-the-lock' case which had been archived as a 'cold case' by his then superior DI Mosely in Leicester. The files were on his desk and he sat down and read them, then reread them. He then returned to his whiteboard and added 'Foxton Locks,' 'Fred Webb,' 'Helen Blake.' He stood back and scratched his head whilst staring at what he'd written.

Chapter Eighteen

It was three days now since he had managed to elude those who were pursuing him. He regarded his dramatic right-hand turn off the A34 as a masterful piece of driving – but then he was, or had been a professional driver almost since the day he left school. 'OK ah wis a wee bit close tae the Atkinson but whit the hell,' he thought to himself. He'd heard the crash and the explosion but hadn't given a thought to the fate of his pursuers. Apart from the American and Mrs O'Rourke he didn't even know who they were. Nor did he care. They were gone and no longer would he be plagued by the irritation they had been.

Following the reckless turn and diversion through East Ilsley, he'd continued to Oxford where much to his annoyance he'd had to stop for petrol again. However, the stop did give him the opportunity to find a café where he enjoyed a full English breakfast – the best breakfast he'd had since Maggie had last cooked for him. He missed her in a strange sort of way. Apart from that very slight twinge of conscience he'd experienced once before, he seemingly didn't have a care in the world. Fortified by the food in his belly, relaxed and with a fresh packet of twenty in his pocket he continued towards Bicester and onto the A43 and Northampton. From there, his plan was to take the A508 to Market Harborough from where it wasn't much more than a stone's throw to Foxton. There was the odd butterfly in the pit of his stomach when he thought of the proximity of Foxton to the devil's tunnel at Saddington, but he had vowed he would never ever commit himself to travelling through that tunnel again, or any other if they could be avoided, as long as he lived. At Foxton he was expecting to renew his acquaintance with his old mate Fred Webb, the Foxton lockkeeper. He was also hoping that Pat Henderson or Wally Whitehead were still plying their trade up and down the Grand Union. He had a cargo he wanted delivering.

And so it was that, on Monday 11th December 1972, a fugitive from justice drove into the carpark behind the Foxton Locks Inn. He was driving a black American Ford Econoline E20 5 litre V8 panel van, allegedly stolen from an American, a traveller in ladies' fashion. The van was carrying a large consignment of weapons trafficked into the UK via the Harrison Network in America, originally destined for the IRA but hijacked by one Duncan 'Jock' McClean, aided and abetted by one Tom Wenzl, with the intention of selling the said weapons to an alternative terrorist organisation after he had been persuaded to do so by the said American. Tom Wenzl was in fact a double-agent and had promised Jock rewards far in excess of what he might have received from the IRA. Not that he was particularly interested, but Jock supposed he might bother to find out who they were, one day. Black September.

'Dae ah care? Nae!' he said aloud as he locked the van. 'It'll be one ay they bloody rock bands!' Although he couldn't begin to understand how even The Beatles would need the sort and quantity of weaponry he was selling. As far as Jock was concerned any purchaser with the right amount of cash would do nicely, thank you!

As always, Fred Webb was in the Waterways office early, glasses on the end of his nose, reading the *Daily Mirror*. The headline on page 8 pronounced 'Ulster Kids Obsessed by Death', not that Fred was particularly interested in 'the Troubles'. He had troubles enough of his own. There had been a short piece on page 2 however that he had been most definitely interested in, under the headline 'Gun Running Suspect Causes Horrific Smash'. As he moved to the sports pages his concentration was interrupted.

'Well the noo, wull ye nae lookie here, ma old pal Fred!'

Fred slowly raised his eyes from the paper, removed his specs and turned to give Jock a long, hard stare.

'I wondered how long it 'ud be afore yo' turned up 'ere agin.' Apparently Fred wasn't too pleased to see Jock.

'Och man, whit's up wi' ye? Are ye nae pleased to see me?'

Fred didn't answer. He licked a gnarled forefinger and flicked the pages back to page 2, He then spun the paper round towards Jock and with the same finger stabbed at a particular article.

Following a fatal road traffic accident on the A34 south of Didcot on Wednesday Thames Valley Police are anxious to trace a 48-year-old man driving a black American Ford Econoline E20 panel van registration 2239-TL New York. The van was last seen at a petrol station in Oxford and is understood to be traveling northwards. The man is wanted in connection with various crimes and is believed to be armed and dangerous. Under no circumstances should members of the public approach the man who is known as Duncan 'Jock' McClean. Any sightings should be reported to Thames Valley Police, your local police station or by dialling 999. All calls will be treated in confidence.

*

Kate Cross was also out early, on her constitutional walk with Byron the Labrador. Most mornings she walked down into Burton Overy to the village shop and bought milk and bread and picked up a newspaper which she very rarely read. Her choice of paper varied from day to day depending on the extent of her success with the cryptic crossword in the previous day's choice of paper. On Monday 11th December she picked up the *Guardian*. Saturday's *Telegraph* had proved to be too much of a challenge. Back at Marsh Cottage, she made coffee and sat down with the paper and scrolled through the pages. It was the inverted commas around the name 'Jock' that caught her eye and caused her to pause and read the piece – twice. She was immediately on the phone to Ben but there was no reply.

*

Meanwhile, Ciara Doyle was laying out the daily newspapers in the Linen Hall Library in Donegall Square. As was her habit she picked up the *Irish Mirror* and idly glanced through it. She replaced it on the rack and went to open up the front doors. Halfway there she stopped dead in her tracks and returned to the newspaper rack and picked the *Irish Mirror* again and this time frantically flicked through the pages and back again eventually stopping at page 2 where she was drawn to a short paragraph, 'Gun Running Suspect Causes Horrific Smash'. Having read it – twice – she was immediately on the phone to her father Michael, who, in turn rang a half-dozen of his paramilitary stalwarts for a meeting at midday.

Chapter Nineteen

After another extremely fitful and restless night with little sleep despite being in a luxuriously appointed suite at the Chesterton Hotel in Bicester, Tom Wenzl showered, shaved and dressed and merely pricked and prodded at what the menu described as 'a hearty traditional English breakfast' as he pushed it around the plate. He picked up a copy of the *Daily Telegraph* from reception and went to the lounge from where he ordered another pot of coffee. When he came upon the police's press release in the paper he almost lost control of his calm and collected outward appearance by knocking over his coffee cup the contents of which spilled onto his trousers scalding his leg. He made a half-hearted apology to the waitress who rushed over to clear up the mess as he returned to his suite.

He removed his trousers and sponged his leg with cold water until the burning sensation had eased. He telephoned down to reception and asked to be connected to the Blackstaff Bar in Belfast. After some buzzing and clicking the connection was made and he could hear the ringing tone. After what seemed like minutes but what in reality was only seconds, the phone was answered.

'Blackstaff, Ciara Doyle speaking.'

'Is Michael there please?'

'Who shall I say is calling?'

'Wenzl. It's urgent,' he insisted. Again, the pause seemed to last forever, but was only a few seconds before Michael was on the line.

'Tom, you're safe!'

'Have you seen the piece in the paper?'

109

'I have, to be sure, in the *Irish Mirror*. What the feck happened?'

Tom proceeded to relate the full details as he had when making his statement to Detective Sergeant Armstrong.

'So, Jock was ripping us off all the time. Have you seen Gerry, my brother? He tailed Jock all the way from here. We know he followed him to Southampton, any idea what happened after that? We haven't heard from him since… When was it, Ciara?'

'The 5th – last Tuesday I think,' Ciara, standing at her father's shoulder responded.

'Did you hear that Tom?' A silence followed. 'Tom, Tom, you still there?'

'Yes sir, I'm still here but I don't know how to tell you this.'

'Tell me what man? C'mon, c'mon straight out with it.'

Tom described the drive from Southampton. Not wishing to incriminate himself he took every care to ensure that his words did nothing to reveal that he and Jock were now in league to rip off the IRA. In his stinted, deliberate and broken delivery he stated that Jock had stolen the Econoline van. The van had then been loaded with a crate from Williams' Shipping Warehouse. He described how he had attempted to follow in the empty Transit van; empty that is apart from Maggie O'Rourke. Doyle interrupted.

'So, let me get this straight, not only has he got away with the shipment you brought in, but he had another one in storage as well?'

'That's about the size of it sir.'

'The feckin' thievin' bastard – I'll wager that Billy Kelly's in on it as well for sure. I'll have Gerry execute them both as soon as I can contact him.'

'That might not be quite that simple,' suggested Tom.

'What the feck you on about?' Michael's voice was raised as he began to rage. Tom was sure the Irishman could be heard down the corridor from his suite. He hesitated before responding.

'There was an accident.'

Tom went on to give the facts to the Nationalist agitator in a statement pretty much identical to the one he'd given to DS Armstrong.

'Are you trying to tell me my brother's dead?'

'I can't see how anyone could have come out of that collision alive. You should have seen the state of those ve-hi-cals! I was lucky to get out alive. If your brother survived it'd have been a bloody miracle!'

Silence. Wenzl wondered if the line had been disconnected, and then it was Ciara who spoke next.

'Tom,' she spluttered, 'daddy's too upset to speak just now. Give me your number and he'll call you back in a while. Stay by the phone!'

It was after lunch that the phone rang in Tom's suite at the Chesterton. It was Ciara.

'We've put out some anonymous feelers which I don't think can be traced back to us. We know for sure that Mrs O'Rourke died. Seems she was having a baby as well. That's too bad. She was a really nice lady – used to come into the Blackstaff with that bloody traitor. Anyway, it seems that Gerry was a survivor and you were right, it was a miracle to be sure that saved him. He was thrown clear when the door exploded from the car, but he wasn't discovered for two days. Fifty yards away in a field, can you believe it? He has very serious injuries and he's in intensive care at John Radcliffe Hospital in Oxford.'

'I'm truly sorry to hear that... I mean not sorry that he survived... sorry that's he's very badly injured.' Tom's sympathy was genuine.

'Dad is going to be getting a platoon together and they'll be coming by ferry from Belfast to Liverpool to meet up with you – should be there within a week. Dad wants to know if you have any idea where your van and the "parcels" might be?'

'Not yet, but I'll be working on it.'

'Oh, and another thing, dad says don't be talking any more to the police. You probably told then too much already.'

'Tell Michael not to worry – I know what I'm doing. So far I've told the cops the truth. They're not interested in me. I've made certain that I'm above suspicion. Their priority is Jock

McClean and then the weapons they suspect are in the van. It's my reckoning that the van and McClean are not that far away from each other.'

'OK, seems the police's priorities are identical to our own then. Be careful Tom. We'll call again when our guys are in Liverpool.'

Tom paced up and down his suite for several minutes. 'Be careful.' Ciara Doyle had said. 'Oh yes ma'am, I will that and no mistake,' he thought out loud. He needed to find Jock. Even more importantly he needed to find the van before the police did and certainly before the bully boys that were on their way from Belfast did. Phase two needed implementing. He rang down to reception and asked for a call to be put through to DS Armstrong at St Aldate's Police Station in Oxford.

'CID, DS Armstrong speaking.'

'Hi there sergeant. Tom Wenzl here. Just a-wonderin' if there's any news on my ve-hi-cal.'

'I'm afraid not yet Mr Wenzl. We have put out an APB I think you call it, and hopefully it won't be too long before we get a sighting. We'll call you when there's any news. You still at the Chesterton?'

'I surely am sergeant – and thank you kindly sir.' Time to make a move he thought.

'What is it about Wenzl's accent? It just doesn't...' Armstrong thought.

Chapter Twenty

In the Waterways office at Foxton Locks, Jock's complexion had turned a ghostly white.

'Och, shite!' was all he could utter, and even that was with a catch in his voice.

'Yo' better sit down afore yo' fall down,' Fred suggested. Fred Webb was the lockkeeper at Foxton and had been so seemingly forever. What he didn't know about all the comings and goings on the Leicester Arm of the Grand Union wasn't worth knowing. He put the kettle on and selected two of the cleaner and least chipped mugs from the shelf above the sink. For the next half-an-hour, over their mugs of tea, Fred brought Jock up to speed with events centred around the abandoned *Emily Rose* and his disappearance, the gun, Helen, the police, all of which had happened almost nine years previously. The subsequent half-an-hour was taken up with Jock's recollection of everything from his perspective during those nine years. Fred couldn't remember when he'd laughed quite so much as he visualised the collision in the Saddington Tunnel between the *Emily Rose* and the *Nancy Blakemore* with Jock being precipitated into *Nancy's* hold.

Jock sat for quite a while in the Waterways Office. The output from the single bar electric heater was hardly producing sufficient warmth to keep the cold draught from around the ill-fitting door and window at bay but despite that, Jock was getting hot under the collar and beads of cold sweat were glistening on his forehead. Eventually, after some hard thinking he spoke.

'Fred ma pal, is the *Emily Rose* still here aboots?'

'She is that, up at Number 8.' Jock recalled that Number 8 was the Foxton Top Lock. Mindful of Fred's earlier discourse he asked if he could take a look 'fur auld time's sake.'

He walked up the towpath beside the Foxton flight and, sure enough, looking very sorry for herself was *Emily Rose*. He climbed aboard and down into the cabin. The air was fetid. He searched down behind the companionway, removed the floorboards to reveal the hidden compartment. Empty! But then he had expected it to be. Helen wasn't stupid. Not bothering to replace the floorboards, he went back into the cabin and rolled a cigarette which he smoked sitting on the bed and reminiscing. He then rolled and smoked a second cigarette.

"Ow yo' a-getting on in there Jock?' It was Fred.

'Och jist a few clothes ah'd left behind. Is the Ariel still on board?'

'I reckon.'

'Gis a hand to get her off wid ye?

With more than a bit of a struggle and with the aid of a length of scaffold board which Fred had days ago fished out of the Top Lock the two men managed to get the motorbike on to the towpath. Jock handed Fred five £20 notes.

'Ah'm relying on ye Fred. There'll be more when we've cracked this wee caper. Nae a bloody word tae anyone. Oh, and there's a black van parked behind the pub. Here's the keys. Ah'll be back tae unload it at Christmas. Perhaps ye'll gae us a hand?' With that, Jock turned on the bike's petrol tap, kicked the Ariel over five or six times and was about to start cursing when, on the seventh kick she started. Fred stuck two fingers in the air by way of a wave goodbye.

It had been more than several years since Jock had ridden a motorcycle. *The excitement, the thrill of the open road, the wind in your hair....*

'It's all bollocks!' thought Jock recalling a Triumph advertisement he'd seen somewhere. 'Ah'm feckin' freezin' ma rocks off here.' But then he was hardly dressed for motorcycling, particularly given that it had begun to rain again. He took the A4304 then the A5 to Hinckley and directly to Ross Motors, a motorcycle dealership. After some sticky negotiating, mainly resulting from the fact that Jock was 'selling for his friend, Ron Nicholls,' a deal was done. A few hours later, the Ariel had been advertised in the classifieds of the local paper at a significantly higher price than the one for which it had been bought. Little did Jock realise that this transaction would possibly provide a lead for those attempting to bring about his ultimate downfall.

From Hinckley he caught the Midland Red 658 service to Leicester – a route he had driven for the bus company more times than he cared to remember. It was like he still knew every stop. At Triangle Motors, a used car dealership, on the outskirts of Leicester, he used the proceeds from the sale of the Ariel to put down a deposit on a Porsche 911 which he would collect the following day. It seemed that being conspicuous was no longer an issue.

Chapter Twenty-One

As soon as Ben and Tina were back home on Tuesday 12th December, Ben telephoned Kate and Stuart and then his mum. He too had now seen the press release and he apprised his mum of what he and Tina were intending to do. He'd already made arrangements with Kate and she had readily agreed that Stuart and herself would move into the cottage's spare room for the weekend, and at any other time Ben, Tina or Hazel required to stay at the Burton Overy cottage.

The sitting room in the Lobster Pot cottage was decidedly chilly. The wood-burning stove was down to its last embers of life. Ben went out to the woodshed. The door was open. 'I'm sure I closed it this morning. Tina wouldn't have opened it, she doesn't bring logs in,' he thought. With a shrug of the shoulders he filled the log basket, closed the shed door and went back indoors to tend to the wood-burner.

Three days later, on Friday 15th December the three of them arrived, in two cars, the MGB and Hazel's new Mercedes-Benz 230SL which she had bought on her release from East Sutton Park. Frank, Hazel's long-time friend and confidante had previously sold the Mini for her when she was sent down. Having dumped their weekend bags in their old rooms, the first stop was to be the Three Greyhounds for something to eat – as soon as Ben could tear himself away from checking the Steinway with a quick burst from Schumann's *Carnival*.

All five piled into Stuart's Austin Maxi and they set off for Great Glen and the Greyhounds. They hadn't driven but 200 yards when Stuart had to take some fairly drastic action to avoid colliding with a maniac who came tearing round a blind bend, on the wrong side of the road, without any lights on.

'Crikey, bloody idiot! Driving it like he stole it!' observed Stuart.

'Glad you saw it, because I didn't. What was it?' asked Ben.

'Couldn't really tell. Some kind of low-slung sports car.'

They arrived at the pub safely for all that Stuart was a bit shaken up by the close encounter. It hadn't changed at all from the way Ben remembered it except in three details; the first, the licensee's name above the door was now 'James D Webster'.

'Jamie?' queried Ben to himself, remembering his old best friend. 'It can't be, surely not?' Secondly, swinging in the wind, the pub sign was new.

The five barged in out of the cold. For all that the place was almost deserted the festive decorations twinkled and... 'Surprise, surprise!' There behind the bar stood Jamie and Diane. There was clearly a lot of catching up to do before any decisions or plans could be made for the following day!

'Jamie! You old bugger!' exclaimed Ben adopting a familiar Midlands' term of endearment.

'Sorry?' responded Jamie. 'Do I know ... is it?... Ben? Well tickle my arse with a feather! Di, look it's Ben and Tina, and...' Jamie struggled to remember the name momentarily, 'Helen.'

'Used to be – it's Hazel now – a long story!' she corrected.

'And you've met Kate and Stuart before' Ben reminded his friends.

'Of course! What're you all doing here? How is everybody? Bugger me!' Jamie's pleasure was absolutely genuine. They all sat around the pub's big table and the evening progressed in the same manner as would any other reunion, with plenty of drinking and reminiscing. Jamie explained how the other change Ben had noted came about.

'When George, the former landlord of the Three Greyhounds had decided to retire, I saw an opportunity to get away from my dad's hosiery business and take over the pub. After all, Diane, my gorgeous girlfriend had been the barmaid here for several years. So, we got married and became the licensees, didn't we Di? We changed the name from the Three Greyhounds to the Old Greyhound. We fell on our feet and found our niche. We're enjoying life aren't we Di?' Jamie continued, 'I was offered a piano for the pub last year, wasn't I Di?' A rhetorical question-cum-statement. 'We need an attraction to bring in some custom. I said at the time, what a shame Ben's away, he could have played for us, didn't I Di?' Ben was beginning to wonder who wore the trousers in this marriage. It seemed Jamie needed Diane's confirmation or approval of everything.

'He did!' Diane's confirmation was forthcoming.

'Ah well, I doubt you could afford me,' Ben retorted.

'Now, I guess you're all hungry' suggested Diane as she passed around copies of the menu.

'It all looks very nice,' observed Kate.

Choices were made and Diane took the order through to the kitchen. The evening wore on with questions and answers; about working in London, commuting, living on the coast and any manner of topics were raised to include contributions from everyone. Every now and again, one or other of 'mine hosts' would retreat behind the bar to serve, but it was a cold, damp December night and even the hardy drinking souls of Great Glen and its environs were few and far between. The food was served and for a while conversation all but ceased whilst meals were appreciatively consumed. The front door opened.

'Aha!' observed Jamie. 'A customer!' and the unmistakably portly figure of George, the erstwhile landlord was revealed once he'd hung up his cap and coat. Jamie served him with a bottle of Guinness and invited him to join the party around the big table. He did and instantly diverted the discourse to the fortunes of Leicester City Football Club. Ben had no interest whatsoever in Association Football; at his school, one had played rugby union! He made an apology and went to the toilet.

'We shouldn't 'ave bin 'eld to a bloody draw at Birmingham last wik. Carry on playing like that'll get us regulated.'

'You mean relegated, you silly old fool,' corrected Jamie.

'Wharever!' George rambled on. 'Any road up, we've got Sheffield bloody United tomorra, they're no great shakes, should be a piece a piss. If the lads keep up winning ways we'll be back t' top o' league next season.' George's assurance was something of an obvious statement even to Ben, who had now returned. However, he was determined to talk about anything but football and was about to launch straight in and discuss the contents of the press release. Then he thought better of it what with George at the table. He came up with a more innocent topic.

'How are you coping with decimal currency Jamie?' Everyone had just about come to terms with the new coinage since the country had abandoned pounds, shillings and pence in 1971. Decimalisation and metrication in general aroused some very mixed opinions which were expressed from all around the table.

'The money's easy,' remarked Stuart. 'Multiples of ten, same as with measurement,' he observed. 'Still,' he continued with an air of mystification, 'why do we still travel miles, drink pints and why do we have CCTV footage and weigh stuff in pounds and ounces?' George, feeling a little put out by the interruption to his exposition on football, demonstrated his general ignorance of decimalisation.

'Don't get it meself. Any road, I reckon you'll lose a fortune missus.' He directed his remark to Hazel. 'All that gold what were in that crate, that's sort o' currency innit? 'Ow does that decimalisate or wharever?' The table went very quiet and there were anxious looks between Ben, his wife and his mother. The facial attitudes of everyone else expressed a mixture of surprise and curiosity. George was referring to the crate that Ken, Ben's father and Hazel's estranged then deceased husband had left at the pub for safe keeping soon after the war.

'So, all that time ago when we came to remove the crate from your stables were you lying when you told me you didn't know what was in it?' demanded Hazel, her voiced raised accusingly. She was clearly irritated.

'Steady on missus' said George. 'I din't know, 'onest I din't, not 'til that bloke turned up, when were it?' he pondered, 'Wednesday, this wick.'

'What bloke?'

'Do yo' remember 'is name Di? Scotch 'e were. 'E came looking for the crate. Said arf of what were in it were 'is, like. It were 'im as told me it were gold. I thought 'e were a-jokin' like! Shame we dint 'ave CCTV – in feet or centiwhatsits – I could a showed you 'im. Turned up in one o' them flash motors – what' d'yo' call 'em… a porch or summat like that.'

'A Porsche, you silly old fool,' corrected Jamie.

Jamie already knew about the crate's contents having assisted with its removal years ago. He sensed the tension building around the table and was regretting having invited George to sit with them. He also had a fair idea that everyone might want to be discussing the press release and the ramifications of the recent road accident that Jock had apparently caused so he took it upon himself to instigate a tactful withdrawal for George. He knew he could rely on Ben to keep him up to speed on developments as his curiosity was as great as anyone's.

'Another Guinness George? Let's go to the bar and leave these good folks to their evening out.' Ben gave Jamie a look that said, 'Thank you'. Diane smiled and leant her ample cleavage across the table as she began to clear it. Kate gave Stuart a withering look which implied 'Keep your eyes off!' Jamie's wife disappeared into the kitchen with the remaining dirty crockery. The others remained sat around the big table. To a casual observer they may have appeared like a mature version of Enid Blyton's *Famous Five*. Reviewing what they knew, what they thought they knew and what they suspected, several theories were expounded, discussed and subsequently ruled out. 'That idea must have been nurtured in the greenhouse of fantasy land!' scoffed Stuart at a suggestion of Kate's. He was obviously getting his own back. But there were certain theories upon which they were all agreed. The open woodshed, the Porsche, the Scotsman asking about gold and if that wasn't enough, the press release which quite categorically and unambiguously stating that Jock McClean was in the country, armed and dangerous – these were far too many incidences to be coincidental. Surely the evidence now was beyond circumstantial and represented a real threat, especially to Hazel.

'Well there we are then,' said Kate. 'We know he's been round here. Can't we just ring the police?'

In unison, the other four intoned just one word – 'No!'

Chapter Twenty-Two

When they arrived back at Marsh Cottage, Kate offered to make cocoa for those who would like some. Ben and Stuart declined, preferring a tot of brandy instead. As they sat with their respective nightcaps, Hazel thought she should take Kate and Stuart into her confidence and share the secret with them. After all, the gold and other precious items from the crate had been a taboo subject for so long until a couple of hours ago. But now, with George having let the cat out of the bag, it only seemed right that Kate and Stuart should be included amongst the five other people in the know. The revelation that Jock had been to the Old Greyhound laying claim to what he considered to be 'his share' was deeply disturbing.

'So,' pondered Ben, 'Jock might have disappeared into thin air in 1964 but he's back from beyond, armed and dangerous, and sooner or later it's highly likely that he'll turn up here.'

'Well, we will have to make sure the police find him before he finds us,' concluded Tina.

'He sounds like a thoroughly disagreeable fellow,' surmised Kate.

'Oh yes! He is certainly that,' confirmed Hazel, 'and worse. He'd sell his own grandmother for a pound.'

'Where do we start then?' asked Stuart.

'You really don't want to get mixed up in this,' said Ben.

'But we are anyway. Just remember it was I who found the narrowboat,'

'We!' corrected Kate.

'OK, we who found the narrowboat and informed the police, so we must also be involved in the search for this illusive

Scotsman,' Stuart insisted. 'What's more, the greater the number there are of us, it'll be easier than it seems.'

'We'll start with a visit to Foxton. Fred might know something.' Hazel had taken charge.

'Tomorrow!' they chorused.

The weather on Saturday 16th December was hardly conducive to investigative excursions and the group looked much less like Ms Blyton's quintet. After an early breakfast they all got into Stuart's Maxi and headed off through Great Glen and down the A6 towards Foxton. Stuart parked the car beside a black van behind the *Foxton Locks Inn* and they all walked around to the pub's frontage on to the canal. Hazel spotted him straightaway. There he was, outside the Waterways Board office, Fred Webb, just as she remembered him, barely looking a day older. Leaving Hazel and Ben to talk to Fred, the others took a walk up the flight of locks. Fred was well wrapped against the elements. He appeared to be almost a permanent fixture, sitting on an Everard's beer crate. As ever, he was leaning back against the wall of the old boathouse on the opposite side of the canal; the building which served as the Waterways office. Engrossed in whittling a stick, he was in a world of his own. Hazel greeted the lockkeeper fondly. He was an old acquaintance, a friend even, after all.

'Hello Fred,' Hazel called as she and Ben crossed the lock to the opposite side of the canal. He looked up from his whittling and his unshaven and grizzled visage broke into a beaming smile. He closed the blade and slipped the knife into his pocket. He squinted at the two people approaching.

'Is that yoursel'? Helen, it can't be? It's been a long time.'

'Yes, it has but I'm now called Hazel – I've changed my name.'

'Aha, you'll still be a-duckin' an' a-divin' then?' Fred chuckled in a knowing sort of way. After a somewhat embarrassing hug, Hazel, sitting on the spare visitors' beer crate, listened intently as Fred delivered what could well have passed as a eulogy for commercial freight traffic on the canal network.

'One o' the last regular commercial boats, the *Nancy Blakemore* came through in October, deliverin' to jam factory up London. It's all bloody pleasure boaters these days. An' 'alf of 'em 'aven't got a bloody clue. I swear one of 'em will barge straight through a gate one o' these days or leave a paddle up or summat else stupid. They runs me ragged some of 'em. No chance of a bit on the side either, if you knows what I means.' Hazel remembered how he and Jock had something of their own private and very lucrative racket going on.

'Still, Waterways Board keeps paying me, but they're now threatenin' to pension me off. Good job I got a little nest egg stashed away, thanks to you an' Jock.' He gave Hazel a wink and a smile.

Ben noticed Stuart walking towards them. He whispered to Ben that Kate and Tina were looking at a particular 'exhibit' up by the disused inclined plane boat- lift. Whilst that piece of genius engineering from the early 1900s was fascinating, the particular exhibit which was attracting Kate and Tina's attention was an old narrowboat. The *Emily Rose* was in grave need of some serious loving care and attention.

'Excuse me butting in Mr Webb,' said Ben, 'but the last time I was here, the first time I met you, I'm sure you promised to sell mum's old boat for her.'

'Cor blimey Helen... sorry Hazel. Is this your boy all growed up an' with a moustache? What's your name again?'

'The name's Ben.' They shook hands.

By now the girls had returned and they were bewildered yet rapt by the conversation that was taking place. Initially, Hazel was visibly agitated at the thought that *Emily Rose* was still at Foxton. Tina took her arm. Kate looked on and was scribbling some notes on the back of an envelope she'd taken from her handbag. In response to Ben's comment Fred continued but it was plain to see that he was uncharacteristically nervous.

'I tried, 'onest to goodness I did. Were in my own interests weren't it? I mean Helen... sorry, your mam said I could keep whatever I got for her. Problem was, nobody'd touch it. Not at any price. Spooked, haunted they reckoned it were. Came through the Saddington wi' nobody on it. Bin involved in a murder enquiry an' all. No, Ben, yes I did. I promised to sell her and gawd knows I tried. Very superstitious, canal folk. Some say Jock must have bin whisked off by the ghost of the headless woman what haunts the tunnel. Others reckon he fell overboard in there and drownded dead. Sometimes, there's a right stink wi' flashing lights an' stuff in that tunnel. They do say it's from that there chemical spillage that 'appened all them years ago when the boat carrying poison an' stuff hit summat underwater and sank They do say it's still toxic. Maybe Jock breathed in some o' that? Anyway, I couldn't get anyone interested in buying the boat at all. So now she sits up by the museum as a piece o' canal history an' myst'ry. That motorbike's a bit o' wartime memorybilly an' all. Still on board where it were left. Can't do any 'arm can it?' Fred was clearly upset at the thought of his having let Hazel down or was it something else?

The lockkeeper's dissertation had captured everyone's imagination but before anyone could offer an answer to his 'can't do any 'arm?' it had begun to rain, and with the wind as cold as it was they all retreated into the pub. Once drinks and sandwiches had been ordered Fred continued with his protracted apologies and explanations.

'I dunno whether there's any truth in it, but canal folks still go on about the headless woman who haunts Saddington Tunnel. I reckon it's a load of ol' tosh me-sel' but then I've knowed boatman arrive here scared out o' their wits saying 'ow they've seen 'er. The bats don't 'elp either. Bloody hundreds of 'em flittin' about and screeching. But we do know for a fact about the chemicals in the water. It were only fifty year ago an' I were not much more than a lad, but I remember my dad who were the lockkeeper here afore me telling how a boat belonging to Fellows, Morton and Clayton 'it summat submerged in the tunnel and sank. It were carrying chemical stuff. Sometimes yo' can see flashing lights down the tunnel and folks reckon it's to do wi' chemicals goin' off or summat. It chucks up a diabolic stink an' all now an' again. I doubt we could 'ave given her away, the old *Emily Rose*.'

'Have the police been back at all, asking questions?' Hazel enquired.

'Nah! I reckon they just wanted someone to bang up just fer appearances sake. Sadly it had to be you Hele… sorry Hazel. I don't reckon them are bothered about finding Jock – but I knows they still think it were Jock what shot the lad that had the motorbike – what were 'is name… Ron somebody? Remember, Waterways blokes pulled what were left of 'is body out of Newton Top Half Mile. Bullet hole in 'is 'ead.'

'Yes I know, I found the gun, a German Luger from World War Two,' said Stuart proudly.

None of the group had previously been aware of much of that which had been disclosed in Fred's diatribe and they sat discussing it whilst he went to the gents.

'I think we should go and take another look at the boat whilst we're here,' suggested Ben.

'And perhaps we could make a detour on the way home and I can show you where the boat ran onto the mud down by the tunnel,' added Stuart.

'Good idea,' acknowledged Ben.

Hazel gave Fred a hug. Despite having let down the woman with whom he had been a very close friend Fred was mightily relieved that during this encounter with her he had managed not to betray Jock by divulging any detail of his visit a few days earlier. After all, he was on Jock's payroll. Even so, Fred really didn't enjoy being caught up in the middle.

'It's been lovely to see you again Fred. Don't go beating yourself up about being unable to get rid of the boat, I don't think it'll matter too much now anyway. You look after yourself and enjoy your retirement. You've earned it!'

With that, the not-so-famous-five walked up the flight to take another look at *Emily Rose*.

'Oh what a sorry sight she is now.' Hazel's observation was tinged with sadness. The paintwork was faded and there were scratches and gouges down the whole length of the hull on the port side. The traditional decorations of roses and castles that she herself had painted were beginning to peel. On board there was an odour of staleness; a fusty smell. Everywhere was dusty and there was an abundance of cobwebs but there were signs on some of the surfaces that the dust had been disturbed. Tina noticed two hand-rolled cigarette ends stubbed out on the cabin sole. The interior of the cabin was pretty much as Hazel remembered it and she had momentary flashbacks to living in the small, cramped space – partial recall, but a few happy memories as well as those she'd rather forget. But then, when she looked at Ben she was overcome with guilt and remorse. She should never have been on the boat in the first place. Stuart and Kate went rooting about in the cargo hold. The cover was worn due to years of weathering and fading by sunlight. It was almost threadbare and beginning to tear or perish in places. Tina was poking about in cupboards, lockers, under cushions and all manner of nooks and crannies. From the potbellied stove she withdrew a partially burnt scrap of paper.

'Well now, will you look at what I've found!' she exclaimed excitedly. Ben looked over her shoulder to see what it was that his wife had discovered. She was holding a smouldered scrap of squared paper, it looked like it had originally been ripped from an exercise book. On the paper, the pencilled scribble could just about be deciphered. '3GH-GG'. Hazel took the paper from Tina and instantly recognised where it might have come from. She immediately went to the hidden compartment behind the companionway steps, except it was no longer hidden. The floorboards covering the hiding place had been removed and not replaced.

'He's been here!' Hazel's statement was quite categorical.

'How do you know? How can you be so sure?' queried Tina

'He's been here!' Hazel reaffirmed. 'Jock used to keep a record of what we sold and the cash that we took and he made notes in a school exercise book with squared paper. Stuart made a further contribution that without any doubt someone, if not Jock had been on board.

'Didn't Fred say the motorbike was still on board? Because it's not here now!'

'And I'm fairly sure that there were some of his clothes still here when we came here before you were sent…' Ben couldn't bring himself to complete the sentence.

'Where are they now?'

'Only me and Jock knew of that secret compartment. It's where he kept his cash and other valuables. Even the police never found it when they did their search. So, it must have been Jock.' Hazel concluded. All were convinced.

The rain had eased a little but the temperature hadn't improved. The wind was bitterly cold. They started on their way back to the car but not before Stuart had gone to great lengths of examining the grass verge where the motorbike might have been unloaded from the boat. At one point it almost looked like he was about to produce a magnifying glass from his overcoat. Kate was giggling.

'What'd you find there Sherlock?' she jested when Stuart caught up with the group.

'You can laugh! I thought there might be tyre marks or something. There was a scaffold plank lying close by though.' On the way back to the car Ben popped into the Inn hoping Fred would still be there. He was.

'Mr Webb, sorry to bother you again but have you seen anyone poking about on *Emily Rose*? It looks as though someone's been aboard fairly recently.' Fred lifted his cap and scratched his head.

'Mr Webb? Blimey, call me Fred for gawd's sake. Can't say I 'ave lad, but then I can't say I 'avent.' This was Fred's dilemma. 'Be honest or say nowt.' He thought. 'There were somebody up by the boat-lift museum only last week. We don't get many visitors this time o' year so I's bound to notice anybody specially when it's chuckin' it down."

'Could it have been Jock?'

'Now there's a question.' Fred was being deliberately obtuse. 'I knows Jock. It might've bin 'im I s'pose. But I can't say. I'd 'ave thought if it were, 'e'd 'ave come down to say hello. We were mates fer a long time yo' know.'

'OK, thanks Fred. If you hear any news of Jock or something else which you think we should know about, can you let us know please?'

'I'll do owt I can to 'elp your mam, don't yo' be a-worryin' on that score.'

Ben ran to catch up with the others. Fred gave him a wave but he was riddled with guilt. He'd already been slipped £100 with a promise of more to come. He couldn't jeopardise that prospect, could he? He wrestled with his guilty conscience.

With everyone back in the car Stuart took the road through Gumley and turned right by the Queen's Head in Saddington village to drive down to the Smeeton Road Bridge where he parked on the verge. Kate stayed in the car and added to the notes on her envelope. The others slipped and slid in the wet grass down the cutting to the bank of the canal where they could clearly see the southeast portal of the tunnel.

'Can you feel it?' asked Hazel.

'I've just gone all goose-pimply,' Tina shivered. Stuart described how, on that Sunday morning, he and Kate were walking the dog and as they crossed over the top of the tunnel on the horse-path they spotted the *Emily Rose* aground on the mud at the side of the canal. A sudden gust of wind seemed to escape from the tunnel, carrying with it a damp smell of effluent or something equally unpleasant. The daylight was fading.

'I don't like it here, there's something unnatural about the feel of the place.'

'Oh come on now Tina! I came through that tunnel a couple of times with Jock on the *Emily Rose* and each time he got the jitters,' recalled Hazel. 'I'll agree that it is something of an eerie experience, but I never saw or felt any ghost, man or woman, with or without a head; just that smell really, well that and the noise of the bats. It must have been the second time we came through, Jock all but "lost it". I told him not to be so stupid. He really was getting paranoid about this tunnel. But then if I remember correctly, the engine did cut out for no reason and then restart just as suddenly.'

'Crikey!' shuddered Tina. 'That is spooky!' – a sentiment with which they all concurred.

The team made their way back up the slippery slope of the cutting to the car and decided they'd done enough for one day and it was time to head home, get warm, and have something to eat. Later that evening they sat around the living room table and took stock of what they had seen, heard and deduced from the day at Foxton. The general consensus was that the evidence gathered on the boat confirmed what they already knew. Jock had indeed been back, probably looking for his money box; the box which Hazel and Ben had appropriated before Hazel went to prison. Ben reported his last final exchange with Fred, and whilst he wouldn't confirm that Jock had been back to the boat, he couldn't rule it out either. The clinching argument however if one was needed was the scrap of paper. '3GH-GG'. This was so obviously a reference to the Three Greyhounds at Great Glen. Had Jock been there as George the ex-landlord had indeed stated? All were agreed he most probably had. What further proof was required?

Discussion then moved on to their respective reactions to the tunnel; it's rumours, myths and legends. Everyone felt that where they had stood, on the canal bank looking at the tunnel portal was hardly an ideal location for a picnic. At the same time none could offer any explanation sufficiently compelling to convince the others one way or another that headless ghosts, bats or chemical pollution had anything to do with Jock's disappearance.

Kate suggested that there was now more than enough evidence of Jock being in the vicinity that they could go to the police and get them to instigate a county-wide search. Hazel was not at all keen on this idea. Were they to involve the police now George's evidence would be critical and the last thing Hazel wanted was any reference to gold. To mention the treasure looted from the Nazis would almost certainly carry with it implications that would be contrary to her interests. Yes, she'd been found guilty of handling stolen goods and served time for it. But handling forty gold bars stolen at the end of the war, not just the handling but selling and keeping the proceeds of the sale was something else altogether. Given Hazel's reluctance, Kate withdrew her suggestion – for the time being. So, what would they do?

Chapter Twenty-Three

'OK ma Yankee pal. It's where ah said it'd be. See ye there in a couple ay days.' The phone went dead and Tom replaced the receiver. He was now in something of a quandary. As far as Michael Doyle and the IRA were concerned he was the good guy – delivering a shipment in person from America in his van. What they were ignorant of was the collusion between himself and McClean; that they had become partners. Jock's sole intention was and always had been to get rich. His gain would be the IRA's loss. Tom on the other hand was motivated from an entirely different perspective and a political one at that. The entire 'stolen' van scenario which he reported to the police, whilst partially truthful, was a scam; a caper by which several consignments of illegally imported weapons could be appropriated and delivered to an organisation with which Tom had sympathy. He wasn't just a sympathiser either. He was connected. In fact he was a member. Now, should he go and liaise with McClean in a couple of days, or should he stay in Bicester and meet the IRA delegation when it arrived from Liverpool? This was Tom's dilemma. He rang reception and requested that a bottle of Jim Beam be sent to his suite. Resolving this predicament would take some serious thought and having developed a predilection for bourbon he felt the bottle might assist him with his deliberations.

*

DC Davies knocked on the door of Marsh Cottage in Burton Overy. The door was opened almost immediately by Stuart Cross. Davies flashed his warrant card.

'Good evening, Mr Cross is it?'

'That's right,' Stuart acknowledged curiously.

'Do you mind if I come in for…' Stuart apologised for his lack of courtesy and without hesitation invited the detective into the cottage.

'How can I help?'

'I'm hoping you may be able to assist us in an enquiry. We've reopened the 'body-in-the-lock' case from about eight years ago. I believe it was you or your wife found the abandoned narrowboat…'

'Yes, that's right, the *Emily Rose* and the gun, don't forget the gun.'

Stuart was quite proud of his 'find'.

'Of course, sir. Anyway, we now believe that our main suspect may be back in the area, and it is in connection with that belief that we would like to speak to Helen Blake. Problem is nobody seems to know where she's gone.' Anxious to please, and happy to be helping the police with their enquires, Stuart provided the DC with the information he was seeking.

'I suppose in one sense, Helen Blake doesn't exist any longer. She changed her name after being released…'

'She wouldn't be going under the name of Hazel Black by any chance?'

'She would indeed.'

'We suspected as much. Do you have an address for her?'

'Not as such, but I know she now lives in Suffolk, a place called Pin Mill. I understand it's not far from Ipswich; tiny by all accounts, a few houses, houseboats and a pub. Shouldn't be hard to find her there, I imagine it's the kind of place where everybody knows everybody else.' DC Davies had made a couple of notes in his pocketbook.

'Thank you very much Mr Cross – you've been very helpful.'

'Only too happy to assist.' And with that Stuart showed the DC to the door.

'If you can think of anything else that might interest us, please give me a call,' Davies said as he handed Stuart his card.

Stuart examined the card and recalling the unanimous decision he had recently been party to, the decision not to involve the police, he wondered if he'd been a little too helpful

The detective sat in his car for a moment and thought to himself that it might be useful to know the whereabouts of Ben Blake as well and saw this as an excuse to drive down to Great Glen to the Old Greyhound rather than disturb Stuart Cross again, not that he had an ulterior motive, of course not! He drove into the pub carpark and went into the bar. To his disappointment it was a man behind the bar and not the voluptuous barmaid from his previous visit

'Good evening sir, what'll be?' Jamie asked. DC Davies took out his warrant card and identified himself.

'I was here the other day and spoke to the helpful young lady behind the bar...'

'Ah yes, Diane, my wife mentioned she'd had a visit from the police.'

Married! More disappointment for Davies!

'I see sir, well I believe you may know about the 'body-in-the-lock' case from about eight years ago?'

'I do indeed. Lock Number 25 Newton Top Lock. I remember it well.'

'We've reason to believe that our main suspect is back in the area and it is in connection with this that we'd like to get in touch with Ben Blake. Do you know Ben Blake, sir?'

'Know him? Blimey, we were at school together. I helped him fish his dead dad out of that lock. I also was best man at his wedding. Oh yes I know Ben.'

'Do you know where I might find him or how I might contact him?'

Jamie was now on the defensive, knowing as much he did. The last thing he wanted would be to incriminate his mate or Hazel.

'He moved away some while ago. I think he now lives in Suffolk but I'm not sure where. He works in London I do know that.' Ray Davies suspected that information was probably being withheld here. But he wasn't too downhearted now he knew how to contact Hazel Black.

'OK sir, I was just passing and I thought I'd pop in on the off chance, good night.'

Next day DI Cartwright summoned DC Davies to his office to learn what he might have discovered. Davies gave a resume of what he'd learned on his visit to rural Leicestershire.

'Well, I can't justify more expense in sending you off on a jolly jaunt to the delights of Norfolk.'

'That's Suffolk, gov," Davies interrupted.

'Isn't it all the same? I'll call the Suffolk Constabulary and get them to send somebody to... where you say?'

'Pin Mill, sir.'

'Sounds lovely, Pin Mill,' he mused. 'We'll get the local plod to interview her.'

Chapter Twenty-Four

Something had been puzzling Ben since the Foxton visit. He drove down to the Old Greyhound to have a chat with Jamie and get his thoughts on the mystery of the missing Ariel.

'Surely it wouldn't have started after all that time would it?' Ben asked.

'It might have. These old bikes had magneto ignition; sort of friction against a magnet and when you kicked it over it would give a good enough spark to fire it up. Built to last they were; reliable. That's one of the reasons why they were used by the army during the war,' Jamie replied.

'So, do you think it's conceivable that Jock or someone managed to get the bike off the boat, kick it into life and ride off?'

'Yes, I reckon that's quite possible.' Jamie seemed very sure of himself.

'I wonder if he's kept it. There can't be too many old Ariels about these days.'

Before returning to Orford, Ben decided to pay his grandparents a visit. They had after all been largely responsible for raising him from a baby until he was almost eleven. His grandparents, Albert and Mabel were now pushing eighty and he owed them both a huge debt of gratitude. It had been Albert that had introduced him to the piano and encouraged him to persevere with it. Not only that, but it was remiss of him not to have paid them a visit in a long while. He collected Tina from the Burton Overy cottage and they drove to Burbage. The plan was to stay the night with his grandparents and return to Suffolk the following day.

Albert and Mabel were delighted to see their grandson and his wife. Mabel instantly started fussing and in no time at all the teapot and best crockery were on the table and a selection box of chocolate biscuits.

'I'd bought these to put on one side for Christmas, but I think it's only right and proper that we should open them now, don't you think Albert? Albert?! It's nearly Christmas anyway.' Tina laughed and Albert grunted his positive response grunt. They sat and chatted about life, work, their new home, the prospect of a great-grandchild, commuting to and from London to work, to the onset of aches and pains which were par for the course for octogenarians and only to be expected according to Mabel. The big issue though was Ben's recent rediscovery of his mother. Both the old folks sat spellbound listening to Ben's account of that Monday in early December and the subsequent developments. Albert was horrified that his daughter-in-law had been convicted of crimes she was not solely to blame for. He took great interest in details of the 'private investigation' which would hopefully discover the whereabouts of the villain who had killed their son Ken, Ben's father.

'The murderer, he who was also the main perpetrator in the black-market racket must be brought to justice.' Albert declared in his most voracious and stentorian tones. He took a bottle of whiskey and two glasses from the cabinet. Mabel and Tina disappeared into the kitchen to prepare some supper. No sooner had Albert taken a couple of sips of the amber nectar than his eyelids grew heavy and he nodded off.

With the women in the kitchen and his grandfather asleep, Ben found the current edition of the *Hinckley Times* on the shelf beneath the coffee table. He flicked through it in a mainly disinterested manner until there in the 'For Sale' advertisements, classified under 'Motorcycles' was an ad that almost jumped off the page and poked him in the eye.

Ariel 'Red Hunter' 350cc. Side valve, pushrod, good condition. Two careful owners. Little used recently. A classic and a bargain. Offers over £200 invited.

Beneath the advertisement was a telephone number. Was this a coincidence? Ben called Tina in from the kitchen and showed her the newspaper. She didn't need to hear the question that Ben was about to pose.

'Yes, ring the number... no, on second thoughts don't. Let Hazel ring. If it's him, she'll surely recognise the voice, be able to get an address as a potential buyer wanting to have a look at it. We can then give the address straight to the police and they can go and arrest him. Simple!' Ben thought about this for a moment.

'But, but if it is him... what is he recognises mum's voice? Wouldn't that scare him off?' Tina considered Ben's question.

'Mmm, I see what you mean. Let's see what Albert thinks.' Before they could fill Albert in on the dilemma Mabel summoned everyone to the table for supper. After the meal was over and Mabel and Tina were clearing up Ben approached his grandfather.

'Grandad, I'd really welcome your advice.' He showed Albert the advertisement and talked him through his deliberations with Tina on what their next step should be.

'If it is Jock, he's hardly likely to recognise your voice. In my opinion, I reckon you should ring as an individual interested in buying the motorbike and try and get a name and address. Your next step after that will depend on the nature of the responses you get, won't it?'

'You're probably right. OK. That's the way ahead then.' Without further ado Ben went into the hallway and referring to the advertisement again, with a piece of paper and pencil to hand, he dialled the number. No answer. He replaced the receiver for a few seconds, picked it up and dialled once more. No answer.

'No one's answering. I'll try again in the morning.' Excited by this new lead in the investigation, Ben phoned his mum and brought her up to speed on the way things had developed. Hazel was anxious that Ben should distance himself from any face-to-face confrontation.

'If you think it's him, that's to say if you reckon whoever answers the phone is Scottish, try and get the address and then get hold of Detective Chief Inspector Mosely at the Leicestershire Constabulary. Let the police take it from there.'

'OK mum, don't worry, I'll do just as you say.'

Ben and Tina spent an intermittent night's sleep in Ben's old bedroom. It brought back memories but at the same time, he was rehearsing his way through the telephone call he would make immediately after breakfast the following morning. He must have dozed off into a deep sleep at some point because Tina had trouble rousing him in response to Mabel's announcement, shouted up the stairs, that breakfast would be on the table within five minutes. She could smell the coffee.

Chapter Twenty-Five

Not without a little trepidation, Ben picked up the receiver and dialled the number in the advertisement. After five rings his call was answered.

'Ross Motors, how can we help?'

'It's not a Scotsman,' he whispered to Tina who had her ear close the receiver.

'I was calling about the Ariel 350 you have advertised in the paper.'

'Yes sir, that's right and still available. Lovely machine and in very good condition for its age. Would you like to come and see it – a test ride perhaps?'

'Could you tell me something of the history; how many previous owners?'

After reeling off the full specifications for this classic motorcycle the man on the phone, who was being very helpful, detailed the information Ben wanted to hear.

'Previous registered owners; let me see, there are two, the British Army and a Ronald Nicholls.'

'You're sure there are no others?'

'Yes sir, quite sure. Now when would you like to come and see the bike?'

Ben instantly decided that he should come clean with the man on the phone as he was being most helpful and it would be unfair to string him along.

'To be honest with you, I don't want to buy the bike. I was hoping it was the Red Hunter that had belonged to a friend of mine who I've lost touch with.'

'Ah, I see. Well we bought the bike – it is a classic you know – from a chap who brought it in and was selling it for his friend Ronald Nicholls, the last registered owner as I mentioned.'

'How long ago was this?'

'Oh, quite recently, only last week. We only just made the copy deadline for this week's edition of the paper.'

'He wasn't a Scotsman by any chance?'

'Well as it happens I believe he was. Could this have been your friend?'

'It certainly sounds like it. I don't suppose he gave you any contact details, address or phone number?'

'Well I'm not sure I should be giving out this information but …let me see now, yes here we are on the receipt. Duncan McClean, Kingsford, Sunnyhill, Burbage.' Ben hastily scribbled the address down.

'Thank you so much. Your assistance is extremely appreciated,' said Ben genuinely.

'You're welcome sir. I hope you find your friend, and if you're ever in the market for a motorcycle…' Ben had replaced the receiver. Not that Ben realised it at the time, but this was another straw on the camel's back of Jock's ultimate downfall. He went and joined the others at the breakfast table and excitedly gave a resume of the telephone conversation.

'That's the address where your mum and dad lived when they were first married, what a coincidence,' said Mabel.

'It's no bloody coincidence,' contradicted Albert. 'This wily Scotsman's hardly going to reveal his whereabouts just like that is he? I bet it's an address he just happened to remember on the spur of the moment I should say.' Ben and Tina were inclined to agree.

'Still,' said Tina, 'it gives us further proof that he's been in the area and recently too. The trail's hotting up, don't you think?' Ben rang his mother with the news which Hazel received with mixed emotions. On the one hand she felt a sense of elation by the confirmation of Jock's recent presence in the area. It was also gratifying to learn that there was now even more circumstantial evidence to support the contention that Jock had been the murderer of Ron Nicholls. Thoroughly upsetting on the other hand was the reminder of the address in Sunnyhill; the address that she and her new husband had shared; the address that she'd unknowingly shared with two dead bodies in an upstairs room; the address that held such happy memories briefly before they had all turned sour; the address where she and her farmer friend Frank Waring had discovered an enormous stockpile of illicit and stolen goods. This was distressing for her in the extreme. Still it was Christmas eve and whilst the momentum in the quest for the elusive Scotsman had made significant strides, greater attention was now required to be devoted to the preparations of a big Christmas Day get-together. Hazel attempted to preoccupy herself on this.

Retribution

Chapter Twenty-Six

Since the publication of the Thames Valley Police's press release and the telephone call from Wenzl, the atmosphere in the Blackstaff Bar had been about as convivial and cordial as might be expected at a gathering of funeral directors with toothache. Amongst the regulars there was a revulsion of feeling, a deep-rooted loathing of the Scotsman who they had considered to be a compatriot, a drinking mate and one of their own. Their contempt for McClean was unmistakable. Such was the bad blood and malice that no one could have been in any doubt whatsoever as to what lay in store for Jock McClean once Michael Doyle's carefully selected platoon of Republicans caught up with him. It was decided that they would take two cars as far as the port and use the ferry crossing between Belfast and Liverpool. Ciara had pre-booked rooms in Liverpool, at the Imperial Hotel in Bourke Street. Michael had insisted that his colleagues were properly attired and that they behaved like gentlemen on the ferry and once they were England. The last thing they wanted would be to draw attention to themselves. So, booted and suited as they were, they could have passed for a group of bible salesmen. Their leader tried to convince himself that he wasn't at all nervous when he saw the neon Guinness advertising on the front of the building. He knew his men would not let him down and let the beer get the better of them – or would they? Michel Doyle found a telephone kiosk and called the Chesterton Hotel in Bicester. He was put through to Tom Wenzl's suite.

'OK, we're in Liverpool. Where are we going?'

'I'm not exactly sure yet.' He didn't want to give any details yet and attempted to buy some time. Since the call from Jock he knew his van was in the agreed location according to the plan. Now he was pinning his hopes on not only getting the cargo moved before revealing the vehicle's whereabouts to the Irish, but also putting as much distance between the IRA and himself as possible. He was very much aware that the realisation of those hopes was entirely dependent on the police not having found the Econoline beforehand.

'Michael, do you have a number I can reach you on? I'll call you the minute I have any news.' He scribbled down the number he was given.

'Don't take too long. My lads here are a handful right enough and I don't want to lose control of them, or them to lose control of themselves whilst they're hanging about here with nothing to do except drink.'

'I understand.' And he genuinely did. He'd witnessed in the past the havoc that a group of beered up Irishmen could create.

Chapter Twenty-Seven

Since he'd delivered the Econoline and its cargo to Foxton Locks, Jock had been holed up with Wally Whitehead in his tiny terraced house in the village of Foxton. Wally had been delighted to see his old mate after such a long time and especially after their encounter in the Saddington Tunnel all those years ago. Back at that time Wally had thought that he'd never see Jock again, given the state of mind that he was in when he walked away from the boat. But here he was, as large as life and twice as ruthless. During the few days that Jock imposed on Wally's hospitality, they had swapped yarns, drunk a lot of whisky, and Jock had regaled Wally with chapter and verse of his Northern Irish exploits. Wally insisted on hearing every little detail, and especially of the relationship with Maggie O'Rourke. Jock had been only too happy to oblige even though what Wally was actually told was a rather lewd and an elaborately embroidered version fabricated from Jock's overimaginative fantasies drawn from 'gentlemen's' magazines of a particular genre. On Christmas eve over breakfast Jock had a proposition for Wally – a proposal that had always been part of Tom and Jock's grand plan.

'Well noo, Wal, ye say ye've nae had a cargo since a run up tae the jam factory in October. Well ah hev one fur ye. Whit's more, it'll pay ye more than jam or any other cargo ye've ever hid.'

Wally's eyes lit up as Jock began to set out the details of what he intended.

'It's nae whit ye'd call strictly legal, but it'll be worth your while and nae mistake, believe me.'

'Aye goo on then, let's be 'avin it,' Wally urged. The prospect of earning a few quid could not be ignored.

'There's a crate and two big wicker baskets in a black van hidden up behind the Locks pub. We load 'em intae *Nancy Blakemore* an' run em up tae Limehouse Basin in London where we transfer 'em intae a ship.'

'Easy – do it wi' me eyes closed!' pronounced Wally. 'Yo' comin' wi' me?'

'Aye, ma sel' and a Yank – unless ah kin ditch him, strange bloke that he is.'

'Great! When d'we start?'

'Aboot midnight tonight.'

'Tonight? But it's Christmas eve!'

'Exactly – tha's the whole point. We cannae let anyone know whit we're aboot, if ye ken whit ah mean.' Jock tapped the side of his nose with his forefinger in the manner intended to convey the secrecy of the mission. 'Ev'rywin will be doin' Christmas and nae bothered wi' us.'

*

After breakfast on Christmas Eve Tom Wenzl checked out of the Chesterton and made his way to the railway station in Bicester. He was all too anxiously aware that the next phase of the plan was scheduled to happen that night. Arriving at the station he consulted the timetables and was dismayed to discover that the journey was not quite as straightforward as he would have liked. The train from Bicester took him to Birmingham Moor Street station from where he would have to walk to Birmingham New Street. Although it was only a short walk he couldn't afford to dawdle if he was to make the connection at New Street to take him to Leicester, which he pronounced 'Lie-cester'. For reasons best known to himself he felt conspicuous. He felt everyone was looking at him. Was it his guilty conscience perhaps, knowing the errand he was on? When he got to Leicester it was approaching lunch time and he decided to give Michael Doyle a call at the

Imperial Hotel in Liverpool – just to let him know it was a matter of merely a few hours before the exact location of the IRA's stolen cache of weapons could be confirmed. He was anxious to let Doyle and his men think he was still loyal to their cause but he didn't want them turning up too soon. The Imperial's receptionist informed Tom that Mr Doyle and his party were all out but she was happy to take a message and make sure that it was passed on. Tom ordered coffee and a sandwich from the station buffet and boarded the train to Market Harborough.

'If there's one thing I can be certain of,' he thought to himself, 'no one will have tailed me given the journey round the park I've taken so far this morning.' The train pulled out of Leicester London Road and it was only a few minutes before it passed through Wigston.

'Hold on,' shouted Tom with a hint of panic. 'I just came through Wigston before I got to Lie-cester. The train's going the wrong way – either that or I'm on the wrong train.' Unsure of what remedy might be available to him he made to rush down the corridor to find the guard only to be calmed down when a local passenger was able to reassure him that he was indeed on the train to Market Harborough. Even then Tom couldn't quite grasp the necessity for the train to double back on itself before heading in the right direction. When the train arrived at Market Harborough he took a cab from the rank and gave Wally Whitehead's address to the cabbie. Finally after what for Tom had seemed a wholly unnecessarily epic journey courtesy of British Rail, the cab – he couldn't get into the habit of referring to cabs as taxis – dropped him at the address in Foxton. Uncertain that he was in the right place he tentatively knocked on the door of the terraced cottage. No answer. He saw the net curtains in the window of the next-door cottage twitch after which the front door opened and there stood Jock. His greeting was sarcastic.

'Och, will ye look who's here, knocking at the wrong door? Get here when you like mon. It's nae that we hev anything important te dae!' He invited Tom in and introduced him to Wally. They strolled the short distance down the road for a bite to eat in the

Shoulder of Mutton pub in Foxton village. Over a couple of pints – English beer, something else Tom hadn't acquired the taste for – they went over the finer points of unloading the cargo from the van and into the *Nancy Blakemore*. Jock ran through the checklist he'd made to ensure they had all that would be required for the trip to Limehouse. Canals, narrowboats, locks and all things pertaining thereto were completely alien to Tom but whilst he tried to appear interested he was nevertheless about as far from enthusiastic at the prospect of the next leg of the weaponry's journey as he would be for a trip across the Sinai Desert on a flea-ridden camel. He begged to be excused from the boat trip but assured Jock that he would get to the location to be present at the point of final sale and see the cargo into the hands of Black September. The three of them walked the towpath to where *Nancy Blakemore* was moored between bridges 62 and 63. Wally proudly showed Tom around the vessel which was his pride and joy. They motored slowly up to the Foxton Locks Inn where Wally skilfully brought the boat alongside the quay just below the bottom lock. This was the exact spot where the crate and the baskets would be slid down a couple of planks from the rear of the van and into the narrowboat's hold; the same hold that held painful memories for Jock. But then, had he not suffered that fall, he wouldn't necessarily have gone to Northern Ireland and this latest criminal venture would not be happening. Provisions and bedding were stowed aboard along with the two camp beds that Fred had loaned to Jock when he handed over the Econoline's keys. Wally checked the engine and filled the diesel tanks.

It was later that Tom decided to tell Jock about Maggie. He didn't appear to be particularly concerned. He certainly wasn't about to shed any tears. There were however some vitriolic exchanges between them when Tom revealed that the IRA's finest from the Blackstaff were in Liverpool awaiting his call with information on the van's location in order that they might recover that which they considered was rightfully theirs.

*

In the John Radcliffe Hospital in Oxford, Gerry Doyle had recovered consciousness and had asked if he could call his brother in Belfast. The phone trolley was wheeled through to him and eventually he had Ciara on the line. She told him about Michael and the group that had gone to Liverpool chasing after the American's van. Gerry wasn't so keen to be reminded of chasing the American's van. He momentarily relived the accident.

'It's like,' he explained to his brother, 'cinefilm playing in my head, over and over – the pursuit, the tailgating, then the suicidal right turn just before the screen goes blank.'

*

At the Imperial Hotel in Liverpool Michael Doyle collected two messages from the receptionist; the first from Tom Wenzl, the second from his daughter. It was only as a result of Wenzl's previous call to the Blackstaff that Michael had become aware that that his brother had been involved in an accident. With the further news now from Ciara he felt obliged to go and visit Gerry. He had to put his family first. With the help of the Hotel's receptionist, he considered the travel options available to him and decided on the train although it would take almost four hours to get there. Later that evening when Michael got back to the Imperial he delivered a graphic description of the accident caused by Jock as described to him by Gerry. His colleagues' sense of anger and outrage was augmented exponentially and Michael was reassured when his men avowed that he could rely on them all 100% to remain sober for the next 48 hours or until such time as his intended plan of revenge for his brother had been affected. Then there was the matter of the recovery of their weapons and dealing with McClean.

Chapter Twenty-Eight

It was after midnight. Two of the three musketeers strolled down towards the canal to wait for the arrival of the Econoline E20. They hadn't expected to encounter the congregation from St Andrew's Christmas Eve Carol Service to be spilling out of the church, so they held back hiding in the shadows for ten minutes until the coast was clear. Tom, who had been given the privilege of driving his van one last time arrived by the canal side where Fred was already waiting. Tom manoeuvred the van into position and he and Fred secured the scaffold boards between the van's sliding side-door and *Nancy Blakemore*'s gunnel. They waited the few minutes it took for the other two to arrive. All were dressed in black and with almost no moonlight the entire operation of sliding the cargo from the van to the boat was completed unseen. Had anyone been listening however, they might have heard some stage-whispered cursing and quite a lot of heaving and grunting. The cache of weapons was aboard. The bottom lock of the Foxton Flight, Number 17, had already been prepared by Fred, and Wally cast off and with just the barest tickle of the throttle, *Nancy* ghosted into the lock, and then with Fred on the gate, rose into the next, Number 16. Wally killed the engine and the boat was made fast at the low water level in the lock and thereby almost concealed from view. This ruse was at Fred's suggestion. He'd also advised that travelling all the way up the flight and on towards the Husbands Bosworth tunnel on a moonless night would be dangerous. Besides which, commercial boats didn't move on Christmas Day. Anyone that did would attract attention. Far better, Fred had insisted, and Wally had been in total agreement, to leave the boat hidden and move early on Boxing day. Narrowboat movements, although few, were not unprecedented on Boxing Day and much less likely to arouse suspicion. The 'Two Boatmen of the Apocalypse' strolled back the way they came and Tom took the van back to its original parking space, locked it, pocketed the keys and wandered back to Wally's cottage for a nightcap of festive cheer.

Knowing that the arms cache was now safely removed from the van and unlikely to fall back into the hands of the IRA Tom felt he could reveal the van's location. So, on Christmas morning he rang the Imperial and the receptionist put him through to Michael Doyle's room.

'Festive greetings Michael!'

'Stuff your bloody festive greeting up your turkey's arse! I'm stuck here, sitting around sucking my thumb, waiting for your call and this bloody hotel's costing a feckin' arm and a leg. Now, where's the feckin' van? My brother's at death's door lying in a hospital bed uncertain that he'll ever walk again, my arms supply chain has been compromised and our organisation's lost a feckin' fortune while the Unionists are walking all over us. Now, where's the van, where are my guns and where's that feckin' devious Scots bastard? His feckin' days are numbered for sure they are.' Once Tom could get a word in, he did.

'The van is parked in the carpark of a pub called the Foxton Locks Inn. I've only just learned that it's been there for days, it's partially hidden up. Foxton is near to Market Har–'

'I'll bloody find it don't you worry.'

'It's not an easy place to get to.' Tom tried to be helpful but Michael didn't need any help.

'You be waiting there for us Wenzl. We're on the way.' It was a threat, not a promise – or was it the promise of a threat – or worse?

Tom wondered how they could be 'on the way' on Christmas Day. Surely there'd be no trains or public transport running would there? He hadn't reckoned on Doyle and his associates stealing a minibus.

Christmas Day for the gunrunning collaborators was spent relaxing and resting up ready for the early start, before first light on Boxing Day. To the enormous surprise of the others, Fred took himself off to the Christmas morning service at St Andrew's. Apparently it was a tradition for the lockkeeper to read a lesson. Later in the day, Jock went off for a drive in the Porsche; the only vehicle he'd ever acquired legally. Apart from getting out of the cottage for a while he needed to deliver a Christmas card. With the card delivered he drove back to Foxton and parked the Porsche next to the Econoline. He carefully locked his car and as he walked back to Wally's cottage he went over the remainder of the plan in his mind. He was reasonably satisfied and confident that all bases were covered. One slight problem he hadn't considered since as yet he was unaware of it, was the minibus full of bible salesmen that arrived in Foxton minutes after he had got back to Wally's.

Christmas Day for Michael Doyle and his IRA compatriots had been a long and tortuous journey from Liverpool to Foxton. Michael had been without sleep since visiting his brother and the driving of the stolen minibus was taken in turns by his colleagues whilst the others tried to sleep. It had been a straightforward trip to Leicester with hardly any traffic but then the expedition had become a little more complicated. They had taken the A6 towards Market Harborough but initially missed the right turn onto the minor road signposted to Foxton. They did find it at the second attempt. Once in the village it hadn't taken but a few minutes to locate the Foxton Locks Inn and, sure enough, the Econoline E20 was concealed in the carpark as Wenzl had said. It was shortly after midnight and with no light pollution it was blacker than that hole in Calcutta. Michael was wide awake by now and he stepped out of the minibus and walked around the van. He tried all the doors but they were locked. He peered through the heavily tinted windows but he could see nothing. The rest of the group had also disgorged themselves from the minibus and were variously stretching, yawning, smoking and urinating against the Porsche parked next to the Econoline. Michael brought the group to order and they gathered around to listen to the plan.

'It's my belief that our weapons are still in the van,' Michael stated.

'Then why don't we just break into the van, hotwire it and drive away?' asked one of the others.

'Because,' and the answer came through gritted teeth and laced with venom, 'this is a twofold mission or had you forgotten you bleedin' eejit? I'm going kill that bastard McClean when he turns up – and he will, to be sure.' Their leader's stated intention was greeted with whole-hearted approval before Michael continued. 'When he's dead we won't need to break into the van then will we, 'cos he'll have the keys and no further use for them!' They all laughed. 'So, from now we'll deploy a watch, in pairs, two hours on, and two hours off. Stay alert and at the first sight of anyone approaching, one of youse come and wake the rest of us. Now where's that feckin' yankee? He's supposed to be here to meet us!' The minibus was tucked away in the far corner of the carpark and all but the two men who were given the first watch clambered back inside. The men on watch were each armed with a Colt M1911 45mm automatic pistol. The stake-out was in place.

Christmas Day at Marsh Cottage in Burton Overy was a riotous affair. Short notice invitations had been extended to friends and sundry relatives. The Greyhound was closed for the day and Jamie and Diane had very kindly offered to look after the catering and supply all the drinks – at cost and for an appropriate level of remuneration, of course. In addition to the 'not-so-famous-five' those present included Albert and Mabel, who by prior arrangement had been collected by Frank Waring who had also picked up his brother Ernie in the Jaguar, and Tina's dad Dennis and Uncle Walter from Aldeburgh. As a special surprise for Ben, Hazel had invited Barrie Sims, his old piano teacher. For all that it was a fairly disparate gathering, it was probably the most festive of all gatherings in Burton Overy that day. The turkey was a monster, the vegetables – a seasonal selection of all that were freshly available, were cooked to perfection. The wine flowed freely and the day was the happiest that Helen could remember since before being incarcerated. There was just one sour moment. It occurred during the game of charades just as Frank was attempting to act out *It's A Wonderful Life*. There was a knock at the door, barely audible given the amount of laughter Frank's charade was generating. Dennis went to answer the door. Parked by the wicket fence was a Porsche 911 with the engine running. A man handed Dennis an envelope and without speaking he turned, got into the Porsche and drove off. Dennis closed the door and re-joined the throng. With a shrug of the shoulders which said 'no idea' he handed the envelope, addressed to Helen Blake, to Hazel and resumed his armchair. Helen opened the envelope. It was a Christmas card. Inside the inscription read *I know where you live and I know where your son lives. I'll be coming for you and to collect my share*. There was no signature. Hazel fell backwards onto the sofa amongst those already sitting there.

'Are you OK mum?' Ben laughed.

'I'm fine Ben' she lied. 'Too much wine!' But Ben knew there was something amiss however he decided not to pursue it there and then. Later perhaps.

Just before midnight with the guests all gone, Hazel, Ben and Tina sat beside the last glowing embers in the inglenook fireplace having a nightcap – not that a nightcap was necessary given the amount that they'd drunk through the course of the day. Hazel handed Ben the card. The colour drained from Ben's face. He took a deep breath and swallowed hard, immediately sober.

'Was it… was it Jock who delivered it?' he looked at his mother as Tina also read the card.

'I don't know. It matters not who delivered it. What matters is he knows where we are.'

'We will not be intimidated with veiled threats like this,' stated Ben defiantly.

Chapter Twenty-Nine

Very early on Boxing Day morning Ben drove the short distance to Great Glen hoping that Dennis and Walter had not yet left their overnight accommodation at the Greyhound. They hadn't. Diane was serving them breakfast.

'Can you describe the man who was at the door delivering the card last night?' Ben was attempting to get a few clues from Dennis.

'I didn't really get a look at him and I couldn't find the switch for the outside light. All I did notice was that he wasn't very tall and he was driving a

dark coloured Porsche. He'd left the engine running.'

A Porsche! Ben's mind was instantly projected back to that Friday almost two weeks ago. Could that have been a Porsche Stuart had to swerve to avoid as he drove them all to the Greyhound that evening before Christmas? This was cause for concern. Dennis saw the worry etched in the expression on Ben's face.

'Is there a problem?' he asked. 'There's something troubling you – I can tell. Is it something I can help with?'

Ben gave Dennis as much information as he felt was necessary to satisfy his curiosity. He didn't want his father-in-law worrying about a situation which now appeared not only to have reversed the roles of the dog and the rabbit but to have given the rabbit a distinct advantage as well. Jock was most definitely hot on their heels.

'Don't you worry Dennis, we'll sort it out. It's just an old acquaintance of mother's who reckons she owes him an outstanding debt from years ago.'

'Well OK, if you're sure. Just remember we're only just down the road in Suffolk if you need any help. Look after my daughter.'

'Oh I will sir, you may be certain of that.'

As Ben drove back to Burton Overy he was vacillating between fear and uncertainty. He informed the others, including Kate and Stuart, of this latest 'coincidence'. They agreed with Ben's interpretation of the evidence in that there could be absolutely no doubt that their safety, even their lives could be in danger. Not only were there the Porsche sightings and the mystery Scotsman in the pub to consider there was now the previous evening's delivery of the Christmas card with its implied malevolent message. Whatever the sender's intentions, and surely it was Jock, there was no doubt that they would unlikely be benevolent, neither honourable nor friendly.

'Well, it's plain as your nose on your face! All we have to do now is inform the police and wait for Jock to come to us rather than we go chasing our backsides looking for him?' Kate was visibly far from happy with this development.

'I don't think it's quite as simple as that.' It was Stuart who had the better grasp of the difficulty.

'That's right,' agreed Hazel. 'It's all to do with the gold. If the police find out about the gold I doubt very much that they'll turn a blind eye and I could very well find myself back inside and I'm not going back to prison at any cost.' Hazel's statement was emphatic.

'So, what do we do? We can't all move house can we?' Kate was decidedly apprehensive and downright uppity.

'Somehow,' suggested Tina, 'we have to lure him into a trap and as far as the police are concerned, we are merely delivering a double murderer to them. This must have nothing whatsoever to do with black-market goods or gold.'

'Perhaps the trap could be baited with gold?' suggested Stuart.

'Good thinking,' said Ben sarcastically.

'OK guys, what's the plan?' Unusually there was a hint of sarcasm in Tina's voice. The situation was causing extreme concern and leading to squabbling. Hazel brought the debate to order.

'Enough now! We must take the initiative before it's too late!'

Yes, it was all very worrying and frustrating and yes, they were all getting very jittery and totally irritated by the constant need to be looking over their shoulders – but for what?

For all that it had been enjoyable, most of the previous day's celebrations had been forgotten. Uppermost in everyone's minds was the veiled threat which the card had contained. The entire team now unanimously believed that sufficient hard evidence had been amassed to convince the police that they should reopen the 'body-in-the-lock' case. Little did they know, until Stuart mentioned his visit from DC Davies, it already had been.

'Hang on a minute!' There was an urgency in the manner Tina suddenly held everyone's attention. 'Where's the paper, you know the one with the press release. Has it been thrown out? The *Telegraph* from two weeks ago?' There were blank looks all round. Ben went to the kitchen cupboard where old newspapers and kindling for the fire were kept. He had a rummage through a stack of papers.

'We're in luck' he shouted through to the living room as he extracted the 11th December edition, folded in such a way to reveal the partially finished crossword. He found the piece.

'Read the police press release Ben' she instructed. 'What colour was the van?' Ben didn't need to read it out.

'Black,' they chorused in unison.

'What did we park next to the last time we went to Foxton?' There was hush before the chorus responded again.

'Oh my god!' It was Kate, who spoke first with a fit of terror in her trembling voice. 'You don't think it was…?'

'Calm down, steady now.' In answer to his wife's question Stuart posed another.

'How many hundreds of black vans are there? Coincidence I'd say.'

'Did anyone spot the make, the model? Was it American?' No one could offer the substantive answer.

'Look,' said Hazel, 'let me give Fred a call. He can go and have a look for us, assuming the van's still there. I'm inclined to agree with Stuart. I bet it's gone by now.'

'But,' chipped in Ben, 'if it is the van in the press release, then I think we can let the police handle it from here.' All were in agreement. Kate was particularly relieved.

*

Earlier that morning, much earlier, Jock and Wally had strolled quite leisurely from Wally's cottage and then down the towpath and over the Rainbow Bridge rather than the road. Not that they realised it at the time, but by taking to the towpath they avoided having to pass the carpark where the van was under IRA surveillance. They walked part way up the flight and boarded the *Nancy Blakemore* where she lay undetected in Lock Number 16. Fred was already there waiting for them and had made the next lock ready. He had more words of caution.

'If yo' want to be' eard, make a noise!' Taking the hint Jock heaved on a bow line and the boat easily slid forward into Number 15. As Fred made each lock ready in turn, *Nancy* pretty well maintained her own momentum as Jock towed the boat through each of the locks in the entire flight, just as a horse would have done back in the day. This avoided disturbing the silent night with the noise of the engine. It wasn't until the boat was clear of Top Lock Number 8 that Wally gingerly turned the key and pressed the starter-button. Passage through the entire Foxton flight had been achieved in silence. As Jock stepped back aboard, he paid Fred off, quite handsomely and Fred pocketed his ill-gotten gains and gave the boat and her crew a wave before returning to the Waterways Office where he hoped his camp-bed was still warm.

Chapter Thirty

Hazel was well aware that Fred was a creature of habit. Even though it was Boxing Day she felt sure that he'd be up and about. As in all those years when she'd been trading with Jock from the *Emily Rose*, Hazel could still visualise him sitting in the Waterways Board office opposite the *Foxton Locks Inn* drinking tea, tinctured with a drizzle of scotch. He'd be sitting by the pathetic excuse for a heater and reading the *Mirror* or watching that television with the troublesome horizontal hold. She dialled the number. After a few rings, the call was answered.

''Ello, Foxton Locks, Fred Webb speakin'.'

'Hello Fred, this is Hazel.'

''Azel? I don't know no 'azel.

'Fred it's Helen, Helen Blake.'

'Oo's 'azel then? Ahh, 'ang on a minit, I remember…' the penny dropped.

'Fred, if you don't mind, is that black van still in the carpark?'

Fred knew full well that the van was still there, just as he knew the cargo had gone, but he didn't want to let Hazel know that he knew what was going on.

'I dunno, I'll 'ave to go an' 'ave a look – 'ang on and I'll call you back, what's the number?'

The Waterways Board office was on the opposite side of the canal to the pub meaning Fred would have to cross over by the bottom lock gate and walk around to the back of the pub. Even so, he thought he'd go and have a look anyway as he hadn't stepped outside yet for the daily inspection of his empire. He pulled on his hat and coat. Halfway across the gate, and although he knew perfectly well, given that he'd seen her go, he noted with satisfaction that the *Nancy Blakemore* was long gone from Lock Number 16. He doubted that anyone ever noticed she'd been there. In the carpark the black van was still where Tom had parked it early on Christmas Day morning after the cargo had been transferred. Intent on looking at the van he failed to notice a minibus full of bible salesmen.

After 20 minutes Fred was back in his office and he rang the number Hazel had given him. She picked up the receiver after just one ring and there were four other pairs of ears all straining to hear the conversation.

''Elen, yes it's still there – bin 'ere over two wiks now.'

'What sort is it?'

'Is it important?'

'Well, yes it is. We think it might be the one which Jock stole – didn't you see the police press release?' Fred feigned ignorance.

'Well I duuno. S'pose I'll 'ave to go an' 'ave a look – 'ang on.'

Hazel cupped the receiver, 'I think poor old Fred's losing it!' The others smiled. Eventually after a further fifteen minutes Fred called Hazel again and was able to determine for her that the black Econoline E20 van, registered in New York was parked in the pub car park. This time he had noticed the minibus, and immediately knew that something sinister was afoot.

'Who left the van there?' Hazel asked.

'Can't say. Promised I wouldn't say – but I reckon yo' can work it out. Yo' dint 'ear it from me now!' Fred emphasised. 'Course I saw the bit in t'*Mirror* couple a wiks back?'

'Be careful Fred, it's trouble, it's dangerous, he's dangerous!'

'Don't yo' be a-worryin' on that score missus. He's gone.'

'What do mean, gone?'

'Just that – gone! Yo' might do better to be a-worryin' about a minibus full of blokes in suits though.'

'Thanks Fred, you're a diamond.'

'Nah, there's better diamonds in a pack o' cards.' The line went dead.

Hazel confirmed to the others the gist of the conversation with Fred although she wasn't quite sure what to make of his comment about blokes in suits..

'So, are we going to ring the police?'

It was unanimously agreed that one of them should make an anonymous call to the local police. Kate went to make more coffee for everyone. As Tina was clearing away the breakfast things, there was a knock at the door. Everyone froze momentarily. Byron started barking. Kate shushed him. Then by silent gestures and facial expressions, everyone understood that, with the exception of Ben, they should all go and lock themselves in their respective bedrooms. The relief at Fred's news of Jock having gone was short lived. Another knock at the door. Ben tiptoed to the door, and engaged the security chain, before opening the door to the extent the chain would allow, half expecting the muzzle of a gun to greet him.

'C'mon mate, open up, it's bloody perishing out here!' It was Jamie.

'Cor blimey Jamie you had us all going there.' Gradually the room refilled, the fresh coffee was made, and Jamie was brought up to speed with recent developments.

'I thought I'd call in for an update. Have you phoned the police yet?' Jamie enquired.

'Not yet. We don't want any of us to be identified. Would you do it?' asked Hazel.

'Hold on a minute, I don't want to get involved either.' But after a little persuasion, Tina had prepared a script.

"*The black Econoline E20 van you're looking for is in the carpark at Foxton Locks Inn.*" That's all you need to say, then put the phone straight down.' Tina looked up the number of the police station in Leicester. She considered the option of the number for the police in Great Glen but decided it was too close to home. Jamie gingerly lifted the receiver then took out his handkerchief and wrapped it around the mouthpiece.

'What're you doing?' Kate was curious.

'Disguising my voice – saw it done in the movies!' He dialled the number.

'Hello, Leicestershire Constabulary, who's calling please?' Jamie ignored the question, recited from the script and replaced the receiver.

'Well done mate.'

'Yes, thanks Jamie. Now we wait for developments, and fingers crossed,' said Hazel. 'I'm going back to Pin Mill for a few days. It's all a bit too hectic here for me.'

Chapter Thirty-One

It was very early in the police station at Kidlington. Boxing Day had barely broken. The DI would rather have been at home with his family.

'It's been almost two bloody weeks!' Cartwright was not having a good day, especially as he'd had to come into work on a bank holiday again. DC Davies, similarly in a foul mood, was on the receiving end of his guvnor's angst.

'We give those country bumpkin swede bashers a simple task – what've they done so far – bugger all that's what. I don't want to lose the scent now after all this time – this is the best lead we've have – my old dad was right – if you want a job doing and doing properly, bloody well do it yourself! Sorry Ray, I don't mean to go on and I'm not having a go at you, but I can't wait any longer. I know it's Christmas and all but do you mind? Get yourself down to Pin Mill and find Helen Blake or Hazel Black whoever she is. She holds the key to all of this.'

'OK guv, no problem. I'll leave early tomorrow.'

Cartwright's phone rang. His DC hovered in anticipation.

'DI Cartwright?'

'Speaking.'

'Leicester police here, Sergeant Cuthbertson. We've just had an anonymous tip off. That American van you're looking for, well according to our anonymous informant, it's behind the Foxton Locks Inn.'

'It is? Is it indeed?' The DI could hardly believe this break. 'But that's great; fantastic! Thanks Sarge. Can you get someone down there to keep an eye on it? We'll get there as soon as possible. Call me if there's any movement, and be careful, the guy who was driving it is armed and dangerous.'

There followed a flurry of excitement. This was the best Christmas present of the year and Boxing Day had suddenly got much better.

'Ray, cancel your trip on the river, we're going on the canal instead!'

With the news of the van being sighted, Cartwright was immediately on the phone to Armstrong. Answerphone! Bugger! He left a message. Cartwright called Cuthbertson back.

'Cancel my previous order. Get a unit to Foxton Locks Inn – armed and as quick as possible? We need to keep that American van under surveillance. Do not attempt to apprehend anyone approaching the van except on my direct order. Understood? We're on the way from here now.'

'I'll do my best. Not sure about armed. We're a bit thin on the ground this morning – it's Christmas you know.'

'I know full well what the bloody date is sergeant – just get that damn van under surveillance now. This is the best chance we've had of catching this villain – God knows we've been after him for long enough. Now move man!' The excitable tone and urgency of the call from the DI left the sergeant in no doubt as to what was required, but it took him the best part of an hour before a team from Leicester was dispatched to Foxton.

Racing out of Kidlington, DC Ray Davies had been studying the road map and was issuing instructions to PC Andy Lewis at the wheel of the Ford Granada Consul GT. DI Cartwright and another PC were sat in the back. The adrenalin was flowing like beer from a barrel at the Policemen's Benevolent Ball.

'Take the A34 then on to the 43 towards Northampton.'

'34 to the 43' was the only response from the advanced driver and traffic PC who was concentrating on manoeuvring with great skill and at excessive speed through the traffic, some of which seemed to be oblivious to the siren and flashing blue lights.

'I reckon we'll be quicker up the new motorway then cut across otherwise we'll get stuffed in Northampton – what d'you reckon guv?'

'You call it Ray,' the DI had every confidence in his DC.

'Did you get that Andy?'

'Got it M1.' The motorway was still something of a novelty. Police traffic officers loved it; a real opportunity to push the big Granadas to their maximum. Once on the MI and at speeds well in excess of 100 mph it didn't take long to reach junction 20.

*

Way over towards East Anglia and beyond, there was the merest hint of pink in the sky as the dawn began to lighten the open countryside that bounded the canal. Daylight was heading their way and with the best part of the next five miles to go being lock free, the first leg was without doubt much easier than it had seemed during the planning. Around the next bend was Honey Pot Farm Bridge Number 26. Wally decided they should tie up for a while and get the stove going. A cup of coffee was long overdue. Wally walked off towards the farmhouse as he had often done in the past. Stopping at a small open shed in the farmyard, he left some small change in the honesty box and returned to the boat with a dozen eggs. The frying pan was on and a fried egg sandwich provided a welcome distraction for a while. When breakfast was over Jock sought Wally's permission to go below and keep his head down. He had seen the north portal of the Husbands Bosworth tunnel looming large. Being well aware of Jock's aversion to tunnels, Wally laughed and conceded to Jock's request on condition he cleared up the breakfast things. When *Nancy* emerged from the 1166 yards of the tunnel the peace and quiet was shattered by the siren of a police car. Obviously, neither Wally nor Jock would have known anything about an anonymous tip-off but as it screamed over the Kilworth Road Bridge, blue lights flashing, in a tearing hurry Jock at least had a shrewd idea. As he came up from below and watched the car go haring off up the A4304 he smiled.

'Whir do ye reckon it might be going Wal? Cos ah reckon Tom's aboot te get a rude awakenin'.' Wally merely smiled and *Nancy Blakemore* pottered on her way south.

*

'Ok Andy A4304 – should be signposted Market Harborough.' Speed was now moderated on the single lane road but Andy Lewis was still pushing it as hard as he could. They all but flew through North Kilworth and over the canal road bridge and completely failed to notice the narrowboat travelling south on the Grand Union.

'Turn left at Lubenham and that'll see us into Foxton.'

'Got it'.

'Oh, and kill the lights and siren,' instructed Cartwright. 'We don't want to announce our arrival.'

'OK, left into Gallowfield Road, turn left, T junction left, Gumley Road, right, right.' Lewis was almost anticipating the directions and swinging the car into the turns with nonchalant effort, spinning the rear end away with an immediate correction of the skid. Then, with an emergency stop the Granada came to a halt where a uniformed sergeant was standing in the middle of the road with the flat of his palm held up, his right arm raised and extended.

'Bloody hell! cursed Cartwright. 'Old school, thinks he's on bloody point-duty!' Three of the Granada's occupants leapt from the car.

'Cuthbertson sir. Couldn't get much of a team together. 'ad to come meself. I 'ave got a couple o' lads down the road. One of 'em's watching the van in the pub car park, the other's watching the two lads who are also watching the van. Don't like the look of it meself sir.'

'You mean there are two other policemen watching the van?'

'No sir, not coppers. They're in suits – look like villains to me. The sergeant continued, 'Like I said sir, I don't like it. A bit further on, in the public carpark there's a minibus with another five or six blokes in it. Every now and then one of 'em gets out and comes and talks to the two on watch. I didn't want you to go charging straight down there and scare this other firm off – s'why I stopped you 'ere.'

'OK, understood – oh, and well done sergeant. Good thinking, and thanks for the rapid response.'

'Only doin' me job sir – bin in the force near on 30 years. Sorry the Super wouldn't let me have more men, oh and we're not armed I'm afraid.'

Cartwright gave the situation a few moments thought.

'Who are these other guys?' Davies, as if reading his guvnor's thoughts asked, 'Do you reckon it could be a firm from the IRA?'

'My thoughts exactly, Ray!' confirmed Cartwright. 'Sergeant Cuthbertson here, doesn't like it, neither do I. This could be dangerous. We desperately need some reinforcements; an armed response unit. If the radio's out of range, see if you can find a phone Ray, drum up some back-up from somewhere. See what you can do.'

It wasn't until Boxing Day morning that the *feckin' Yankee* had deigned reluctantly to show his face down by his van in the pub carpark. Ted Reilly, one of Doyle's men on watch spotted him approaching and went to the minibus to alert Michael Doyle. Wenzl drifted into the carpark as if on an incoming tide of an uncertain future. Did he really think he could blag his way out of what he knew full well was a very tricky situation?

'Ah, morning Michael.'

'Don't you be a "Morning Michael" me, you useless piece of shite!' Doyle spat on the ground.

'I'm sorry Michael. How's Gerry doing?' At the thought of his brother Michael's attitude hardened even further. It never occurred to him that Wenzl might also have been traumatised given his close encounter with the Grim Reaper. Doyle's sense of sympathy was firmly enclosed in a matchbox along with his sense of humour.

'Is all our weaponry still in the van?'

'Sorry Michael, I don't know.'

'What the feck d'you mean, you don't know?'

'Sorry Michael. I really don't know.'

'Well have you not looked, you festering arsehole?'

'I'm not sure where the keys are.'

'Oh bejesus, you really are the biggest waste o' feckin' space?'

Tom patted his pockets and made a good show of having lost or misplaced them. Doyle began stabbing his finger into Wenzl's chest. It was becoming ugly. 'C'mon you… you… total feckin' dickhead.' The finger stabbing became more vigorous – pushing and shoving.

Meanwhile Cartwright, who had crept down the hill to the pub was witnessing this highly charged confrontation from a discreet distance. He was trying to make sense of what was occurring and who the principal players in this particular drama were. He had read Armstrong's report and was aware of the chain of events. But not having met Wenzl before, whereas Armstrong had, he could only assume that the guy in the baseball cap with ears like wingnuts was the American who had been driving the Transit involved in the accident. He was also assuming that the other fellow was a member of the IRA cell looking to recover what Jock had stolen. Even as he was thinking about what to do next four other heavies then joined the scene from upstage and they weren't just 'extras' either. Each of them was armed. Cartwright recognised some of the weaponry; an M1 Carbine, a Thompson submachine gun, a Garand semi-automatic. Cartwright's heart was pounding. He felt sure it could be heard yards away. His uncertain interpretation of the scene vied with confusion and panic for a space in a now very turbulent area of his brain normally reserved for rational thought and action. He backpedalled to where Davies, just back from the phone box, and the uniformed officers were gathered.

'The way I see it,' Cartwright suggested, 'is that either there's about to be an execution by firing squad down there or we rush in and save the American's life by arresting him and hoping the IRA will back off. Now, bearing in mind there's some very serious firepower down there, what does anyone else think? Ray?'

'We can't just stand by and watched a bloke get shot, even if he is an American gangster.'

'What say you, sergeant?'

'I'm usually on traffic or running the front desk. This is all a bit out of my depth here.'

'OK, understood. Anyone else?' Andy Lewis had joined the gathering.

'Why don't I give it the beans, siren on and gun the car down there? That might put the wind up 'em enough for you to wade in and get the Yank out. They won't know we're only just a few coppers. With a bit of luck they might think it's the riot squad and a van full of armed police and decide to leg it.'

'Ray, what's the news of the armed unit?'

'They reckon at least half-an-hour guv.'

'We might not have five minutes never mind half-an-hour. OK Andy, we'll go with your plan since it's the only one we've got!'

Back in the car park, Wenzl had miraculously found the keys which had been in his pocket the whole time. He'd been frog-marched over to the van and forced to unlock it. When Doyle took a look inside his reaction was maniacal, frenzied and violent. He struck Wenzl with the butt of his M1911. Wenzl fell to the ground in a heap like the proverbial sack. Two or three men pulled him back to his feet and his wrists were roughly bound behind his back. Wenzl stood very unsteadily and blood was running from the wound at the back of his head and soaking into the collar of his Harrington jacket. The heavy mob with their artillery had sauntered back to the minibus. Doyle and Reilly remained facing Wenzl with weapons raised.

In that instant, the strident two-tone scream of the Granada's siren split the air and Lewis performed a spectacular handbrake turn, skidding to a halt centre stage. Cartwright's five-strong force charged the scene like whirling dervishes; uniformed men with batons raised, yelling and shouting, attempting to give the impression that there were more than just five of them. But this wasn't the scene they'd been expecting. Cartwright's magnificent five were relieved to see that the situation was not quite as intimidating or potentially suicidal as they just got a glimpse of Doyle and Reilly running off in the direction of the minibus which was already on the move. Both of the armed men turned and let off a couple of random rounds as they clambered aboard the bus. Unfortunately, one of Cuthbertson's lads caught a ricochet in the upper arm, but apart from that there were no other police casualties. Wenzl had collapsed and lay blubbing and bleeding on the ground.

'Let 'em go!' instructed the DI as the minibus sped away, 'but get the number.' Cuthbertson had taken the first-aid kit from the Granada and was administering treatment to Wenzl's wound which was not actually as bad as it had initially appeared. He'd certainly have a headache though. His wrists were untied but immediately handcuffed and he was bundled unceremoniously into the Granada. PC Lewis had taken a look in the Econoline and confirmed it was empty apart from Wenzl's small suitcase. This he collected and placed in the boot of the Granada. Cartwright thanked Sergeant Cuthbertson and his 'lads' for their assistance and promised he would recommend to the Leicester superintendent that they be awarded a commendation.

'Well done, sarge. Now get your man to casualty and you get back to your desk. Too much excitement's not good for a man of your age,' he joked. The Granada left to make its way back to Kidlington. Fred Webb had watched the whole event from an obscure vantage point on the swing bridge at the bottom of the flight.

'Well done Andy. Good plan!' Cartwright congratulated his driver. 'Couldn't have come up with a better one myself!' he jested. Lewis drove back to Kidlington at a rather more sedate pace. Davies was on the radio to the base dispatcher. When they arrived, Wenzl was placed in a cell whilst back in his office the DI and his DC reassessed the situation. After a few moments, the phone rang.

'Cartwright.'

'Armstrong, sir. I only just got your message.' Although Cartwright had initially been annoyed that his subordinate in St Aldate's police station had not been there earlier in the day, his demeanour now, given the way things had turned out was conducive to a fairly pleasant exchange. They each briefed the other.

'We found the American's van but there's no need for you to let him know. He knows already! He's banged up here in the cells. What's more, and a country mile from the cock and bull he gave you of being the innocent victim of vehicle theft, I reckon he's involved up to his back teeth in whatever's going on here. We'll hopefully know more when we've interviewed him.'

'Oh, right-oh, I see,' Armstrong responded. 'Any sign of your villain, Jock McClean?'

'Nah! Crafty bugger's long gone, and the guns and stuff with him. As I've said, I'm hoping we can get some sense out of the American. We also need a country-wide BOLO for a Volkswagen T2 8-seat minibus registration DKA 493L – believed stolen in Liverpool. The occupants, unless they've ditched it, may look like a Sunday School teachers' convention but believe me they're anything but – far from it. They're IRA terrorists and armed with more guns than John Wayne had at the Alamo. Now, can you get someone over to Foxton and bring that van in, and while you're at it, check out the Porsche the van's parked next to. I'm not convinced that's kosher either.' Cartwright beckoned Davies over.

'OK Ray, as you were, Pin Mill for you. Get yourself to Norfolk, That's enough excitement for one day.'

'Suffolk, sir,' Davies interrupted,

'Wherever, Suffolk then, and bring me Helen Blake or Hazel Black. Either will do!'

*

As had become customary in recent years, the period between Christmas and New Year was one during which the media, newspapers, magazines and television liked to look back at newsworthy or other memorable events that had happened throughout the previous twelve months. The following day, Kate, having given up on the *Telegraph* crossword was idly browsing through a supplement entitled 'Review of 1972'. The majority of what she read made pretty grim reading even just skipping through the headlines. 'Coal Rationing and the Miners' strike'. 'Destruction of the British Embassy in Dublin in an Anti-British Protest'. 'IRA Attack on the 16th Parachute Brigade at Aldershot'. 'Riot at the Saltley Coke Depot by Striking Miners'. 'Belfast Marches Against Direct Rule; 100,000 Protestors'. 'Roy Jenkins Resigns as Deputy-Leader of the Labour Party Over Plans For a Referendum on Membership Of The EEC'. 'Enquiry Into the "Bloody Sunday" Massacre in Northern Ireland'. 'Twelve Power Stations Shut Down Due to Fuel Shortages'. 'Black-outs'. 'Miners Riot as Police Attempt to Stop Oil Deliveries to Power Stations'. 'IRA Ceasefire Followed By The Ceasefire Being Abandoned and More Deaths'. 'British Army Clashes with Protestant Ulster Defence Troops'. 'Government in Dublin Passes Strict Anti-terrorist Laws'. 'Civil Rights Marchers Shot Dead'. 'Heath Government Freezes Wages'. 'Home Secretary Reginald Maudling Quits in Corruption Scandal'.

'Why oh why has everything been so depressing this year?' Kate was talking to Byron but the dog didn't appear to be that interested.

'Oh now, this is more like it. "Women rush to buy the first issue of *Cosmopolitan* a Monthly Magazine Promising Articles on Life, Love, Sex and Money".'

Byron cocked an ear briefly, yawned, farted and went back to sleep.

Chapter Thirty-Two

DI Cartwright sat in his office twiddling a pencil and thinking. He was looking at his whiteboard which hadn't helped reconcile or order his thinking at all since the arrest of Wenzl and the IRA's tactical withdrawal. He felt quite despondent. It seemed that Jock had slipped from the top of the wanted priority league and become side-lined as yet again he'd escaped from the DI's grasp somehow. The coffee in his mug had long since gone cold and he had resorted to a glass from the bottle he kept in the bottom drawer of his filing cabinet; the bottle for those difficult moments; those tricky situations which required a little inspirational guidance. He picked up Wenzl's suitcase and placed it on a table. One of the catches was broken and the other one was locked but didn't take much opening. He removed the contents of the case, spare clothes mostly, some clean, some not so clean, some in serious need of laundering. The bag of toilet requisites contained nothing out of the ordinary, razor, toothbrush and the like. What did intrigue the DI was why there should have been a paperback book in a foreign language which he didn't recognise. As he tried to make head or tail of the book, he took a further look at the case and found it had a removable lining in the bottom. Cartwright removed the lining and amongst the items concealed were various pieces of paper and several American and English bank notes. Of much greater interest were three passports; a green one issued by the USA, a navy-blue one, issued in Lebanon and a second navy-blue one issued in Northern Ireland. This discovery prompted a need for his glass to be topped up. Cartwright looked at each of the passports in turn. 'I think Tom Wenzl, Ahmed abu Mousa and Dermot O'Donnell have got some explaining to do.'

The following morning the DI was at his desk, early yet again. He sat there, in a quandary staring at the three passports when his telephone rang.

'Cartwright,' he announced, not really welcoming the interruption.

'This is Doug Armstrong sir. I was hoping you'd be in. I think you'll like this!' The DS's upbeat prophecy did little to lighten the DI's mood.

'I've had the vehicles at Foxton checked. I got onto Interpol about the black van, the Econoline E20 and I heard back from the New York Police Department that it was reported stolen by the owner, a Louis Winston, on Wednesday 29th November.'

'Now, why doesn't that surprise me?'

'Sorry sir?'

'Never mind, for now anyway. What about the other, a Porsche wasn't it?'

'Yes sir a Porsche 111. You'll love this.' Armstrong could hardly contain his excitement.

'I doubt it – go on let's hear it.'

'Registered owner, Duncan McClean of 214 Church Street, Burbage. Seems he bought it only a couple of weeks ago. From a dealer in Leicester, Triangle Motors. Dealer says he paid cash.' Cartwright took a deep breath and punched the air with his clenched fist as he exhaled. 'Alleluia!'

'Sorry sir? Is something wrong?'

'I'll say there is – you wouldn't believe the half of it.' The DI gave the DS a run-down on the three passports and his gut feelings.

'So, our Jock owns a Porsche – legitimately acquired and paid for, must be the first honest thing he's ever done. Look, Doug, is there any chance you could get down here to Kidlington, I could really use some experienced assistance on this. I'd rather not, but I reckon I'm going to have to call in the Counter Terrorism Unit.'

'Blimey! Oh no, not Alex Simons? Let's hope we can avoid that. OK, I'll have a word with my Super first, shouldn't be a problem and I'll be with you in an hour.'

As soon as Cartwright had replaced the receiver in its cradle, the phone rang again.

'Cartwright.'

'Ray Davies, guv. I've got Hazel Black and I'm bringing her in. Should be with you in two or three hours.'

'Well done Ray. What a case this is turning out to be!'

After lunch, DS Doug Armstrong and DI Cartwright – no one ever used his first name – sat at the table in an interview room. Opposite sat an individual who until earlier that day had been known as Tom Wenzl, a traveller in ladies' fashions; an American – or was he? The detectives were hoping they would find out exactly who he was.

'Good afternoon Tom – or should I call you Ahmed? Or Dermot perhaps? Which would you prefer?'

'No comment.'

'Well whoever you are, we have reason to believe that you are connected with or to one or more terrorist organisations. Is this correct?'

'No comment.'

'Now c'mon Tom,' Armstrong had previously dealt with him after the accident and thought by playing 'good cop' he might be able to get somewhere.

'Why were you asking the police to locate your van when you knew all along where it was?'

'No comment.'

'Well you now know that we have located your van, your Econoline E20. You were there when we located it! It's now in the police pound in Oxford, except it's not actually your van is it?'

'No comment.'

'You stole this van in New York on 29th November, didn't you? Came over here on the *QEII* which arrived at Southampton on 8th December.'

'No comment.'

'The van actually belongs to a guy named Louis Winston doesn't it?'

'Louis lent it to me.'

'Ah now that's better. Maybe we can get somewhere. Did he know you were coming to England with it?'

'Yes sir.'

'Did he know what you would be carrying?'

'Yes sir, I told him. Ladies' fashion garments. I work for Oscar de la Renta.'

'Did you tell Louis about the other stuff?'

'What other stuff?'

'The stuff under the dresses, under the frocks.'

'I don't know anything about any other stuff under the frocks.'

'So, you weren't illegally importing guns and other weapons for the IRA?'

'No sir I was not, most definitely not. I was carrying only ladies' fashionwear for Oscar de la Renta.' Cartwright took over the questioning.

'Who was in the Ford Cortina you were following on the night of the accident?'

'I don't know.'

'It wasn't your IRA contact then?'

'I do not have IRA contact.'

'We don't believe you. We think you're lying. We think you were illegally bringing weapons into the UK for supply to the IRA. We think you were collaborating with a Scotsman, Jock McClean, to supply arms to an unlawful terrorist organisation. Am I right?' Cartwright delivered each line slowly and deliberately, every one a little more vociferously than the previous.

'No comment.'

'Do you know or have you ever met Jock McClean?'

'No sir, I do not and I have not.'

'You're a liar! You are lying and I am losing my patience.'

The intensity of the interrogation was becoming highly charged yet the suspect remained calm and collected, showing no signs of agitation or discomfort despite the increasing aggression with which the questions were being posed.

'Why do you have an American passport?'

'I am American.'

'OK, the why do you have a British passport issued in Northern Ireland?'

'I have dual citizenship for work with Oscar de la Renta.'

'Why Northern Ireland? Why a different name? What are you hiding?'

'No comment.'

'What is your nationality? Are you American, or British or perhaps you're Lebanese?' The last of the three options offered by the DCI touched a nerve as it prompted a very forthright and indignant response.

'I am not Lebanese. I am a citizen of Palestine. Palestine is a territory over which no actual foreign sovereignty is exercised…'

'So, your real name is in fact Ahmed abu Mousa or is it Ali-bloody-baba?' Cartwright interrupted the diatribe which seemed about to swell into a declamation of party-political proportions. To the detectives' surprise abu Mousa rose to his feet smartly followed by Armstrong who did similarly.

'Please remain seated!' Armstrong instructed but to no avail. The rant continued. The fake American accent was dropped. Ahmed abu Mousa's effusion took on a valedictory ring to it, almost as if he knew what lay in store for him.

'I am a supporter of Fatah. My brother was murdered by Israelis in Jordan during the Six-Day War in 1967. I support the PLO. I fight in a civil war in Jordan. The Jordanian army forced the PLO and Fatah into Lebanon. I live in Palestine. 4052 Ibrahim Al Khatib Street, Gaza, Palestine. I am a member of Black September at the Olympic Games. Revenge for my brother. I demand political asylum.' He sat down.

Neither Armstrong nor Cartwright knew very much, if anything at all about the political situation in the Middle East although Cartwright could vaguely recall reading something about the murder of Wasfi-al-Tel the Jordanian Prime Minister in 1970.

He also seemed to recollect that it was a terrorist organisation calling itself Black September who were responsible. Far more recently, just a few months earlier in fact at the Munich Olympic Games the whole world was outraged when members of Black September held eleven Israeli athletes hostage before eventually massacring them and murdering a German policeman. Was this man, Ahmed abu Mousa, the man sitting across the table from them a member of Black September – perhaps the most extremist militant terrorist organisation in recent times? Has he just confessed? The two detectives looked at each other wearing expressions of absolute incredulity. Cartwright decided he did need help. This was all way above his pay-grade.

'Take him back to his cell!' ordered Cartwright. The uniformed constable, PC Colin Harvey, who had been present in the interview room throughout the interrogation stepped forward and took hold of abu Mousa's arm. As he was about to be escorted back to a cell Mousa asked if he might have his suitcase. He needed a change of clothes. Knowing exactly what the contents of the suitcase were, Cartwright felt that the request was entirely reasonable, and as the detective in charge of the investigation, he wasn't about to be accused of denying anyone a basic human right. After all the man now known as Ahmed abu Mousa had not been charged, as yet. He was merely 'assisting police with their enquiries' at this stage; enquiries into the whereabouts of Jock McClean, a murder suspect, believed to be a member of the IRA. But, and as happened now and again, the investigation had uncovered something far bigger. Besides which, were abu Mousa to be charged Cartwright wasn't entirely sure what the charge should be.

Cartwright and Armstrong returned to CID and Cartwright's office. Both of them resorted to the liquid comfort from the bottom drawer of the filing cabinet. Cartwright picked up the phone.

'Could you put me through to Detective Chief Superintendent Alex Simons please?' The DCS was the fearsome and unpopular Commander of the Counter Terrorist Unit.

Chapter Thirty-Three

Later in the day DC Ray Davies arrived back at Kidlington accompanied by an extremely well-dressed and very attractive fifty-something year old woman, Helen Blake also known as Hazel Black. Davies knocked on Cartwright's office door.

'Come in!'

'I'm back guv – hello sir.'

'Ms Blake – excuse me, Ms Black. I'm Detective Inspector Cartwright, leading the investigation into the various activities of a Duncan McClean. This is Detective Sergeant Armstrong, and Detective Constable Davies, you've already met of course, and I'm sure he's not stopped talking to you all the way from Norfolk…'

'Suffolk,' corrected Davies.

'Yes, of course. Thank you so much for sparing the time and coming in to see us. We believe you may be in a position to assist us in our enquiries. I'm sorry, how rude of me, Ray, get Ms Black a chair. Would you like a cup of tea perhaps? Ray, pop and get Ms Black a cuppa…'

'It's OK Detective Inspector, thank you anyway, and please call me Hazel.' Cartwright was slightly flustered. He had never been particularly comfortable interviewing women and especially women as attractive as this one. He could even now feel himself blushing, much to the amusement of Armstrong and Davies.

'Now then, Hazel, could you begin by telling us everything you know about Jock McClean, how you got to know him and how your relationship with him lead to you being sentenced to, what was it now, seven years at East Sutton Park.'

For the next two hours Hazel provided a detailed account of her life since the end of WWII. The black-market, her husband's involvement and subsequent disappearance. The birth of her son, Ben, and how she abandoned him to take off with Jock on a narrowboat. She was close to tears when she related the manner in which her husband had been murdered and his body discovered by her son. The three detectives were most attentive with the DC taking notes, and the DS and DI posing questions and requesting further and better particulars with regard to some of what they were being told.

'You actually witnessed McClean murder your estranged husband?'

'I did. We'd just taken the boat from Foxton and had entered Lock Number 25, the Newton Top Half-Mile Lock. Ken, my ex-husband had been waiting for us and came on board. He and Jock were arguing over something – might even have been me they were arguing about – I don't know. Anyway, the argument developed into a fight and Jock hit Ken over the head with a winch handle several times and Ken fell overboard into the lock.'

'Did he fall or was he pushed?'

'Bit of both really.'

'When was this?'

'Late July or early August 1962. I don't remember the exact date but his funeral was August 23rd.'

'Why didn't you report it at the time?'

'I thought I'd incriminate myself, with what we, me and Jock that is, what we'd been up to trading black-market goods and stolen property and such. But I did eventually, to a Detective Chief Inspector Mosely.'

'Yes, I remember. Mosely was my boss in Leicester.'

'I thought I recognised you,' Hazel observed with a smile. Cartwright blushed again.

'And it was as a result of what you told Mosely that you were charged – you pleaded guilty I think?'

'Yes I did. Well, I was, wasn't I?' Hazel was quite prepared to be open and truthful – up to a point.

'I understand you're a wealthy woman Hazel.'

'I'm comfortable thank you.'

'Where'd your money come from?'

'War Bonds.'

'I see.' Armstrong said, in such a manner that it was obvious that he didn't believe her.

'Well, I think we're nearly done, is here anything else you can tell us?'

'Do you know about the other murders?' Hazel wondered.

'Go on,' Cartwright encouraged her,

'Well, there was Ron, Ron Nicholls, used to work with Jock on the buses. He got shot. Then there were the two blokes that lived upstairs when me and Ken were first married. I'm not sure, but I'm pretty certain Jock bumped them off as well.'

'We're aware of Ron Nicholls, but it's the first we've heard of the other two. Do you remember their names?

'I never knew their names, never even spoke to them really, two men living together – I didn't like to interfere. You know what I mean?'

'When did you last see Jock, Hazel?'

'When I left the boat in that July or August. I can't remember exactly.'

'In 1962 you mean?

'Yes, that's right. But he's here again, he's around somewhere, and I'm frightened. He's threatening us.'

'What makes you think he's around? What are you frightened of? How is he threatening you?'

'I received a Christmas card. Delivered by hand. My son's father-in-law answered the door but couldn't recognise who it was that delivered it. He was a small man apparently. He'd driven to my cottage in a Porsche. We were having a Christmas Party. And then a bloke in a Porsche, a bloke with a Scottish accent had been to our local pub, the Old Greyhound in Great Glen asking for something my husband had left there for me after the war.' Hazel was all too well aware that she had to be careful and not give the game away with regard to the Nazi gold.

'Have you still got the Christmas card?' Armstrong asked adopting an avuncular attitude.

Hazel reached into her handbag, pulled out the card and handed it over to Cartwright. The DI read the inscription inside the card.

'I know where you live and I know where your son lives. I'll be coming for you and to collect my share.'

'Yes, I see what you mean. It does sound threatening doesn't it? What do you think he means *collect my share*? Share of what?'

'Well I can only imagine he means some money he left on the boat. You know the boat was found abandoned? Well after it had been taken back to Foxton I went and saw Fred…'

'Fred?'

'Yes sorry, Fred Webb the lockkeeper. We were very good friends. I wanted another look at the boat, you know, for old times' sake, and collect a few things I'd left aboard. Well I also found a box of cash, not a lot, can't remember exactly how much, about a thousand I think. Well I wasn't going to leave it there was I? I reckoned he owed me that at least. Maybe that's what he means?'

'Yes maybe. What was it that your husband had left for you in the pub? Could that have been what he was after?'

'I shouldn't think so, it was a box, just a few trinkets, a bit of jewellery that's all.'

'Well, look Hazel, you've been very helpful. You've given us some further leads to follow up. Don't worry too much about Jock turning up to claim whatever it is he thinks you have that belongs to him. We know about the Porsche, and it's still in the car park at the Foxton Locks Inn where we've got it under surveillance for when he comes to collect it. We're that close…' he indicated a small space between his thumb and forefinger, '… to making an arrest and then Jock will be going away for a very, very, long time.' Cartwright placed a heavy emphasis on the second *very*.

Ray Davies escorted Hazel from the office and at her request he was only too happy to drive her to Burton Overy rather than

Pin Mill. It was so much nearer for one thing and maybe that barmaid would be on duty in the Old Greyhound.

The DI and DS took to the bottle again.

'Do you believe her?'

'I want to. She's had a rough time, seven years? Even if she was paroled after five, a bit excessive if you ask me. But while I'm sure her story is mostly true, I'm not so sure about the trinkets and jewellery. There's probably more to it than that. As for the cash, if he can afford to buy a Porsche I can't see how Jock would be worrying about a thousand. What's more, how could Mosely have missed a box of cash when he searched the *Emily Rose*?' Armstrong was more than prepared to give her the benefit of the doubt.

'She may not be giving us the whole truth, but I don't think she's got anything else that will help us get to Jock.' Cartwright nodded his agreement.

'Can I leave it to you Doug, to get in touch with Leicester, or I suppose Hinckley would be more appropriate. Let's see if we can get any more on "the two blokes upstairs". Oh, and make sure our Leicester chums keep a twenty-four-hour watch on that Porsche.'

They were about to leave when the phone rang.

'Cartwright.'

'Alex Simons, Cartwright. You rang me.'

'Yes sir!'

*

Hazel was mightily relieved to have got her interview with the police over and hopefully done with once and for all. It was an even greater relief to have learned that the police were well and truly on the case and that Jock would be apprehended before very much longer. Ray Davies had been the perfect gentleman driving her back to Burton but he declined Hazel's invitation to come in for coffee opting to call in at the pub instead. This set an alarm bell ringing in Hazel's head. Was he making further enquiries about what she had told the police; that it was nothing more than a box of trinkets and jewellery she wondered. Ben and the rest listened carefully as his mother recounted her inquisition, and there was relief all round.

'Call me paranoid if you like,' Hazel said to Ben, 'but the detective who drove me home has gone to the Greyhound. Be a love Ben, run down there, make an excuse about wanting to see Jamie or whatever but I'll not sleep easily unless I know for sure he's not digging around for information about the crate or its contents.'

Ben obliged without question. He returned about an hour later.

'You're paranoid mum!' he laughed. 'I had a quick half with him, the detective, and all he was interested in was Diane's frontage.

Chapter Thirty-Four

Since leaving Foxton during the early hours of Boxing Day, the *Nancy Blakemore* had made steady progress southwards and having encountered no other traffic on the canal they had reached Long Buckby Wharf by 29th December. Having seen the police car speeding over the Kilworth Road Bridge three days earlier, Jock could only assume that the balloon had gone up back at Foxton, but there again he might have been wrong. Perhaps the police had been called to some other incident. Either way, he was only mildly concerned. Wally, for his part was merely the boatman; an accessory maybe, but his primary role in the business was to deliver his cargo to Limehouse Basin in London's East End. Wally was blessed with a fairly happy-go-lucky disposition and Jock's reaction whenever they encountered a tunnel gave him a great deal of amusement. He had derived enormous satisfaction from winding Jock up earlier in the day when they made passage through the Crick Tunnel. At almost a mile long and only a few inches wider than the boat, it wasn't unknown for the occasional brick to fall from the tunnel roof and Wally would compound Jock's dread of tunnels by banging on the cabin roof, claiming another fallen brick and scaring him half to death. With time on their side and not wishing to arrive at Limehouse before the planned rendezvous, they decided to stay the night at Long Buckby where they could sample the delights of the New Inn if indeed there were any delights to be sampled.

*

'Is that the *Oxford Mail*?' PC Phil Doherty was on the phone. 'Could you put me through to the news desk please?'

'News desk.'

'What'll you pay for the hottest exclusive you've ever had?'

A deal was negotiated and the evening edition of the paper carried the following article beneath the reporter's fairly pathetic pun.

Terror Suspect 'Locked' Up!
Munich Massacre Man Held.
Following an anonymous tip-off from a member of the public, Thames Valley police with a detachment from the Leicester Constabulary raided a pub car park at local beauty spot Foxton Locks where a stolen van believed to be carrying a shipment of guns was due to be collected by an IRA gang. The IRA made off empty-handed in a stolen minibus but not before shots were fired and a police constable wounded. The van actually proved to be empty with the weapons cache having been diverted to another terrorist cause by an IRA deserter and the main suspect in a multiple murder enquiry. A man believed at the time to be American and the importer of the weapons was taken away for questioning. Under interrogation by senior detectives at Kidlington, the American admitted to being Palestinian and a member of the notorious Black September terrorist organisation who were responsible for the massacre of Israeli athletes at the Munich Olympics earlier this year. The incident has been referred to the Counter Terrorism Unit under Detective Chief Superintendent Alex Simons.

The following day every national daily in the land carried the story and most of them had made it the lead article on the front page. The telephones at Thames Valley police headquarters did not stop ringing all day and Alex Simons was not a happy man.

'Cartwright, I'm holding you personally responsible to find out which blasted idiot leaked this to the press. We'll have the whole of the bloody Black September organisation in the country attempting to rescue one of their own I shouldn't wonder!'

*

Before continuing their 'voyage' down the Grand Union canal, Jock went to buy some provisions from the shop by Buckby Top Lock Number 7. Passing by the newsstand he couldn't help but notice the billboard. 'Black September Suspect in Custody – IRA Escape'. Along with the bread, milk and bacon, he bought a copy of the *Daily Mirror*. Back on the *Nancy Blakemore* over a mug of tea Jock read the front-page report out loud to Wally whose reading skills were somewhat limited.

'Ah ken tha' polis car was on its way tae Foxton. Ah'm reckoning we were dead lucky tae get awa' wi' it when we did Wal! Ah'll jist goo back an' gi' Fred a bell. Mebbe he kin tell us more.' Jock clambered back onto the wharf's quayside and made his way over to the phone box.

'Fred, is it yersel' Fred? It's me Jock. After we left on Boxing Day did ye see whit happened wi' IRA an' polis?'

'I did that Jock. I watched the 'ole thing from a-top o' swing bridge. Tom took a right beatin' from one o' IRA lads then t'cavalry arrived, bloody siren a-goin' fit to wake the dead. IRA scarpered shootin' as they went – med off in a minibus. Tom got took away in the police car. I guess yo's seen t'papers?'

'Aye, jist a wee while ago. Ah knew there wis summat nae quite right wi' that Tom but ah'd niver wid 'ave thought he wis Black September. Ah'll be beggared! Anyway, Fred, ma wee pal, kin ye keep an eye on ma Porsche please? I dinnae ken when ah'll be back fer it.'

'There's already somebody keeping an eye on it – twenty-four hours a day. If I was yo' Jock, an' I'm glad I ain't, I'd forget it. If yo' come back for it yo'll be nicked. Tell yo' what, gis a ring now and again an' if the coast's clear I can let yo' know.'

'Och thanks a million Fred. That's another one I owe ye. Sees ye soon, eh?'

Jock returned to the boat and was grateful that Wally had the kettle on the boil. He needed coffee; more importantly coffee with a dram to go with it. After several more 'wee drams' Jock slept soundly all night.

*

At Thames Valley Police Headquarters Ahmed abu Mousa, in handcuffs, had been led into an interview room by PC Phil Doherty who remained, standing guard. Already present in the room were Detective Chief Superintendent Alex Simons of the Counter Terrorist Unit and Detective Inspector Cartwright. Wearing full dress uniform and a very grave expression, Simons invited Mousa to sit down.

'I'll remain standing if you don't mind, please?'

'As you wish'. Simons proceeded to caution him. 'You have the right to remain silent but anything you do say may be taken down and later given in evidence. Do you understand?' Mousa was clearly intent on exercising his right to remain silent and said nothing. He merely nodded to confirm his understanding of the caution. The DCS continued.

'Use or threats of action both in this country and outside the United Kingdom which are designed to influence any international government organisation or to intimidate the public in an attempt to advance a political, religious or ideological cause are regarded as acts of terrorism contrary to the Prevention of Terrorism Act 1972.' Cartwright felt that the DCS's pontification was perhaps a little over the top and had his doubts whether abu Mousa fully understood or even cared. Simons continued.

'You are charged under the aforementioned Act in that you illegally imported guns and other weapons from America for use by a known terrorist organisation namely the Provisional Irish Republican Army.' At the mention of the IRA abu Mousa reacted.

'Not for the IRA. The guns were for Black September. I am a Palestinian – a member of the Palestine Liberation Organisation.'

'Oh I see. So you admit that you belong to a terrorist organisation?'

'No comment.'

'Before you were brought here on 26th December you met with Michael Doyle and other members of the IRA at Foxton. Is that correct?

'No comment.'

'Your van, or rather the van you stole in New York was used to carry guns and other weapons into the United Kingdom for use by the IRA.' Cartwright was satisfied that the head of the Counter Terrorism Unit had clearly been listening and making notes when he had briefed him.

'The van was then subject to an elaborate plot whereby that consignment which was intended for the IRA was hijacked with the intention of supplying another terrorist organisation. Is that correct?

'No comment.'

'Where are the guns and weapons now?'

'No comment.'

'Do you admit to being part of the Black September Organisation that held eleven Israeli athletes hostage during the Olympic Games in Munich?'

'No comment.'

Do you admit that you were part of the organisation that then massacred the Israeli hostages and also murdered a German policeman?'

'No comment.'

'Did you post, or do you know who posted a letter bomb to the Israeli embassy in London that killed an Israeli diplomat in September last year?'

'No comment'

Simons was becoming increasingly exasperated by the lack of any manner of response and indicated to Cartwright that they should step outside briefly for a consultation.

'This is getting us nowhere. And I'm flying a bit of kite since none of the weapons have been recovered yet. What's going on there Cartwright?'

'We believe we know who has the cache sir. We're pretty sure it's in the hands of a Scotsman, also believed to be an IRA member, but more likely acting independently as a mercenary. We've been after him for a while now – wanted for at least two, possibly more murders.' Cartwright didn't wish to admit that Jock had been on the wanted list for eight years.

'OK, well bloody well get on with it. I'm going to have our man Mousa moved to somewhere secure in the meantime. I'll also see if our German friends want to get involved. But CTU will take it from here.'

'I understand sir, thank you sir.' They both returned to the interview room where Ahmed abu Mousa was still standing to attention, hands cuffed behind his back with PC Doherty on guard. Simons didn't sit down to address the prisoner.

'You will be taken to a maximum-security installation pending further enquiries.' He nodded an acknowledgement to Cartwright and marched out of the room.

'OK constable,' sighed the DI, and with some relief, 'take him back to his cell.'

'Sir!'

*

'Newsdesk please…. Yes, hello. Would you be interested in buying an exclusive?' Philip Doherty was on the phone again, this time directly to the *Times*.

*

As DS Armstrong arrived back at St Aldate's police station in Oxford the station's desk sergeant had just finished a telephone call.

'Doug, that was the landlord of the Turners Arms, a pub in Blackthorn – a village just off the A41. Apparently, the minibus used in the incident at Foxton has been abandoned in the car park there.

'Have we got the registration number?' The sergeant referred to his notes.

'I'm fairly certain it's the one guv – a VW T2 8-seater DKA 493L?'

'Yep, that's the one. Let's get a forensic team over to it…'

'Hang on guv that's not all. Seems the minibus crew swapped their vehicle for two cars, stolen from the same pub car park.'

'How long ago?'

'About half-an-hour.'

'Ring the pub and let 'em know I'm on my way!'

When Armstrong arrived, the small village pub, obviously a popular place, was busy with Sunday lunchtime regulars. He bought himself a pint of bitter and waited until the landlord was on top of serving a backlog of customers and had a spare moment to talk to the DS. Armstrong made notes. The landlord clearly remembered two Irishmen, although he couldn't identify whether they were from Northern Ireland or the Republic being unable to distinguish between the accents.

'They came into the pub on the day after Boxing Day, had a couple of pints and left.'

'Is there anything else you can remember about them; could you give a description?'

'Not really. Just an ordinary couple of blokes, dressed in black suits, wearing black ties. I thought they might be on their way to a funeral or just come from church or something. Perfectly respectable. I did notice they came in a minibus though.'

'What about the cars that were reported a stolen from your car park?'

'Well, that's it innit? The more I thought about it the more it made sense. They were casing the place weren't they. Two of my regulars, Bob and Dave, there they are at the bar now.' The landlord indicated two 'town and country' types perched on bar stools, obviously familiar with the barmaid. 'They're both in here almost every night, and lunchtimes at weekends. They spend a fair bit between them. Small pub like this depends on its regulars. Bob drives up from Kingswood, and Dave lives out at Piddington. Well, sometime last night, Bob's Cortina went and Dave's Capri – he hadn't had it long – cost him a fortune dinnit? Both fairly new motors as well.' The landlord went back behind the bar to deal with the growing number of thirsty customers. Armstrong walked over to have a word with the two victims of car theft. Having taken their details he resumed his seat by the fireplace to finish his pint. He picked up a newspaper that had been left behind. The *Sunday Times*. The headline on the front page screamed at him. 'Terrorist Arrested in Black September/IRA Showdown'. The article that followed gave a comprehensive report of DCS Simons' interrogation of Ahmed abu Mousa. Armstrong was incensed and rushed straight back to his office and put in a call to Cartwright.

'Yes Doug, I've seen it. We've got a serious leak here and when I find out who it is he'll be back on the worst beat on the patch if not kicked off the force all together – and that's if Simons doesn't have my guts for garters first.'

*

In a layby overlooking open countryside not far from Weston-on-the-Green Michael Doyle and Ted Reilly were sitting in a blue Ford Capri 3000E. Ted was gazing out of the window, smoking. Michael was reading the *Sunday Times*.

'So it seems Tom's not Tom. He's feckin' Ahmed is he? Well, he won't know who he is, or his arse from his elbow when I get to him. Feckin' festering double crossing bastard that he is. I reckon Ted, that if they're going to transfer him to a maximum-security nick, that'll be our chance. Now, where?'

'Gartree,' said Ted in an absentminded sort of way. 'It's the nearest.'

'Where's that?'

'Not far away. It's close to where we've just come from, near Market Harborough.'

'OK, Let's go take a look. We'll drive the route that the police are likely to take. Look, there's a map on the back seat. That's handy! Let's have a look. We'll go as soon as I've been to see Gerry.'

*

Kate had also bought the *Sunday Times* and was reading the article based on the leaked information.

'You all need to read this,' she shouted with an incredulous sense of urgency to no one in particular but intending that everyone in the house should hear. In the kitchen Tina was preparing lunch. Hazel was upstairs, Ben was rattling up and down scales and arpeggios on the piano and Stuart was out in the garden with Byron. Everyone heard the shout and they all gathered around the article.

'I don't believe it!' There was an air of exasperation in Ben's exclamation.

'No mention of Jock – is the terrorist stuff more important?' His question was rhetorical.

'Maybe I shouldn't, but I'm inclined to ring that Detective Cartwright and find out what's going on. Seems obvious to me that this Mousa bloke and Jock were in league. They've got one of them but not the other, and it's the other one that's our problem.' Hazel sat fidgeting, patently uncomfortable with the latest development

'Give it another day or so mum,' Ben urged. 'His Porsche is under surveillance and surely he'll be back for it sooner or later.'

'Yes, perhaps you're right,' Hazel conceded. 'Let's hope it's sooner, eh?'

*

At the John Ratcliffe Infirmary, Gerry Doyle was no longer on the critical list but still in intensive care. Michael filled him in on the developments in the situation thus far but his brother uttered but two words.

'Get Brian!'

Chapter Thirty-Five

The crew of the *Nancy Blakemore* became victims of an involuntary intemperance during the New Year celebrations in the New Inn at Long Buckby. Despite their earlier misgivings the delights offered by the pub were plentiful and Jock, as always was the life and soul of the party, aided and abetted by Wally who couldn't remember the last occasion he'd had such a good time. For all that, they hadn't quite lost sight of what they were about; to deliver a stolen cargo of guns, ammunition and explosives to an extremist terrorist organisation. Despite the forces of law, order and counter-terrorism being hard on their heels, neither Jock nor Wally seemed unduly concerned. The mission may have been uppermost in their minds initially but as the party continued into the early hours the consequences of this particular delivery were dissolving further in every pint.

When they eventually came to on New Year's Day, notwithstanding the excesses of the previous evening, the stove was stoked, the pan was on, and *Nancy Blakemore* was on the way. Sore heads there may have been but they were both fully focused again. Once they had cleared Lock Number 13, the Buckby Bottom, it had been an easy, straightforward, lock-free run up to Blisworth and the junction with the Northampton Arm, although the weather hadn't helped. It was here that they had planned on staying the night. Wally brought the boat gently to a stop a few yards under the A43 road bridge and made her secure to metal mooring stakes in the towpath. The day had been grey and cold with patchy fog and now it was almost dark but reassuringly warm in the boatman's cabin. Jock and Wally were thawing out over a cup of tea.

'Ah've had an idea an' ah reckon wi' this wee wheeze we kin lead the polis up the garden path.' Wally was listening, curious to learn what Jock had in mind.

'They wicker baskets have got they posh frocks hiding the guns an' stuff.

We'll go an' sell 'em. Wit, wi' their designer labels an' all we can make a few quid too. Wit d'ye reckon Wal?'

''ow does that lead police up the garden path?'

'They frocks are connected tae Wenzl an' his wicker baskets. We'll find a pub close tae the new Motorway and let whoever might be interested or even wint tae buy 'em think we're on our way tae north, up the M1. We kin tip off the polis and they'll be off in the wrong direction. Genius dae ye nae think?'

'I s'pose it could work; buy us a bit o' time.'

So it was that that evening, two men walked into the Compass Inn in nearby Milton Malsor, each of them incongruously carrying an armful of ladies' fashions by the Dominican design guru Oscar de la Renta. To Wally's way of thinking, this plan was not quite as cunning as Jock thought. Even Wally could detect the fundamental flaws inherent in the idea. Firstly, the pub, remote as it was, would be all but empty the night after New Year's Eve celebrations and what customers there were would hardly be the sort likely to be interested. Secondly, what were two men, so obviously bargees, doing with women's clothing? Undaunted, they sat and had a pint anyway. So, what was it about Jock? How on earth did he always manage to come out of any situation smelling of roses? Just as Wally was about to get up and leave, a fellow came into the bar wearing an air of gullibility and a dark brown suit. Seeing Jock and Wally, he minced over towards them.

'Excuse me boys, but I appear to have taken a wrong turn somewhere. Could you direct me to the northbound M1 motorway please?'

'Och, for sure sir, We're just goin' up the motorway oursel's from a ladies' fashion convention in London. Ye'll need tae tek the A43 to junction 15. It's nae far!'

'Ooh, ladies' fashion convention you say?'

'Aye. We've got a few surplus garments here. Might ye be interested? We could dae ye a bonny price, so we could.'

Wally just sat there opened mouthed in total disbelief at Jock's patter. After another five minutes of blarney of the Scottish variety and another round of drinks, including a gin and tonic for the dark brown suit, they were loading Oscar de la Renta's summer collection into the boot of a white Jaguar XJ6 and £50 better off.

Wally could not believe it nor could he stop laughing.

'I've never seen owt like it, you crafty ole bugger.'

On the way back to the boat, they managed to find some old pieces of sacking in the yard at the junction to replace the cargo's more sophisticated covering it had enjoyed since leaving the USA. It was perhaps as well that Jock didn't know the real value of ladies' designer fashion wear. Had he done so he surely would not have let it go for so far below the retail price. Unusual for this particular Scotsman.

From a phone box in Blisworth Jock dialled the number for the Thames Valley Police in Kidlington. When the call was answered he put on his best BBC announcer's voice.

'There's a white Jaguar XJ6 travelling north on the M1 motorway driven by a man in a dark-brown suit. He has ladies' fashion garments in his car which are believed to be stolen.'

He immediately replaced the receiver.

Thirty minutes later the white Jaguar XJ6 and the dark-brown suit pulled into the Blue Boar at Watford Gap, a popular yet infamous night spot. The Blue Boar was not just a service station and cafe. Ever since the motorway had opened, it was the place to be seen, always full of young men, taking a break from speed trialling their customised cars or motorcycles up and down this section of the motorway. Almost invariably they would be accompanied by their trend-setting girlfriends and random hangers-on, all of whom were dedicated followers of fashion. Mr Dark-Brown Suit easily sold on his recently acquired garments and quadrupled his initial outlay in no time at all. An off-duty policeman, Eric King out for an evening with his girlfriend happened to notice the label in one of the dresses and made a note.

*

The following morning Jock faced his demon; another tunnel. Not just any tunnel, but one of the longest on the entire canal network at one and three-quarters of a mile. As they came under the Blisworth Mill Bridge and the north portal of the tunnel hove into view Jock was overcome with a fit of terror, his blood turning to iced water.

'Wally, Wally ma best pal. Wull ye nae stop the boat please? Ah cannae dae it! Nae, I wullnae dae it!' Jock was absolutely adamant. The Blisworth Tunnel held no demons for Wally and whilst he just could not understand the mortal dread that Jock experienced, he did have another flashback to just over nine years ago and the Saddington incident. He smiled to himself.

'OK yo' wimp. Yo're nowt but a big girl's blouse. Mebbe I'll get yo' one o' they dark brown suits or 'appen we should 'ave kept one o' them frocks back for yo'.' He was roaring with laughter. 'I'll meet yo' at t'other end.' He pulled over and into the bank and allowed Jock to jump ashore to follow the well-worn path over Blisworth Hill. About an hour later he was back on board as the *Nancy Blakemore* glided in to Stoke Bruerne.

*

When PC Eric King signed on for his shift on Tuesday morning he took out his pocketbook and referred to the note he'd made the previous evening. 'White Jaguar XJ6 – dark-brown suit – Oscar de la Renta'.

'Does this name mean anything to you Gordon?' His good friend and mentor, Gordon Almey previously a regular PC stationed in Hinckley was now, after almost thirty years' service, a Detective Constable at the Hinckley Road station in Leicester.

'Don't think so, why?'

'Bloke in a brown suit was knocking out this Oscar de la Renta fashion label gear at the Blue Boar last night. I reckon it were all knockoffs.'

'Leave it wi' me son. I'll 'ave a word.'

Chapter Thirty-Six

'Ciara, can you find a number for Brian O'Connor?' Michael Doyle was on the phone to his daughter at the Blackstaff Bar in Belfast. Brian had been one of the IRA's men in London for many years and one of the army's most trusted foot soldiers. He'd been one of the kingpins in the so-called Kilburn Battalion of the IRA. It was this group that had claimed responsibility for planting a bomb in the roof of the men's toilets in the restaurant at the top of the Post Office Tower in London in 1971. Brian O'Connor was an unassuming character, well-read, an intellectual even. He was also an expert marksman, a sniper with extraordinary ability.

*

Detective Chief Superintendent Simons had made arrangements with the Governor of Gartree regarding the transfer of Ahmed abu Mousa who was to be held in maximum-security on remand pending trial. DI Cartwright had been ordered to organise the transport. The DI went in search of Andy Lewis. He'd been very impressed with his driving skills and initiative and he was always keen to give young officers an opportunity to prove themselves and climb the career ladder. He found Lewis in the canteen.

'We're going to move the "Sheikh of bloody Araby" tomorrow and I'm leaving the transport details to you.'

'Thank you sir; won't let you down sir.'

'I reckon on a motorcycle escort, the "Black Maria" with one driver and two guards from the prison then you and me in the Granada. What d'you think?'

'Should cover it sir. Same route as when we went to Foxton?'

'You're in charge!'

'Thank you, sir. What's the ETD?'

'Early – 0600 hours.'

'Sir!'

Taking a keen interest in this conversation whilst in the queue for a cup of tea was PC Phil Doherty.

*

After visiting his brother Gerry and ringing his daughter Ciara, Doyle and Reilly drove the route they were banking on the police taking when Ahmed abu Mousa would be transferred to Gartree Prison. Neither Michael nor Ted had noticed on the map how close the prison was to Foxton. They were fairly confident that the convoy conveying the prisoner would take the A4304 and make the left turn just before Lubbenham, then follow the two miles long Foxton Road across Mill Hill, then right, on to Gallowfield Road for the last mile-and-a-half to the prison. There wasn't really a practical alternative. Ted and Michael drove slowly past the formidable looking prison building, with its high double fencing and razor wire They continued on into Market Harborough. They parked up and considered their options. Together they poured over the map again.

'The Foxton Road across Mill Hill is favourite,' concluded Michael. 'I'll admit it looks fairly straight and there's not much cover, but it's rural and it's more than probable it'll be almost deserted with little if any traffic. I reckon it'll do.' Ted Reilly went and found a phone box and made the first of three telephone calls. It was to Brian O'Connor.

'Be on the next train to Market Harborough. We'll meet you at the station. The second call was to Michael Doyle's informant, Phil Doherty. The final call was to one of their own at the Coach and Horses in Kibworth Harcourt where the rest of IRA 'bible salesmen' were staying. The stolen Ford Cortina

2000E was parked in an old stable block behind a row of laurel and holly hedging in the car park.

'Be ready. It's tomorrow morning. Just be prepared and keep off the booze tonight it's an early start. Oh, and we'll need a Land Rover, one with a winch on the front if possible, just in case. We'll be back as soon as we've collected Brian from the station.' Michael parked the Capri by the station and together he and Ted went and sat in the Peacock in St Mary's Place while they waited for Brian's train to arrive.

*

The fog on New Year's Day had taken a couple of days to dissipate and a high-pressure system was now dominating the weather. As the convoy left Kidlington, on the dot of 6 am the temperature was just a few degrees above freezing. As dawn broke the day looked like it held the prospect of some sunshine for a change. Leading the convoy was PC Colin Harvey on a T6 Triumph Thunderbird, nicknamed SAINT – 'stops anything in no time'. Following the motorcycle was a black Ford Transit; the Mariah. Inside the back was a secure cage. The 'Paddy Wagon' as it was sometimes so called was named after the police vans in New York which rounded up mainly drunken Irishmen at the turn of the century. The Irishmen they were to encounter on this trip would be stone-cold sober. Bringing up the rear were Cartwright and Lewis in the Granada. Lewis had estimated that the seventy mile trip would take about an hour-and-a-half.

Doyle and his team had dressed down for the occasion and were now in camouflage fatigues with balaclavas ready to wear if required. By 7 am they were in position. Brian O'Connor had arrived at Market Harborough station the previous afternoon as instructed. He carried a golf bag inside which was concealed the preferred tool of his trade; a Remington M21A sniper rifle fitted with a Zeiss ZF42 telescopic sight. This was Brian's favourite weapon which, with its high precision, accuracy and reliability, firing high ballistic centre-fire cartridges had a range of about 800 yards. Brian had concealed himself in long grass, some 400 yards from the road and about a half-mile along the route to Foxton from the A4304, just over the brow of Mill Hill. He had an uninterrupted view of Foxton Road. Doyle and Reilly, both armed with Thompson submachine guns were sitting in the stolen Ford Capri 3000E facing south, partially concealed on the side of the road just below the junction with Welland Avenue. The rest of the squad, all carrying side-arms at least, were divided between the Ford Cortina 2000E and the recently acquired Series III Land Rover. With its four-wheel drive, 88-inch wheel-base, traction tyres, crash bars and a 'Rhino' heavy-duty winch capable of pulling 13500lbs, just in case. It was well suited for what Doyle had planned. With their vehicles tucked out of sight in the track leading to Holmes Farm, the ambush was set.

*

The call which Jock had made anonymously to Kidlington had been referred to DC Ray Davies. Using his initiative, as Cartwright had often instructed him to, Davies had put in calls to several police stations for any information on stolen ladies' designer fashion wear and struck lucky when he rang Hinckley Road. The Oscar de la Renta label witnessed by PC King at the Blue Boar was the link. DS Armstrong had been the first to hear of this label when the man they then knew as Tom Wenzl made his statement after the road accident in early December. Since then, the name had become familiar in Kidlington. DC Davies had made the connection immediately after the anonymous tip-off and he soon struck lucky with his speculative calls. The call to the Hinckley Road nick jarred DC Almey's memory of what PC Eric King had said earlier. Almey was instructed to issue a BOLO for a white Jaguar XJ6. It hadn't taken long before Mr Dark-brown suit, real name Justin Quigley had been apprehended back at the Blue Boar. He'd been brought in for questioning and was now sitting opposite DC Gordon Almey in an interview room. It seemed Mr Quigley had something of a penchant for the boy-racers who congregated at the M1 service station. Justin, or Mr Whip-it-in, whip-it-out and wipe-it, as he became referred to by Almey's 'lads', readily admitted it was not at all unusual for him to be offering the latest in men's and ladies' fashions at discount prices, acquired from spurious sources. He was cautioned, charged with handling stolen goods and released on bail pending further investigation. Was the Oscar de la Renta label to become another step on the road to Jock's downfall?

Chapter Thirty-Seven

PC Colin Harvey on his Triumph Thunderbird turned left into Foxton Road, closely followed by the Black Mariah and the Ford Granada. Lewis glanced in his rear-view mirror and noticed a Land Rover had pulled out of a farm gate and was now fifty yards behind him. Up ahead and in the long grass in prone position Brian O'Connor took aim, breathing slowly and deeply, his forefinger caressed the trigger of his Remington M21A. He squeezed. The report of the shot rang out over the open countryside and the Triumph fell away from beneath PC Harvey. The centre-firing cartridge had pierced the Colin Harvey's crash helmet and the bullet had entered the frontal lobe of his cerebrum killing him instantly. Still partially astride his bike, the Thunderbird and rider skidded another 100 yards up the road before coming to a halt with the bike's 650cc engine still revving hard. PC Reg Alwyn threw every ounce of his strength into standing on the brake pedal of the Black Mariah. The prison officers and the handcuffed Ahmed abu Mousa inside were precipitated into the front of the cage by the force of the forward momentum. The van ran into the Triumph and its fallen rider. Lewis felt the massive shunt to the rear of the Granada from the Land Rover and fought to control it but was unable to prevent the car from being propelled forwards and rammed into the back of the van. The impact was such that driver Lewis, and passenger Cartwright were knocked unconscious. The Granada was then hauled back away from the rear of the Mariah by the Land Rover's winch. In the same instant the shot had been fired the Ford Capri with its 0 to 60 mph in eight seconds capability roared down the road from

Foxton to the pile-up. Ted Reilly and Michael Doyle, with their Thompsons at the ready stood over the scene while one of the men from the Cortina attached a sizeable piece of Semtex to the buckled rear doors of the van. They took cover as the pentaerythritol tetranitrate fuse exploded and the blast of the plastic explosive blew the doors thirty feet into the air. Flocks of startled birds took flight and scattered in all directions. Doyle and Reilly fired their semi-automatics mercilessly strafing the open end of the Mariah instantly killing two prison officers and Ahmed abu Mousa. With their mission complete the IRA platoon, less one, drove off in their respective stolen vehicles leaving the scene of carnage in Foxton Road. The daily papers on 4 January all carried the story on the front page. The tabloids particularly had sensationalist banner headlines, 'Four Dead in Terrorist Massacre'.

By the time DI Cartwright regained consciousness the IRA gang were miles away on the A4304 heading towards Market Harborough and then on the A6 northbound. Cartwright had a nasty gash to his forehead and his ribs were extremely sore from where he'd been impacted into the dashboard and the broken windscreen. Steam was still hissing out of the Granada's fractured radiator as Cartwright managed to struggle from the wreckage of the car and limp around to the driver's side. Lewis was still unconscious and Cartwright's attempts to extricate his driver from the twisted metal that had until minutes ago been a prestigious motorcar were futile. He peered into the back of the van. He didn't need to look any closer to know that the bodies in a contorted heap were dead. PC Reg Alwyn had been lucky. He was dazed and traumatised but managed to climb down from the van. He was unscathed. He walked the few steps forward and bent over the dead body of his colleague; the body he had almost run over. He wept. The silent tears ran down his face like molten grief. The sound of the tractor roused Cartwright. A farmer was heading up Foxton Road towards the village. The DI urged him to get to a phone as quickly as he could.

Brian O'Connor remained in his position in the long grass. He watched and he waited. He watched the tractor disappear up the road into the village. He waited. He watched a detective make further attempts and fail to extract his driver from the front of the Granada. He watched the coroner's ambulance arrive and take away the dead bodies. He waited. He watched the ambulance arrive and take away the detective and his driver and the driver of the Black Mariah. He then waited until the Triumph Bonneville, the Granada and the Mariah had all been cleared away by a variety of breakdown vehicles. He packed away the Remington in the golf-bag, got to his feet, dusted himself down and made his way back towards the A6 where he thumbed a lift to Market Harborough Station.

Having been ministered unto in the Accident and Emergency department of Kettering General Hospital Cartwright had been discharged and although he had been advised against it, he was back at his desk in Kidlington the next morning. The Union flag that normally flew from the building was at half-mast. Detective Chief Superintendent Simons was in high dudgeon, furiously intent on getting revenge for this fiasco and the resulting stain on his reputation. He had to lay the blame on someone, somehow.

'How in the name of God did the IRA cell know our movements? As I've said before, there is a serious leak in this station and when I find out who it is he will be spending the rest of his life behind bars!' Cartwright agreed but his response was riddled with despondency; his levels of enthusiasm and optimism barely above zero. Seeing that the DI was consumed by depression, Simons stormed off to shout at some other poor unsuspecting individual.

Cartwright was wishing that he'd taken the A & E doctor's advice and decided to go home. As he passed the front desk the sergeant offered his sympathy.

'They were good lads, good lads they were, more than can be said for one or two we've got. Bloody Doherty for one.

Hasn't shown up for his shift. He must know we're short after yesterday. I've sent someone round to his flat. He's not there – makes you wonder doesn't it?' Cartwright had mentally noted the sergeant's comments.'

'Keep me posted sarge. I'm off to see Andy Lewis.'

'Give him my best. Get a good rest yourself as well gov'. Good lad that Andy Lewis, good lad!'

*

It was later that day that DC Davies was reporting the significance of the Oscar de la Renta connection with DI Cartwright. They had known that some of his dresses and other garments were covering the weapons in the wicker baskets. Now they'd turned up at the Blue Boar thanks to Jason Quigley, the man in the dark brown suit, the man arrested and released on bail. Cartwright rang DC Almey at Hinckley Road.

'Gordon, can you get Quigley back in for further questioning. I reckon he might be able to give us a clue as to our Jock's whereabouts.'

*

DS Armstrong had gone to visit Gerry Doyle in the hope that he might be able to extract some useful information from him. When he arrived at the John Radcliffe Hospital in Oxford he managed to have a word with the consultant orthopaedic surgeon.

'We managed a partial fix of his femur, although between me and you it's been a bit of a bodge. The fractures were so severe we didn't really have much material to get pins into. Maybe, when he's in better shape we might look at an artificial hip and femoral neck.' From Armstrong's expression the surgeon could see that an explanation was required. 'That's the ball at the top of the thigh-bone which fits into the hip socket. There's precious little chance he'll walk again until we've fitted some spare parts. On the positive side I understand from the medical registrar that the ruptured spleen has been satisfactorily sorted.'

'OK, thanks doc. Don't rush things. As far as we're concerned it's one less terrorist on the streets for the time being. Is it OK if I go and see him, there are a couple of questions I need answers to.'

Gerry Doyle was in a private room outside which a young uniformed police constable sat reading the *New Musical Express*. Armstrong flashed his warrant card and the constable immediately stood bolt upright to attention.

'Easy lad. Any problems? No one made a rescue attempt?'

'No sir, 'fraid not. It's dead boring this. I'd much rather be on the beat.'

'It's a cushy detail this is. Make the most of it.'

Armstrong entered the room. Doyle eyed him suspiciously.

'What'd you want?'

'C'mon now Gerry, that's no way to speak to a visitor.'

And that was about as far as the conversation went. To every other question, the answer was the same. 'No comment.' The only positive response came from Armstrong's mention of the name McClean. It clearly touched a nerve.

'He was supposed to be one of us. He was one of us, alongside my brother in Belfast. Michael even saw him take on an RUC man during a riot and shoot him dead.'

That was good enough for Armstrong. He had at least got confirmation of something.

*

With the horror of the Blisworth Tunnel avoided, a few quid made on the dresses, Jock was of a cheerful and optimistic disposition as the *Nancy Blakemore* started her descent through the Stoke Bruerne flight of seven locks.

'What're yo' so bleedin' chirpy about this mornin'? enquired Wally who was in a less genial frame of mind.

'Nae more tunnels and we've gi'en polis the bums' rush. Full steam ahead now pal, payday awaits!'

The weather had improved with some periods of sunshine but the daytime temperatures didn't rise many degrees above freezing, but mercifully it was dry. Jock and Wally would take turn and turn about on the helm or huddled in-front of the potbellied stove in the boatman's cabin. There was little opportunity to keep warm by moving about and the cold was debilitating. Progress towards their destination at Limehouse Basin was slow even though they had encountered no other traffic. With daylight hours at a premium the distance travelled on any one day was restricted. It was unsafe to travel in the dark but they were now ten days into the trip and they pushed on to Marsworth Junction, on the edge of the Chilterns. Despite having been cold throughout the day they were both in good spirits when they turned in, having spent several hours in the Grand Junction Inn totally unaware of what had occurred the previous morning.

Chapter Thirty-Eight

The residents and guests at Marsh Cottage in Burton Overy were studying the front pages of various newspapers, comparing and contrasting what they were reading. Although the heat they had all been feeling over Christmas had cooled somewhat with the spotlight no longer focused on Jock McClean, Ben suggested that perhaps they could give the police a few pointers since from the 'famous five's' perception the police had lost direction and were barking up the wrong tree.

'Look, I am as outraged as the next person that three innocent people are dead; murdered by terrorists. What were they after, these terrorists? Retaliation, that's what! Nothing more than a reprisal against another terrorist organisation! I mean, Ahmed what's his name is a self-confessed member of a group of political extremists; a member of the group that massacred the Israeli athletes in Munich. Perhaps he deserved to die. If I knew more about the problems in the Middle East with one country invading another and empire building with innocent civilians being dispossessed and stuff like that, I might be able to understand what motivates these militant gangs. But then, isn't the IRA just as bad as Black September? Isn't it all about different religious beliefs, Protestants, Catholics, Arabs, Jews, Muslims? Why do they feel the need to kill each other? Are there really Hitler-type characters out there that the world needs to be rid of?'

Ben's rhetoric continued as the rest sat around with their heads bowed. He was in full flow and getting himself into something of a state.

'Now Jock…,' the rant went on, 'well, I'll tell you, Jock is motivated purely and simply by greed. He's a one-man terrorist organisation. Sure, he'll support the IRA one minute but only until Black September, or some Middle Eastern left-wing radicals or Islamist fundamentalists offer him more money. He'd sell his soul to the highest bidder. Jock is not trying to change the world. Jock is only looking after number one – himself. If that involves murdering someone that gets in his way, well…' He'd said his piece. Hazel, with tears in her eyes was compelled to make a contribution by way of clarifying some of her son's points.

'Ken, your dad Ben, was at school together with Jock. They left school and went to war together. They had no choice in the matter. Together they saw a means of turning a brutal, savage situation, a situation that neither of them wanted to be in, to their advantage; the black market. It was probably a bit of a laugh at first, but it became much more than that. Everywhere, people were having to make do, to go without. But not Jock and Ken. I think Ken could see where it was leading. Maybe he had a degree of integrity, of honesty, with higher moral principles than Jock. Maybe that's why Ken got out. Why did I get involved? I don't know. It made life exciting somehow, easier, and it was, all easier than it seemed. True I made a lot of money, illegally. I allowed myself to come under Jock's influence and money was the motivation. I regret the whole blasted thing now and if I could change it, I would have done so by now. I paid for what I did. I knew it was wrong and I paid for it with five years in prison. If I could have my life over again…But I never did anyone any harm. I never…' She looked at Ben and burst into tears through which she managed to utter 'except Ben.'

The gathering was sitting uncomfortably, pensive, pondering on Ben's analysis and Hazel's confession. It was Tina who spoke next, always one to put any situation into a rational context.

'Whatever has happened, has happened, and we can't go back. If Helen, as she was then, had a debt to society it is settled. What we must avoid is anyone, by which I mean Jock, now interfering. Let him get on with whatever it is that compels him to do what he does. If he's on the wrong side of the law, then let the law deal with him. He'll get what he deserves sooner or later. Jock seems to think that Hazel owes him. She doesn't, and we're not going to allow him to blight her life any more than we'll allow him to blight ours. If we can give the law a few clues or assist the police in putting Jock behind bars, then obviously we will. If we can't help, then we'll just get on as best we can and hope that justice will be served.'

'Let's go down the pub,' suggested Stuart.

*

A PC from Hinckley Road had been dispatched to bring Quigley back in for further questioning but he wasn't at his home address. However, spotting a white Jaguar XJ6 had not been difficult and it wasn't too long before Justin Quigley was again helping police with their enquiries. He'd been brought into Hinckley Road but DC Gordon Almey thought that DS Armstrong or even DI Cartwright should lead the questioning rather than himself. Quigley was placed in a cell but the door was left unlocked and he was given a cup of tea and a ginger biscuit. The DC made contact with his superiors in the Thames Valley force and in the event both Armstrong and Cartwright turned up to meet the man in the dark-brown suit.

'So, Mr Quigley, do you have a lot of dealings in the fashion industry?

'Well, not really Officer. I like to see young people looking nicely turned out. Trouble is, fashionable clothes are so expensive, aren't they? I can tell you know this from the cut of your suit. So, if I can help, I do. I do have one or two contacts in the rag trade you know.'

'Let me understand this clearly, are you saying your contacts supply you with stolen clothing.'

'Ooh, Officer how could you suggest such a thing? Certainly not. Quigley was quite indignant. 'I have principles you know.' He continued with his affected effusion.

'Let me explain. Occasionally during the manufacturing process, certain garments are flawed; a dropped stitch here or a pulled thread there. I get offered these seconds, they call it "cabbage" in the trade, you know, at significantly reduced prices. It's all totally legit. I can show you receipts if you like.'

'I don't think that'll be necessary. Now what about the dresses and other garments that you sold on Monday night, New Year's Day, at the Blue Boar. Where did they come from?'

'Oh, I do like the Blue Boar. I get a real thrill going there. Have you ever driven a Jaguar XJ6 up and down the M1 Officer? It's a real turn on especially if one then gets lucky. There's always a lovely party going on at the Boar.'

'Yes I'm sure!' Cartwright was finding this interview quite entertaining and trying to keep it serious was becoming difficult.

'Let's get back to the dresses in question if we may. Now, New Year's Day?'

'Let me see… Ooh yes, I remember now. I'd driven down the M1 ever so fast you know, and when I decided to come back I got lost – couldn't find the northbound slip road so I stopped in this pub to ask for directions.

'Which pub?' asked Armstrong.

'Oh I don't know, I go into so many. I think it was called the Compass, near Junction 15, to the south of Northampton. Anyway, there were these two old boys sitting there with a pile of dresses. I was curious so I decided to ask them the way. Ever so helpful one of them, quite good looking as well with a moustache like Clarke Gable had in that film *Gone With The Wind* – have you seen it? Ooh I do like that film, so romantic and everything! Anyway, he gives me directions and it turns out I wasn't as lost as I thought I was. He sees me eyeing up the dresses and he says they've just come from a fashion convention and I says oh have you, you know curious like, and he says as how they've got these dresses – frocks he called them – surplus. He could tell I was interested. Anyway I had a look and well, blow me,' he giggled, 'it's all top quality gear, they're all from Oscar de la Renta, you know the Dominican fashion designer.

Anyway he says he'd do me a bonny price and I says...'
Armstrong interrupted.

'A bonny price, you're sure he said a bonny price?'

'Oh yes, Scotch he were. I could tell by his accent. I've been to Scotland. Have you been to Scotland, lovely it is, especially in the autumn. Anyway, I offers him fifty quid like and he accepts it and buys me a gin and tonic. Do you have any idea how much dresses like those are worth?... A small fortune they are you know. Anyway...' And as Justin continued waxing lyrically, both detectives were struggling with suppressing their amusement.

'What about the other man?'

'He just sat there, rough looking chap in a dirty flat cap. Never said a word. Anyway, I finished my gin and tonic, put the dresses in the Jag and drove straight to the Blue Boar. It was heaving with lots of young men, some with their girlfriends, some with their... well, you know. I sold every last one in no time at all and got my money back at least four times over.'

'Did you not think it was strange – two men in a pub with a load of dresses?'

'Well, now you mention it, I suppose it was a bit queer, if you know what I mean! They were a bit scruffy.'

'Did it not occur to you that the dresses might have been stolen? Didn't you ask where these two scruffy blokes might have got a wardrobe full of designer dresses from?'

'Well, ask no questions, hear no lies I always say.'

'OK, Mr Quigley. Thank you. You've been very helpful.'

'Am I in trouble? Am I under arrest?'

'No, you're free to go although you will have to answer the "handling stolen goods" charge. But since you've been so cooperative, we'll put a good word in for you – oh and we might need you to attend an identity parade.'

'Ooh, an identity parade. I love a parade, how exciting!'

After Justin Quigley had left, Cartwright and Armstrong collapsed into paroxysms of laughter.

'It has to be, doesn't it?' asked Armstrong.

'Hell of a coincidence if it isn't!' suggested Cartwright.

'Has to be! A Scotsman? Oscar de la Renta dresses? It must be, no doubt about it in my mind!'

They went into the CID room and studied the map on the wall. Junction 15.

'What're you doing down there, Jock? Cartwright mused.

'Gordon, have you got a contact in Northampton?'

'Alf Smithson – if he's still there.'

'Give him a shout, get him on the line for me can you please?'

A WPC brought in a tray, with coffee and biscuits. Armstrong lit a cigarette and the phone rang. Cartwright snatched up the receiver.

'Cartwright.'

'DC Alf Smithson, guv. Gordon says you'd like a word.'

Cartwright briefed him.

'Call me at Thames Valley, Kidlington if you get anything.'

'Will do guv.'

They hadn't been back in Kidlington very long and as the DI and DS were going over the latest pieces of intelligence the phone rang. It was Smithson and he'd come up trumps. Acting on Cartwright's request, he'd been to the Compass and managed to get descriptions of the two 'scruffy' men, one with a Scots accent and a Clarke Gable moustache, the other a sullen, silent type, in a dirty flat cap. The pub landlord had not only remembered the men he also recollected that they'd met up with a bloke in a dark brown suit, and that they'd had four pints of bitter and a gin and tonic.

'According to the landlord,' Alf reported, 'they looked like a couple of bargees. Apparently, as the pub is so close to the Grand Union canal, the Compass gets a lot of canal-folk in and the landlord recognises the type.'

'Bloody well done Alf!' complimented Cartwright.

Excitement and an air of anticipated success in the CID office had been in short supply since before Christmas but the last phone call to the DI had lifted the blanket of gloom and optimism abounded. Speculative theories were being bandied about between the various ranks in CID that no one had noticed the eavesdropper at the open door.

'How come we hadn't made the connection. Bloody hell, it's so obvious. Talk about can't see the wood for the bloody trees. They're on a narrowboat. Jock spent several years on a narrowboat. Pushed one of his victims off a narrowboat and dumped the body of another into the canal. He was at Foxton. His Porsche is still at Foxton. Where's Foxton? On the Grand bloody Union! I'd bet my pension that the cache of weapons, irrespective of whoever it might or might not be intended for, be it Black September, the IRA or the bloody Maidenhead Young Wives Bondage Association, it's on a bloody narrowboat somewhere down the bloody Grand Union. The designer dresses were covering weapons in the baskets in Ahmed's van and Jock sold them to Quigley!' Cartwright was all but dancing around the room. Delight spreading across his face.

'We've got you this time Mr Jock bloody McClean!' he confidently pronounced. The euphoria didn't last long though.

'Cartwright? Simons here. Have you sorted out that leak yet? Just get your bloody finger out will you!' The DI replaced the receiver and immediately picked it up again.

'Ray? Find Phil Doherty and arrest him.'

'Guv?'

'You heard! I want him charged and banged up here for obstructing the police in the execution of their duties, accomplice to conspiracy and murder, and that's just for starters. If you can think of anything else to charge him with, do it! Then bring in what's his name, the lockkeeper from Foxton.'

'Sir!'

Chapter Thirty-Nine

By the weekend, the *Nancy Blakemore* had passed through Hemel Hempstead and Watford. At Uxbridge they met up with Pat Henderson on the *Sheldrake* just as she was leaving the Slough Arm, empty, having delivered a load of coal to Slough power station.

'Bugger!' Jock cursed. This was one of the last people he would have wanted to run into. It had been Pat with the *Sheldrake* that had offered him a tow to Foxton, that day he was loitering with *Emily Rose* north of the Saddington Tunnel.

'Eh up then, Wally, who's your new crew? Nah, I don't believe it! Bloody hell, Jock! 'Aven't seen yo' in years. ''Ow yo' keeping?'

'Och, Pat, nae so bad thanks. How's yersel'?'

The two boats rafted together whilst Pat and Wally exchanged a bit of bargee banter. Then, out of the blue, Pat remarked, 'I see that terrorist got 'is comeuppance.'

'Who wis that then,' asked Jock

'Ain't yo' seen the papers? That bloody foreigner, Black September bloke, 'im what shot them Israeli athletes at 'lympics.'

'Aye, well good riddance eh?'

'Yo, yer right there. Seems he nicked a load o' guns an' stuff from the IRA; another murdering bunch. The IRA got 'im when 'e was bein' transferred from nick in Kidlington to prison. Copper an' two screws bought it an' all. Now the cops are after the IRA blokes what did it.'

'Did the paper say anything aboot where the guns wis?'

'Nah, they ain't sure.' Pat answered.

Jock stepped into the companionway down to the boatman's cabin out of sight and was frantically making gestures to Wally to move on. Any longer spent talking to Pat and there'd be all manner of awkward questions he'd rather not have to fend off.

'Ok then Pat, must get off. Got to get this lot to Limehouse.'

'Right oh ol' mate. What yo' carryin'?'

''Tis a load ay machine parts, so it is.' Jock butted in with the answer.

After the boats had moved on their respective ways, Jock came very close to thumping Wally.

'Didnae I tell ye that this wis all very hush hush? Ye stupid wee bastard! That gobshite'll be tellin' everyone he's seen me on the way tae Limehouse. Everyone 'cludin' polis will now ken we're goin' tae Limehouse.'

'Sorry Jock, I wasn't thinking.'

*

After the ambush and massacre of Ahmed abu Mousa, Michael Doyle and his IRA contingent in three stolen vehicles took three diverse routes back to the Coach and Horses in Kibworth Harcourt where the intention was to lie low for a few days to see how the situation might develop now the Arab, the double-agent, had been dispatched. Michael also didn't want to move too far from Oxford whilst Gerry, his brother remained in hospital at the Radcliffe. The priority now was getting the guns and McClean. Where McClean was so would the guns be. He wouldn't have had time to dispose of them yet, surely? Well, that was Doyle's thinking.

*

DI Cartwright had driven to Kettering General where PC Andy Lewis was recovering from the injuries he had sustained during the ambush. Happily, all his major organs were intact and the cuts, abrasions and lacerations were not critical although he had been warned that his facial good looks might be compromised when the stitches were removed. Apart from some severe bruising he was in better shape than could have been expected. This was certainly confirmed when Cartwright arrived and showed him photographs of the carnage which had been taken by the police photographer. Lewis wasn't exactly feeling sorry for himself. Whatever he was feeling was guilt. He was surprised yet pleased that the DI had taken the trouble to visit him.

'I'm so sorry sir. I let you down.'

'Don't be so bloody silly. It wasn't your fault. There was absolutely nothing you could have done to have prevented it.'

'The minute I noticed that Land Rover pull out behind us I should have realised what was about to happen.'

'Now look, stop it, and that's an order! If anyone's to blame it's me. I should have known that there was a risk involved after newspaper reports of confidential interviews started to appear. We have a serious leak at Kidlington and I'll bet my pension that that is where the IRA got their tip-off from.'

Cartwright bet his pension quite frequently and so far he hadn't lost it!

'Do you have any ideas? Lewis asked.

'I'm pretty certain I know who it is.' Cartwright answered confidently. 'I'd better plug the leak before too long or DCS Simons'll have me back on point duty.'

Chapter Forty

It was the start of the new working week. The weather was grim and reflected in Jock's expression. He'd been worrying about having met with Pat Henderson. Pat had a reputation on the Grand Union for being unable to keep anything to himself, always one for gossip and tittle-tattle. It was almost a racing certainty that the police and the IRA would get to hear of Henderson's encounter with Whitehead. That would inevitably lead to *Nancy Blakemore*'s destination being revealed. What was not so sure was who would get to him first, the police or the IRA. Either way, it was not a prospect Jock welcomed. A contingency plan was needed urgently.

'When ye hev tae make choices, be sure tae choose the right win, eh Wally?'

'What yo' bletherin' on about now?'

Jock tried to explain to Wally how, as a result of his indiscretion, his careless, idle chat with Pat, the mission which had been meticulously planned to the point of infallibility was now in a state of uncertainty. So far, the whole operation had gone according to plan, right from the Braemar Lodge and the liaison with Billy Kelly at the Williams' Shipping Warehouse. OK there had been one or two minor amendments which had required improvising on the hoof. For one, it had never been intended that Tom should have taken pity on Maggie O'Rourke and bring her along for the ride. What had he been thinking of? It was just too bad that she and the baby had died. Secondly, being tailed by a third party, someone that Jock could only presume had been a member of the IRA, well, that had not been anticipated. The smash between the lorry and the Ford Cortina;

the resulting explosion, well, it was no more than was deserved. As far as Jock was concerned whoever had been following him shouldn't have been sticking his nose in! It was a pity though that Tom's full colours had been revealed. Tom, or Ahmed as he would have become known in the fullness of time was a key player in the game, the crucial link with the paymaster. If the *Nancy Blakemore* could get to Limehouse before being apprehended the final negotiations and transfer of cargo would now be all down to Jock. He could hardly delegate any of it to Wally.

Having heard Jock's explanation Wally was most apologetic.

'Well look Jock, I knowed it were an illegal job but I never knowed it were all to do wi' international terrorism. I want to get the whole bloody caper done as much as you, an' as quickly as possible. I reckon I've got a chart down below. Never bother wi' it normally going to Limehouse, I've done it so many times. But there might be an alternative place, nearer here where we can drop the stuff off, then the coppers'll 'ave a long wait at Limehouse 'cos I'll 'ave turned round and buggered off back up north. What do you reckon?

'Och aye, it could work if we kin get in touch wi' ship we're s'posed to load.' Jock took the tiller while Wally went below to find the chart. He returned after a few minutes and they laid out a dog-eared, tattered and torn chart of the Grand Union's London Ring on the cabin's coach-roof. Wally took the lead in proposing a revision; a rather more expedient scheme.

'Now if we was goin' to Limehouse, we'd turn left just up here after Bulls Bridge and onto the Paddington Arm, then it's a straightforward easy run, past Wembley, North Kensington, past Lord's cricket ground, skirt the edge of Regent's Park, there's a couple o' locks at Camden, oh yeh, an then the Islington Tunnel then straight down the East End into Poplar and Limehouse Basin.' Wally had traced the route on the chart with his finger, and Jock had paid close attention.

'Aye, ah ken! Ah've made the trip maself in the past. Dinnae forget, Ah've been a boatman!' Wally acknowledged the gentle rebuke.

'Easy run that, we'd do it easy in three days and be there two days early for the drop. But, if we carry on ahead at Bulls Bridge junction we could go down 'ere to Brentford where t'cut meets t'Thames.' Jock had never followed this route before and was studiously looking at the chart.

'There's twelve locks but we could do it two days, then while everyone and anyone's looking for us in Limehouse we'll be down here, bloody miles away.' Wally folded the chart with almost a triumphant look on his face having provided what he obviously considered to be a credible alternative to the original plan; the plan which as it stood was almost certain to be doomed.

Jock scratched his head.

'Assuming we kin let 'em know in time, Kin the ship we're s'posed tae meet at Limehouse on Friday get all the way upriver to Brentford?'

'Dunno! Depends on what sort o' ship it is. There's a lot o' bridges to get under and depending on t'tide, water might not be deep enough. All depends on t'ship.'

Jock had no idea. All of sudden, the glimmer of hope that Wally's alternative plan had shone was extinguished. He was mindful of an old saying of his mother's; "The light that burns twice as bright burns for half as long". 'Ain't that the truth!' he thought. They were rapidly approaching the Paddington Arm junction. It was make-your-mind-up time.

'Kin we tie up at junction while we make a decision?' And they did; tie up at least. There were many issues to be resolved if plan B was to become operational. Not least amongst these issues was communicating with whoever it was would be taking delivery and handing over the money. Were the intended recipients of Jock and Wally's shipment already at Limehouse? If they weren't going to arrive until Thursday or even Friday, plan B was a nonstarter. What was the name of their ship? Or was it a boat? He couldn't remember. Had he written it down somewhere? Surely he would have written it down. He went below and frantically searched through his bag, throwing what few possessions and items of clothing he had all over the cabin. There in a side pocket of his bag he found his wallet. Inside the wallet, alongside a significant wedge of banknotes there was a scrap of paper. *Thurs 11 Jan. 6pm 'Samson'*. That had to be it – the *Samson*.

'Wally, wid there be an office or a harbourmaster or summat similar at Limehouse? I need tae find oot if our boat's there the noo.'

'Yo' could ring the Basin office,' Wally suggested. 'D'yo want the number?'

'Aye, I cannae ring 'em wi'oot it yer dafty.' Jock stepped ashore and found a phone box. He dialled the number. When the line was answered he put on his best BBC voice.

'Sorry to bother you sir, but could you tell me has the *Samson* arrived yet? We're due to make a delivery.'

''Ang on there cock, I'll just 'ave a butcher's at the ole berthing sheet 'ere'.

'Aye, he soonds like one ay they diamond cockney geezers.' Jock said to himself.

'Not 'ere' yet cock. We're expecting the *Samson* on Wednesday evenin' around 'igh water, abaht 1830. That's abaht half-six to you. Seems he wants to load and shove orf at 'igh water Thursday, that'll be abaht 7.'

'OK sir thanks for your help'.

'No worries cock!'

Jock was back aboard the *Nancy Blakemore*.

'Could I tek another look at they chart there Wally.'

After further consideration and hoping that they'd covered every eventuality

Plan B was hatched. The *Nancy Blakemore* would proceed to Brentford and into the Thames, but rather than go all the way to Limehouse they'd berth at St Katherine's Dock barely a stone's throw down river from Tower Bridge, about a mile-and-a-half mile upstream from Limehouse Basin. All it needed was to somehow get a massage to *Samson* about the change of loading arrangements. Jock went back to the phone box and rang the diamond geezer again.

'Hello again sir, I rang a few minutes ago regarding the *Samson*. I've been speaking with the freight forwarding company and they've decided they want *Samson* to come into St Katherine's Dock for some reason – something to do with loading facilities I believe. Would you be so awfully kind as the redirect *Samson* when she gets to you on Wednesday?'

'OK cock, I've made a note 'ere for my oppo, I'm on afternoons on Wednesday so's it'll 'ave to be 'im 'as passes on the message.'

'We appreciate your help sir, thank you so much.'

'No worries cock!'

As Jock walked back to the *Nancy Blakemore* he was thinking along the lines of 'What a jolly fine fellow '– or something similar.

So, Wally looked at his tide tables; columns of figures, dates, heights, times, highs, lows and suchlike, a complete mystery to Jock. Wally determined that they needed to be out of the canal and on to the river by 6am on Wednesday to maximise on the benefit of the ebb-tide all the way to St Katherine's Dock. They would then be berthed and ready to trans-ship the cargo that evening and any police presence would be concentrated in the wrong place. He then had another brainwave. Get in touch with the IRA! Let them know that their weapons would be at Limehouse Basin and then they could keep the police occupied and vice versa. With all the anxiety of the previous hour resolved, *Nancy Blakemore* pottered on and worked her way down the six locks in the Hanwell Flight to the Hanwell Bottom Lock Number 97 where they picked up a berth and spent a subdued evening in the Fox.

Chapter Forty-One

Spread out over DI Cartwright's desk was a British Waterways map of the Grand Union Canal, which he was finding quite illuminating. A knock at the door heralded the arrival of DC Ray Davies and Fred Webb.

'Good morning Mr Webb. I'm Detective Inspector Cartwright and I'm leading the investigation into the murders of Ronald Nicholls, Kenneth Blake and probably two, maybe three others. Our prime suspect is also wanted in connection with theft, illegal dealings in firearms and for associating with terrorist organisations. We believe you may be able to assist us in our enquiries.'

'Oh, do yo 'now? What makes yo' think I can 'elp? I knows nowt!'

'Do you know a Scotsman, a certain Duncan McClean?'

'Jock? I've knowed 'im fer years. But I ain't seen 'im in a long time. Fust met 'im mebbe twenty year since when 'e ad the *Emily Rose*. She's at Foxton now as part o' t' museum exhibits. 'E gave us a bottle o' scotch first time 'e came through Foxton flight and we got to know each other. I knows all the boatman what come up and down the Leicester Arm. I bin lockkeeper since me dad retired, must be forty-odd year ago.'

'You say you haven't seen him for a long time. When did you last see him?'

Fred put a gnarled finger to his grizzled chin in a 'thinking-about-it' sort of pose.

'I reckon that must a bin round autumn-time in 1963, or mebbe it were 64. Strange it were.'

'Go on.'

'Well I reckon 'im an' 'elen must've 'ad a fallin' out.'

'That'd be Helen Blake, yes?'

'That's right. D'you know 'elen, lovely lady, 'elen. Got very fond of 'er I did. They'd bin runnin' a bit of a dodgy shop, sellin' stuff off the boat. Booze and fags mainly, an' customers were usually boatmen. Mebbe I shun't 'ave let 'im do it, but I 'ad a soft spot fer 'elen. Any road up, I reckon they 'ad a bust up, cos one day 'e just shoved off toward Kilby Wharf. 'E said 'e'd be back after a few days, an' that's the strange bit – he weren't but 'is boat, *Emily Rose* was, wi'out 'im. Pat Henderson, he's boatman on *Sheldrake* said 'ow 'e'd seed 'im by Taylor's Lock Number 20 waitin' fer a new impeller fer 'is water pump. An' that were it. Boat were on the mud just through t' Saddington. It were 'azzard to navigation, so I 'ad to get it towed to Foxton, and there's where it's bin since. We 'ad police all over it – I think the 'tective's name were Mosel – summat like that any way.

'Yes it was, Detective Inspector Moseley. I was a DC then and worked with him. I was there when *Emily Rose* was towed off the mud near the Saddington Tunnel.'

'Ah well, yous'll know all about it then. Jock 'ad disappeared, and no one know'd where. Then last month, 'elen and 'er lad, she's changed 'er name, you know, since she came out of prison – she were in for all that sellin' dodgy fags an' stuff – should a bin Jock what got banged up not 'elen, if y'ask me – any road, she came to Foxton and wanted another look at *Emily Rose*. I thought it were a bit unusual like, but I were glad to see 'er. I reckon she wanted to show ole *Emily* to her lad. Then Wally Whitehead shows up wi' *Nancy Blakemore*. I 'adn't seen Wally nor 'is boat since autumn last. 'E said 'e 'adn't 'ad a load fer ages. I reckon Jock might 'ave 'ad summat to do wi' that, but I never see'd 'im. 'Part from that, I can't really 'elp. Oh, there is summat else. I did see a minibus full o' blokes in suits, aroun' Christmas. They was parked behind t'pub. There were also a black van there for a while an' I did see a couple suits arguing wi' another bloke over it. Oh yeah an' a flash motor, a Porsche.'

'Well, thanks Fred, if you don't mind me calling you Fred?'

'I bin called worser,' he grinned.

'For your information Fred, the "blokes in suits" as you call them were in fact the members of the IRA that shot and killed Ahmed abu Mousa, from another terrorist organisation. They also killed a policeman and two prison guards. You must have read about it in the paper.'

'Really? Well bugger me!'

'Indeed!'

'And the Porsche is registered to Duncan McClean – your man Jock. So, your suspicion of his being involved in something is not far from the truth.'

'Really? Well bugger me!' Fred's feigned incredulity did seem to be pulling the wool.

DI Cartwright had been picking out the places Fred referred to on the map. He then asked,

'If Jock and Wally were delivering a load where would it be to, do you think?'

'Ah well that'd depend on t'load. Could be any one o' several places. I can tell you though, back in t'day Jock used to go down t'London to pick stuff up. Limehouse Basin I reckon it were. If 'e's goin' to centre o' London, it'll be Limehouse for sure. But 'e's just as likely t'be going north to Leicester or down to Buckby Junction then up to Birmingham or onto the Oxford, 'ard to say, I'd say.' The DI's finger had been tracing the possibilities which Fred was offering but Cartwright was shrewd enough to know that Fred was just casting red herrings about.

'But your best guess, Fred?'

'Limehouse – but don't yo' go blamin' me if I's wrong!'

'Brilliant, OK, thanks very much Fred, you've been a great help. DC Davies here will give you a ride back to Foxton, he's becoming quite familiar with the route.'

Cartwright went directly to the bottom drawer of the filing cabinet, poured himself a stiff one, and studied the chart plotting out the route and various interception points on a passage to Limehouse.

When Fred got back to Foxton he needed a drink and went straight to the Foxton Locks Inn. As he crossed the bottom lock he could see the *Sheldrake* moored up by the Rainbow Bridge. Pat Henderson was already in the pub.

'Ey up Fred. Yo'll niver guess 'oo I seen on Sat'day.'

'I dunno, let me 'ave a go.' Fred adopted his 'thinking-about-it' pose for a few seconds. 'Jock McClean!'

'Bloody 'ell! 'Ow d'yo' know that – yo' psychic or summat?'

'I knows cos cops 'ave bin askin' – pulled us in "to assist in their enquires", he intoned in his imitated Oxford English.

'Mebbe I should gi' em a ring?' Pat asked. Fred then realised, perhaps he'd said too much.

Chapter Forty-Two

Phil Doherty wasn't really cut out to be a policeman. Even as a schoolboy he'd been more adept at breaking the law rather than upholding it. He never had aspirations to join the police force and as a teenager he'd drifted from one unskilled job to another. When his irate mother, fed up with him lying about at home pointed out to her son that she'd seen it advertised that the police were recruiting, he'd thought 'Why not?' The starting salary of around £1300 wasn't that bad, a pension, uniform and other perks were sufficient incentive. When he arrived at the Police Training facility in Droitwich, he had to be dragged off 'kicking and screaming' to the barber shop to get his 'Beatles' hairstyle cut to regulation standard and he felt that he'd actually joined the military rather than the police, and began to have second thoughts. Even so, he stuck at the training course and was looking forward to the day he qualified; the day he'd have 'power'. What he had perhaps failed to recognise was that the day he was sworn in, along with the 'power' came an enormous burden of responsibility. Whereas when had been a member of the public he could just have walked away from any illegal situation, as a police constable, in or out of uniform, on or off duty, society looked toward members of the police force to set an example. After he'd qualified it wasn't too long before his superiors had him down as a loner; certainly not a team player. He was a malingerer who didn't take kindly to so many aspects of the job. Too often when he was supposed to be pounding the beat, Doherty would be hiding up somewhere out of the way. Self-disciplined and conscientious he was not and that had been the main reason he'd been given the role of custody constable; a role where the duty sergeant could keep an eye on him. Doherty soon discovered though that this was an easy duty and that there were ways and means in which, from his 'inside' position he could easily augment his annual salary. By keeping his eyes and ears open, all manner of confidential 'intelligence' came his way and he soon learned how to use it to his advantage.

Snippets of information to the press in return for a backhander were simple and uncomplicated. But, having given Michael Doyle the tip-off regarding the detail of Ahmed abu Mousa's transfer to Gartree Prison, Doherty had begun to understand that he was now involved on the periphery of terrorist activity. This was heavy stuff. Not at all like taking a bribe for turning a blind-eye to some fairly insignificant transgression. He was in way over his head. He'd also become aware that he was suspected of leaking information to the press. Colleagues in the station had 'sent him to Coventry' and he wasn't anticipating the Chief Constable recommending him for a promotion either. So, when Michael Doyle offered him an 'opportunity' Doherty, a Catholic, thought 'in for a penny'... What's to lose?

So it was that he was on his way to Kibworth Harcourt and the Coach and Horses. Not only was he to receive £250 for information supplied so far, but he was also in a position to point the IRA in the right direction to recover their stolen weaponry. Although they had never met, Doherty was greeted with open arms like a long-lost brother. A bottle of Jameson's was opened and toasts to almost everything and anything were being proposed by the time the third bottle was down to its last dribble.

Michael had been able to glean the information he was waiting for from Phil Doherty, now the IRA's latest recruit. Michael was also impressed by the way in which Doherty had used his initiative and brought along a British Waterways chart of the

Grand Union. Limehouse had for several years been a dropping off point for illegal weapons coming into the UK, destined for the IRA in Belfast. In fact, had it not been McClean himself who had delivered to Limehouse, by narrowboat, shipments of all manner of armaments he had acquired during WWII? Was that not how McClean and Doyle's brother Gerry had become acquainted? Yes, it was as Michael knew very well. And now it was all shaping up nicely.

'Have you still got your uniform?' Doyle asked Doherty.

'Yes, I've not been dismissed yet. I reckon my dishonourable discharge, arrest and prison sentence won't be that long coming. So, the deal is that I help you guys out and in return, I get to escape back to Belfast with you.'

'And for sure you will, you will. Right then, get you down to Limehouse Basin and have a sniff around. Should be easy for you to access everywhere and anywhere in your uniform. We need to know the name of the canal boat bringing our weapons down and when they're expected. We can then arrange one hell of a reception committee, party, and a feckin' hanging!' We'll be ready to roll as soon as we get your call. We're putting a great deal of faith in you, don't let us down. Don't feck it up. If you do it'll be the last thing you ever do! Good luck!

*

DC Gordon Almey answered the phone on his desk at Hinckley Road Police Station in Leicester.

'The bloke yo' are a-looking fer will be at Limehouse Basin in the next couple o' days.' That was all. The line went dead. The DC immediately relayed the message to DI Cartwright in Kidlington.

*

It was 0400 hours on Wednesday 10th January. Jock and Wally had been up and about for half-an-hour, neither of them had been able to sleep anyway. With the engine started and ticking over and navigation lights on, they cast off. The darkness was dimly illuminated by the loom of the streetlights of civilisation as they got closer to Brentford and the Osterley Lock Number 98. Switching on the boat's single headlight they could see the gates were against them meaning there was probably a boat ahead travelling in the same direction. Wally flicked the light off and Jock stepped ashore and prepared the lock which they then passed through without incident. Even at this ungodly hour road traffic was rushing towards London along the recently opened M4 motorway as they passed under the bridge and on towards Clitheroe's Lock Number 99. As they anticipated, the gates were closed. This time, Wally made the jump ashore to prepare the lock and *Nancy Blakemore* was coaxed in by Jock and, much to Wally's surprise, she never touched the sides. The canal was now fairly well lit up by Brentford's lights on both sides. On the helm, Jock could just make out the boat ahead as she disappeared into Lock Number 100. Wally was back aboard.

'In one way Jock, I'm glad to see us 'as got company up ahead cos there's summat I forget to do.'

'Ay, an' whit might that be?' Jock was slightly panicked by this confession.

'Well this 'ere Thames Lock is allus manned by a lockkeeper and at this time o' year and this time o' day I think I's s'posed to have booked it. T'ain't quite the same as regalar locks as yo'll see. Still, wi' boat up ahead, I bet 'e'll 'ave remembered to book, so us should be all right, ar kid, we can just tag on behind 'im.' And once they had worked through Lock Number 100, Jock understood what his skipper had told him about the locks. There were the comparatively enormous River Thames locks. Brentford Locks Numbers 101 A & B. Two wide locks separated by a central island on which there was a small shelter for the lockkeeper. Both Jock and Wally recognised the boat up front. It was the *Damselfly*, another one of the few remaining commercial boats. Up until recently, the *Damselfly* had always been accompanied by her sister ship the *Mayfly*, but with commercial loads by narrowboat becoming a way of life since consigned to historical nostalgia, the *Mayfly* had been pensioned off, converted, and now spending her retirement as a holiday pleasure-boat.

It was almost high water and in consequence, there was very little difference, if any, between the height of the water in the canal, in the lock or in the Thames, so working through the lock was merely a case of opening the gates. Sneaking in on the transom of the boat ahead would not be an issue. They didn't have to wait for the level in the lock to equalise one way or the other. Even so, Jock was on the helm and holding back. The gates were open and the lockkeeper was waving them through. As they eased their way into the lock Wally asked the lockkeeper to call St Katherine's with *Nancy's* ETA.

'Ah dinnae want tae get too close to Nick,' Jock explained to Wally. They both knew Nick of course – Nick 'the Greek' Kavvadias, the boatman on *Damselfly*. She would, without doubt be heading to Limehouse Basin. It had been a regular monthly run for her for several years. Nick had only acquired the boat and the contract to move aggregate two years ago when *Damselfly's* previous owner had retired. But, he had already become well-known by the Grand Union fraternity as a larger than life character in every respect.

'It's probably best Nick dinnae ken we're astern of him otherwise 'e'll be asking questions when we turn intae St Katherine's. What'd ye reckon Wal?'

By now, Wally was all too well aware and didn't need reminding of the confidentiality of this trip and could only agree with Jock's reckoning.

The tide was just about on the turn and already *Nancy Blakemore* could feel the benefit of the ebb. Jock had throttled back but even at just above tick-over they were making a steady four knots. To the right there was a mist hanging over Kew Gardens and they were soon under Kew Bridge and rushing downstream towards Chiswick Bridge. Travelling eastwards, the first hints of daylight were giving the sky a very slight orange glow through the light pollution of the city. From the right and the left, wider than any canal Jock had navigated, and getting wider, the lights from the banks of the river were reflected on the water which for all that it was now ebbing quite quickly appeared still and calm on the surface. The engine was purring quietly above idling as *Nancy* made rapid progress. They'd been travelling in silence until Wally voiced the concern he'd been chewing over.

'When us git there, an' ship arrives, 'ow does we get t'cargo unloaded from 'ere and loaded onto there? It's bloody heavy!' Not only was this a masterful understatement from Wally, it was a matter that had also crossed Jock's mind.

'Dinnae fret yerself aboot that yet. We'll worry aboot it when time comes. Ah'm sure there'll be a way.'

Jock's previous trips to Limehouse with the *Emily Rose* all those years ago had been by way of the Paddington Arm. The Thames was a new experience for Jock he was distracted and intrigued by the sights. The many riverside pubs and historical waterside wharves and warehouses all held a particular fascination. With the tide now pushing them along even faster it was agreed that they would defer breakfast until they were safely tucked away in St Katherine's Dock. There would be plenty of time for whatever needed to be done before the *Samson* was due. With the bends in the river snaking their way forever eastwards towards the centre of London Jock was getting excited.

'I think I'd better tek-over, Jock. Look yo're not concentratin,' steering bananas, one side o' river t' t'other. Yo're s'posed to keep right. Jus' like on any cana... Whoa – look, watchout!' Wally grabbed the tiller and by just a few inches managed to get the head of the boat hard to port and avoid being swept onto a moored pair of lighters.

'Bloody 'ell mate that were close. It's one thing boating on t'non-tidal canal. On tidal Thames mate, it's summat else, spec'ly when yo' ain't done tidal afore.'

Jock was more than relieved to hand over the helm to Wally. He could now give all his attention to taking in the sights with the early morning sounds of the Capital waking and coming to life.

They swept under Hammersmith and Putney Bridges. The stern light of the *Damselfly* could still be made out ahead and the amount of river traffic was increasing in both directions. It wasn't long before they were passing under the Battersea and Albert Bridges and trains could be seen arriving and departing Victoria Station over the Grosvenor Railway Bridge. After Vauxhall and Lambeth Bridges Jock was rapt by the sight of the Houses of Parliament on the left, and, the cherry on top, the tower at the north end of the Palace of Westminster. Big Ben began the Westminster chimes as the overture to striking 8 as they passed under the bridge. As they came round the right-hand bend and under the Waterloo Bridge Jock stood there, his lower jaw dropped, mouth wide open at the sight in the distance of London's most iconic landmark, Tower Bridge. After they had cleared Blackfriars, Southwark and London Bridges Wally had eased the throttle right back to tick-over and forward progress was purely a factor of the increasing rate of the ebb tide.

'Now's the bloody tricky bit.' Wally was looking anxious. From tick-over he engaged full-astern.

'I can't afford to get swept past the lock at St Katherine's and I gotta turn head-to-tide to shape up for t' lock.'

As any boatman knows, a U-turn in a seventy-two-foot long boat with the tide doing the opposite to what you would like, not to mention being in a congested waterway, represents a challenge of Herculean proportions even for the most experienced. Approaching Tower Bridge, Wally pushed the tiller hard to starboard and *Nancy Blakemore*'s stern swung out on the tide and she drifted under the bridge broadside on to the current. The pedestrians walking over the bridge might have glanced down at this spectacular manoeuvre, but they wouldn't have witnessed the vicissitude of Wally's anal sphincter! The call to St Katherine's had obviously been made and Wally heaved a sigh of relief to see the outer lock gates were open and the lock was empty. As *Nancy* came clear downstream of the bridge's roadway Wally gunned the engine ahead. The sudden burst of forward momentum almost threw Jock overboard. The boat surged forward. Jock looked up and saw the river wall rapidly approaching dead-ahead. Surely a looming disaster about to happen, Jock looked for something against which to brace himself ready for the collision. The opening to the lock was yards to starboard. Wally eased the throttle right back and with the help of the tide the *Nancy Blakemore* glided into the lock with her backside just kissing the starboard lock gate as, with a burst astern from the engine, she came to rest, just fitting into the lock. The outer gates closed. Heart rates gradually decelerated.

'Bugger me!' panted Wally.

'You've done that before!' complimented the lockkeeper.

Chapter Forty-Three

With no new developments on the McClean front the 'famous five' had resumed what amounted to as near a 'normal' existence as was possible. Hazel had returned to Pin Mill and taken up painting watercolour riverscapes with the Winsor & Newton set she'd received as a Christmas gift from Tina. It was something she'd always fancied having a go at and now she was a lady of leisure she had nothing better to do. Such was the scenery the opportunities for landscape artists on the banks of the River Orwell were bountiful as they were beautiful irrespective of whether the artist was a member of the Royal Academy of Arts or a complete novice. Ben and Tina were back at the Lobster Pot, their cottage in Orford and living the lives of well-educated young professionals. Kate and Stuart remained in residence at Marsh Cottage, maintaining a friendly relationship with Jamie and Diane at the Old Greyhound. Every day Kate would scour the daily newspaper of her choice for any news of Jock, the IRA or Black September. Surely there would be something to report in the aftermath of the Foxton Road massacre?

*

On Wednesday 10th January Phil Doherty was loaned the Ford Capri, the one which had been stolen by Michael Doyle, and he took the A6 as far as Luton and then the M1 motorway to Staples Corner from where he got on to the A5, Edgware Road. His knowledge of London was sketchy at best but he found the junction into Maygrove Road just before the railway bridge in Kilburn. Michael had arranged for Sean O'Donnell, a leading light in the so-called Kilburn Battalion of the IRA to liaise with Doherty and lend assistance if and when it was required. Phil was right on the pre-arranged time and, sure enough, readily recognisable and as described by Michael, there was Sean in the distinctive flat cap.

'Now it's probably better for you to let me drive, then I'm not forever giving you directions.'

'Pleased to meet you too!' Phil was just a bit miffed that Sean hadn't bothered with the normal courtesy of a proper greeting, but then Sean didn't like policemen, especially bent ones. Phil attempted to engage Sean in small-talk but was rewarded with little if any response. They were now through Kilburn and Maida Vale, into Edgware Road and had turned left at Marble Arch into Oxford Street.

'Has Michael briefed you on what this is all about, because I can fill you in with all the details of…' Sean interrupted whilst giving a lady driver the benefit of some Gaelic sign language as she impeded his right turn into Charing Cross Road.

'I know what we're doing and where we're going.' The journey continued in silence. Left into The Strand, right Arundel Street, left onto the Victoria Embankment. Phil sat taking in the sights whilst secretly admiring Sean's driving skills and knowledge of London streets. He'd only ever been to London once before and that was when he was a child and his gran had taken him to the British Museum. They were now into Upper Thames Street, Tower Hill, East Smithfield.

'Nearly there.' Sean had broken the silence. 'I'm thinking that we'll park in Goodhart Place which is right by the entrance to the basin. We should have a good vantage point from there.' And, there it was – Limehouse Basin. Sean parked up and they got out of the car. Sean rolled a cigarette and Phil strolled over towards the lock. He could see that there were not many vessels in the basin, but then it was January after all. There were a few pleasure boats and yachts moored up and then he spotted a narrowboat.

'Sean, I think they're here already. Look, there's the narrowboat and there's smoke coming out the chimney.

They'll be waiting for the boat that's coming to collect the guns – our guns.' Phil directed Sean's line of sight over towards a narrowboat. Sure enough, there it was. 'That must be it. *The Damselfly.'* Two characters could be made out on the quay beside the boat, adjusting the mooring lines.

'I have to phone Michael. How long do you suppose before the other boat arrives?'

'Well now, look you, it can't be much after low water now. The gates won't operate until,' he looked at his watch in a knowing sort of way, 'until four o'clock this afternoon at the earliest so no one is going to be coming in or going out 'til then.'

Sean's knowledge of London streets may well have been impressive but he knew little of the waterways network. At the north end of the Basin there was access to both the Regent's Canal and the Limehouse Cut which led on to the River Lee Navigation. Neither were tide dependent to the same extent as the Thames, and a narrowboat could quite easily slip away unnoticed.

Phil went off to find a telephone box and left Sean to keep an eye on the narrowboat.

*

Even as Phil Doherty was on the phone to Michael Doyle in Kibworth Harcourt, DI Cartwright, DS Armstrong and DCI Simons were in an unmarked police Ford Granada driven by DC Davies, on their way to Limehouse from the Thames Valley Force's headquarters in Kidlington. Prior to setting off Armstrong had called the Metropolitan Police Force's station in West India Dock Road and the Thames River Police headquarters in Wapping High Street. The officer in charge of both forces had been fully apprised with a resume of the recent history of the assassination of Ahmed abu Mousa and massacre of a police constable and two prison officers. Forewarning his 'Old Bill' colleagues Armstrong had stressed the importance of an armed unit being in attendance given the expectation that cells from both the IRA and Black September would likely be attempting to reclaim the stolen cache of weapons which was believed to be on the narrowboat. He had indeed laboured the point that this was likely to be a Counter Terrorism incident and the Head of CTU would be there. He went on to inform them of the outstanding murder charges the Leicestershire Constabulary were intending to bring against McClean. Simons took some comfort from the knowledge that both of these police stations were within a stone's throw of Limehouse Basin and they had given an assurance that they were now on standby and ready for action if and when required. It was also gratifying to know that the police launch *Patrick Colquhoun* would be cruising up and down the river in the vicinity of the entrance to the Basin.

The Granada from Kidlington had made excellent time down the new M40 to the Beaconsfield Bypass which was as far as the motorway had been completed. It was then on the A40 through the centre of London to Whitechapel that they would have preferred a marked car with lights and siren. However they arrived mid-afternoon and parked in Northey Street. Little did they know that parked just opposite them, across the short channel from the lock and into the Basin was a Ford Capri stolen from a pub in Blackthorn. The detectives got out of the car. On this occasion none of them was wearing a suit; casual, practical clothing being the order of the day. They gathered around the boot of the car and each of them put on a bulletproof vest. Such protective clothing was not standard issue and only came out for special occasions. This was deemed such an occasion and for all that the vests were bulky and constricting to a certain degree, they all agreed that not to wear one would be a poor decision.

*

It wouldn't be long before the light started to fade. A Series III Land Rover and a Ford Cortina 2000E were following the same route as had been taken by a Ford Capri earlier in the day. Groups of men, in twos and threes from the Kilburn area were making their way by bus and London Underground towards London's East End. They all had a rendezvous in the Old Ship, a pub in Barnes Street in Limehouse.

*

Under way and making way up the River Thames on the rising flood tide was the *Samson*, a fifty-foot workboat. On the starboard bank were the chimneys of the West Thurrock Power Station. The skipper, Sam Reynolds and his son Joe, the deckhand, had no idea what the cargo was they were collecting. All they had been told was two baskets and a crate. They had already received a message via the Marine Band VHF Radio amending their original itinerary instructions. Given *Samson* still had some way to go, they were on the edge of the VHF's range and there had been interference on the frequency and the transmission from the harbourmaster's office at Limehouse had been broken. Still, Sam was pretty sure he now had to lock in at St Katherine's, not Limehouse. It wasn't a big deal, although the lock at Limehouse made for a much easier entrance, and once through you were in open water rather than the confines of the smaller basins at St Kat's.

*

By 0900 *Nancy Blakemore* was snug against the quay in the west basin of St Katherine's Dock which, apart from a couple of laid-up Thames barges, was empty. There would be plenty of room for *Samson* to lay alongside. Jock and Wally had had a fairly restful day since their arrival but were now becoming just slightly agitated, and wanted to get the job over and done with. Jock could then get on with the rest of his life and at the top of that agenda, he hoped, was his own personal prize and share of Nazi gold.

*

Officers from West India Dock Road were on high alert. They had been joined by colleagues from the Counter Terrorism Unit and they were all in the briefing room listening to Detective Inspector Cartwright.

'Our intelligence is based on that gathered by detectives from the Thames Valley force. Initially it came from information arising from a road traffic accident which took place in the early hours of December 9th on our patch. As a result of further investigation, a known multi-murder suspect, Duncan McClean was discovered to be involved. It was almost ten years ago when I was a DC with the Leicestershire Constabulary and within their jurisdiction that the murders were committed. Subsequently, approximately one month ago, a statement made by an individual, believed at that time to be an American and involved in the RTA revealed that McClean was a member of the IRA for which organisation he was running guns illegally imported from America. McClean's involvement with the IRA has been confirmed by Gerald Doyle, brother of Michael Doyle. Both the Doyle brothers are known to us. Gerald, is a member of the Kilburn Battalion of the IRA and was also involved in the December 9th RTA. He is still in hospital in Oxford and under guard although it's unlikely he'll ever walk again. Now, it turns out that the American is, or more accurately was in fact a Palestinian and a member of the extreme political terrorist organisation known as Black September. He'd persuaded McClean to sell the cache of weapons he was known to be carrying in a stolen van, to Black September. The IRA got wind of this and at the same time, they too discovered that the American wasn't an IRA sympathiser but a Palestinian. A group led by Michael Doyle came over from Belfast in an attempt to recover their weapons and execute the two traitors, McClean and abu Mousa, the Palestinian. We managed to snatch abu Mousa and he was arrested for terrorism offences which he admitted. When we were transferring him to high security at

Gartree, we were ambushed by the IRA, abu Mousa was shot and killed, as were two prison officers and one of our own. My driver is still in hospital. Somehow McClean got away with the weapons. We believe he's in a narrowboat and he's now here in Limehouse Basin waiting for his Black September contact to collect. We suspect that the IRA may be aware of this and they'll be turning up to conclude their unfinished business. Gentlemen, we may have a terrorist war on our hands but I am anxious that we should avoid any shooting if possible. My guess is that it'll be a waiting game. Stay alert! We certainly want McClean alive. Chief Superintendent Simons will brief you on deployment in a few moments. Are there any questions?'

'Will the river police be involved?'

'How will we recognise the suspects?'

'How many are we expecting?'

Several other questions were posed mainly focused on who would be collecting the weapons and how. DS Armstrong responded to the questions but generally his answers did little to alleviate the tension which had begun to mount. DCS Simons concluded the briefing by issuing instructions on how and where various units would be positioned.

Chapter Forty-Four

In the fading daylight the floodlights were on and reflected in the ranks of brand- new cars at the Ford Motor Works at Dagenham.

'Look at that lot Joe,' Sam was gesturing over towards the factory through the starboard side of the wheelhouse windows. 'Escorts, Capris, Cortinas, hundreds of 'em. Not surprising the roads are getting more and more congested is it?'

The *Samson* was making steady progress on the tide upriver. They were soon passed Dagenham and into Woolwich Reach. A few ships could be seen in the Royal Victoria Dock but nothing like the number there would have been back in the day.

'D'you want to give Limehouse a shout Dad, just to confirm we're now due into St Kat's?' Joe suggested.

'Good idea son. Have you checked the hydraulic oil in the Hiab?'

The *Samson* was fitted with a Swedish built Hiab 'knuckle' crane on the afterdeck. With a twelve ton lift capability it made loading and unloading as easy as child's play. Sam picked up the receiver from his 'Sailor' RT144 VHF.

'Limehouse, Limehouse, this is *Samson*, *Samson*, over…'

'*Samson*, this is Limehouse, over…'

'Limehouse, can you confirm your previous transmission please? Over…'

'*Samson* you are to proceed direct to St Katherine's. You are not required to dock at Limehouse, your itinerary is amended, over…'

'Limehouse, this is *Samson*. All understood thank you, over…'

'*Samson* I reckon somebody knew summat we didn't and it's p'raps as well, given the number o' Ole Bill crawling all over the place, Summat's about to kick off by the look of it. Best you keep clear of 'ere I'd say. Keep a lookout for *Patrick Colquhoun* underway close to the Basin. Limehouse out.'

As *Samson* steamed passed Greenwich and rounded the Isle of Dogs, Sam could just make out the navigation lights on *Patrick Colquhoun,* which seemed to be stemming the tide, standing a short way off the Limehouse Basin Lock.

'Sure looks like there's some kind of trouble.' Sam said, and he gave the police launch a wide berth.

Neither Phil Doherty and Sean O'Donnell saw *Samson* cruise by. They were both in the Old Ship being briefed by Michael Doyle along with the rest of the Republican contingent which, swollen by the Kilburn Battalion now stood at around fifty strong. The pub was packed. The landlord was happy.

Sam had retuned the 'Sailor' VHF to channel 80.

'St Kathrine's, St Katherine's this is *Samson*, over...'

'*Samson,* we're ready for you. When you're through the lock wait for the lifting bridge and proceed round to the west basin on your port side. You're to raft up alongside the *Nancy Blakemore* for trans-shipment of cargo, over...'

'All understood thank you. *Samson* out.'

Whilst *Samson* was manoeuvring alongside *Nancy Blakemore* and making fast, the battalion of the Irish Republican Army were also manoeuvring into position unaware that the combined forces of law and order already had.

Jock and Wally offered a warm greeting to Sam and Joe and when the hand-shaking was all done they got down to business.

'If we get loaded straight way now, we don't have to worry about it later. We want to be away at the top of the tide in the morning'

'Aye, suits us fine, eh Wally?' Jock and Wally folded back the tarpaulin to reveal the cargo; two enormous wicker baskets and a similarly sized reinforced packing case. Joe was on the hydraulic controls of *Samson*'s Hiab. The crane swung over the hold of the *Nancy Blakemore* and the straps attached to the shackle on the wire were gently lowered onto the first of the baskets. Wally wrapped the straps under the basket and back to the shackle. *Samson*'s engine gave a bit of a grunt as the hydraulic pump took the strain and lifted the basket clear and swung it over to lower it into *Samson*'s hold. The operation was repeated three times, although on the third lift, the suspended weight of the crate caused *Samson* to list quite alarmingly to starboard, but it was safely landed on the lower deck of the boat's hold. The crane was returned to its 'stowed' position, the hatch cover on *Samson*'s hold was secured and locked, with two heavy-duty padlocks. *Nancy Blakemore*'s hold was left uncovered at Wally's suggestion. Leaving the hold open revealing its emptiness would prevent prying eyes and deter would-be thieves. With the entire transfer completed inside forty minutes and the boats locked and secured, the four made off to the Dickens Inn. Once settled around a table with their drinks Sam handed Jock an envelope inside which was a banker's draft for $50,000.

By the time Jock and company were onto their fourth pint, the situation at Limehouse Basin was becoming tedious for those watching and waiting particularly so as it had started to rain, not heavily but that dense type of drizzle that soon has you wet through. Many of the Kilburn Battalion had got bored and gone back to the pub and it was only Michael Doyle and his diehards that remained, still sharply focused on the narrowboat. High tide had come and gone and Sean O'Connell advised that there would be no more movements through the lock until around 4 am on Friday morning. There had been no boats enter or leave the basin whilst they'd been watching. Surely this was the right boat?

'Why don't I go and have a look?' Ted Reilly asked. 'I'm sure getting fed up with this hanging about!'

'I think that goes for all of us. OK Ted, carefully as you go.' Dressed in black from head to foot and in his black balaclava Ted crept along the quay towards the boat.

'I think I saw movement sir,' one of the CTU officers whispered in Armstrong's ear.

'Yes, I think you're right. I saw it too. Pass the word.'

Anxious faces amongst the police peered into the darkness but visibility was now reduced by the drizzle. Ted was at the stern of the boat and he deftly climbed aboard. The doors into the boatman's cabin were unlocked. He gently pulled one slightly ajar. Apart from the dull glow from the potbellied stove he could see nothing in the gloom. He delicately pushed the door closed and carefully stepped back onto the quay. Making his way forward he untied one of the ropes fastening the tarpaulin cover over the boat's hold but again there was insufficient light to see very much.

'What's he doing?' Armstrong audibly wondered.

'Dunno guv – looks like there's no one on board and I'm guessing it's too dark for him to make out whether or not the guns are in the hold. Look he's creeping back down the quay.'

Ted made his way back to where Michael and the rest were concealed behind six-foot high stacks of bricks. Ted reported the negative findings from his reconnaissance.

'I couldn't bloody see. Does anyone have a feckin' flashlight?'

Ted crept back along the quay for a second time, this time with a torch. He went straight to the hold and switching the light on, he climbed inside. He found himself standing on a heap of aggregate. He moved further forward. Another heap of aggregate. 'The guns must be hidden underneath all this feckin' gravel,' he muttered to himself. He began to scrape top of the pile away but there was nothing to find except more aggregate; thirty tons of it to be exact, in four neat heaps just as the mechanical shovel had loaded it.

A solitary figure came ambling down the quay wearing a heavy-duty waterproof coat and also carrying a torch, Limehouse Basin's nightwatchman.

'Who the blazes is this?' Armstrong and his team of ten from the Counter Terrorism Unit were watching intently from their vantage point further along the quay.

'Is it your man McClean?' someone enquired.

'Hard to say – might be – just stay put for a minute, let's see what he does.'

Onboard the boat Ted had heard the footsteps and had made his way back to the opening in the tarpaulin. The watchman flashed his light at the untied corner of the cover and as he bent down to resecure the rope he received a mighty blow to the back of his skull from Ted's torch. The nightwatchman crumpled in a heap and Ted leapt from the boat on top of him and beat him about the head several more times. As he stood to get his breath back, he signalled to the stacks of bricks with his torch and several figures emerged and cautiously approached Ted and the comatose figure lying on the quay. They didn't appear to be carrying firearms.

'Go, go go!' Cartwright bellowed and the first two of the police units burst from their hiding places, charging the IRA cohorts who, taken by complete surprise, turned to face the rank and file of police with truncheons drawn bearing down on them. All hell broke loose and in the ensuing pandemonium the initial confusion and uproar became a frenzied affray of ferocious fist-fights and brawling. This was not just any ordinary public-bar fracas either. Three or four of the Irishmen had now armed themselves with pickaxe handles which they were wielding wildly. Quite a few connected with policemen who were instantly laid out cold. The IRA's aggression was fearsome. Hostilities had continued for several minutes and several shots were heard. One unfortunate police officer fell to the ground. Fearing an all-out gun battle, Cartwright sent a second wave of police reinforcements to join the skirmish and the IRA were now hopelessly outnumbered. With their superior numbers the police managed to forcibly drag one or two from the thick of the fray and restrain them in handcuffs. But still the Irish maintained a bloodthirsty offensive. Simons had seen enough and ordered his elite Counter Terrorist Unit to fire a warning volley out over the basin. At once the Irish realised the hopelessness of their situation and the contingent of Nationalist Republicans had little alternative than to capitulate. They were forced to kneel with their hands on their heads. Five officers from Simons' Unit covered the kneeling group with their Heckler & Koch MP5 submachine guns whilst other colleagues removed balaclavas and snapped on handcuffs. The Republicans were then 'patted down' and relieved of any weapons they were carrying. With one or two token gestures of resistance, they were all loaded into an unmarked 'paddy-wagon' which had been parked out of sight behind stacks of oil drums. One individual had been singled out. He was handed over to DI Cartwright who instantly recognised the face of Phil Doherty. The constable who was shot had a gunshot wound to his abdomen and he, together with the unconscious nightwatchman were rushed away by ambulance to the Royal London Hospital. A second ambulance took care of the walking wounded from amongst the ranks of the police. A third took away those members of the IRA requiring hospital treatment, under an armed guard provided by three CTU officers. An extremely anxious looking Doherty was handed over to two of DCS Simons' unit.

'Well that was all a monumental cock-up!' DCS Simons was not impressed.

'Oh, I don't know,' reasoned Cartwright. 'We've taken about a dozen IRA terrorists off the street, including those who murdered Ahmed abu Mousa, PC Colin Harvey and two prison officers and we've identified the leak at Kidlington and plugged it.' Cartwright gestured towards the forlorn figure of Phil Doherty, who had now been handcuffed to the stern rail of the narrowboat.

'Well, OK that's as maybe but our intelligence was sadly lacking. How come we didn't know there was a bloody nightwatchman? Why hadn't he been warned to keep clear? As for the rest of it, we've got the wrong bloody boat, we've failed recover the stolen weapons, Black September never turned up and I don't suppose you've got your man McClean have you? What's more we're all bloody cold and soaking wet through!'

Cartwright had to concede. Yes, perhaps it had been a cock-up but not of the monumental variety. With that, the remaining members of the various police forces were stood down and returned to West India Dock Road.

The rain was now persistent. The pools of blood left by the gash to the nightwatchman's head and the gunshot wound had been washed away. It was just after midnight. Strolling back down the quay from a night out at his brother's restaurant on Commercial Road, slightly inebriated, were Nick Kavvadias and his crew Dmitri Konstantinos. They climbed aboard the *Damselfly* and went below blissfully unaware of the attention their thirty tons of aggregate had attracted.

Upriver, in St Katherine's Dock, Jock and Wally, Sam and Joe had returned from the Dickens Inn at a respectable time given that *Samson* needed to make an early start the next day. Although Jock knew full well where *Samson* would be bound with her new cargo he hadn't mentioned it. He'd made his delivery and been paid his first instalment. There was nothing more to be said other than 'Sees ye there in a week or so then!' He and Wally would spend Thursday 'on the town' in London. Jock would cash his banker's draft, pay off Wally and get on his own way to conclude the current project and then on to unfinished business. Wally let Jock know that he would make an early start on Friday to give the *Nancy Blakemore* the benefit of the last three hours of the morning flood, lock into the canal and work her way back to Foxton. Jock didn't seem to be that bothered.

Chapter Forty-Five

At the same time as *Samson* let go her mooring lines, Kate was also up early and in the kitchen at the Burton Overy cottage. She'd just put the kettle on and would make Stuart a cup of tea before she walked Byron down into the village to collect a newspaper.

*

Jock and Wally had walked round from their berth to the lock to look on as *Samson* eased through and moved into the mainstream of the river and headed east towards the North Sea and dawn's twilight.

'Ah'm thinking we deserve a foo fried breakfast. Whit say ye Wal?'

*

Stuart had the pan on by the time Kate returned from the paper shop. As she opened the front door she was greeted by the enticing smells of frying bacon and sat at the living room table to browse through the paper whilst waiting for her breakfast. Having become frustrated at her inability to finish cryptic crosswords in the broadsheet newspapers, Kate had today opted for the *Daily Mirror* and a piece on page 4 attracted her attention.

Police High Hopes Pebble Dashed

A riot broke out during a joint operation last night in which police forces from Thames Valley and London's East End were thwarted in their attempt to arrest known IRA terrorist Duncan McClean wanted in connection with at least two murders in 1964. Police had also been hopeful of recovering a large cache of illegal weapons, ammunition and explosives thought to be destined for UK based terrorist cells. A carefully planned ambush was mounted at Limehouse Basin on the River Thames where it was expected that the arsenal would be delivered by McClean in a narrowboat. In the event the boat which had been under surveillance turned out to be carrying aggregate. However, twelve members of the IRA were arrested and are being held at West India Dock Road Police Station. It is believed that six of the arrested men were responsible for the recent killing of a police motorcyclist, two prison officers and the self-confessed Black September terrorist Ahmed abu Mousa. A police officer and a nightwatchman were admitted to the Royal London hospital with non-life-threatening injuries sustained in during the riot.

The article totally suppressed her appetite and being of a slightly nervous disposition since becoming involved with the 'Jock problem' she felt the urgent need to let Ben and Hazel know that the slippery Scotsman had evaded the police yet again. She was immediately on the phone.

*

Fred Webb was eating his breakfast in the Waterways Board office at Foxton. A regular *Mirror* reader, he too took great interest in the piece on page 4.

' Yo' crafty ol' bugger, Jock. I dunno 'ow yo' manage to get away wi' it,' he thought. 'I 'ope 'e's not coming back 'ere for 'is car. That'll undo 'im!'

*

DI Cartwright was back at his desk in Kidlington and he was hopeful that Jock would do exactly as popular conjecture was suggesting. Surely the Porsche would now lure Jock back to Foxton?

*

Before driving from Pin Mill to Burton Overy, Hazel telephoned Cartwright to quiz him on what had been reported in the paper. She was curious to know what had gone wrong when he had been so confident that the police would get their man this time.

'Strictly between you and I Hazel, we weren't properly prepared. Had we taken the time and trouble to watch Foxton more closely when we knew the stolen van was there, we might have seen the weapons loaded onto a boat, if in fact they were. If they had been loaded onto a boat, we'd have known the name of the boat and we could have had it tailed all the way to wherever it went. We wouldn't have then wasted a lot of time and resources watching thirty tons of innocent aggregate. My guess now is that the weapons are long gone. Where? I have no idea, but I guess they'll show up sooner or later. As for Jock – well I just don't know. I've never ever come across anyone with such a knack for completely disappearing. I'm sorry this is no comfort to you at all, but you are now a target in the sense that you have something he wants; something he believes you have that belongs to him. I'm therefore going to recommend that you and your family move into one of our safe houses.'

'Now hold it right there, Inspector. There's no way in the world that I nor Ben nor the rest of us are going to be intimidated by this pipsqueak of a Scotsman to the extent that we have to move. I know him, remember. If he turns up, or should I say when, I can deal with him. I'm not frightened of him.'

'Well if you're sure. At least can we have you all in one place and I'll make sure there's a discreet police presence keeping your house under surveillance twenty-four hours a day.'

'OK if you must. But we will be permitted to carry on with our lives as normal I hope?'

'Of course. One straw I am grasping at is that he'll be going back to collect his car from Foxton, you know the Porsche. If he does, we'll have him.'

'Well I hope you're right.'

That Friday evening at opening time just three of them were in the *Old Greyhound* at Great Glen. Ben needed to go home to Orford to pick up Tina and he needed a change of clothes and some other stuff before he could drive over to Leicestershire. He hoped to arrive at the pub before closing time. Hazel passed on the detail of her dialogue with the DI to Kate and Stuart. Kate took little comfort from it.

*

On Friday morning, and as Wally had intimated, *Nancy Blakemore* left St Katherine's Dock and was taking the last of the flood tide on the Thames up to Brentford where she would lock into the Grand Union and make passage back to Foxton. Wally was on his own and with £1000 in his pocket he was happy and perfectly content to enjoy his own company, but then he was richer than he'd ever been before.

*

It was something Wally had said, likening Jock to a cat with nine lives, that gave him cause to think. 'The polis have ne'er seen me. They dinnae ken whit ah look like,' he thought to himself. 'They may hev a description ay sorts, but ah kin come up wi' a disguise.' He decided to ring Fred.

'Is ma Porsche OK?

'No! The cops still 'ave a twenty-four hour guard on it. They'll nab yo' the minute you come back.'

'Och, bugger!' He was beginning to regret his decision to buy the Porsche. His thoughts went back to early December and inconspicuous motors.

'OK Fred, now here's whit ah'm gangin' tae dae.' After listening to Jock for a few minutes Fred was completely mystified. But then he was Fred, hardly a man of the world. Fred was a man of the canals.

'What's he mean, keys under the wheel arch for Wally?'

After a few minutes more on the phone Jock picked up his bag and walked towards Tower Hill Underground Station. He boarded a Circle Line train to Liverpool Street Station. Alighting at Liverpool Street he left the station and went in search of a complete outfit of new clothes. He bought a couple of spare casual shirts, a woollen hat, a red waterproof sailing-coat, deck shoes and boots suitable for the coast. He also bought toiletries, a towel and a holdall in which he could carry everything. Returning to the station he found the gent's toilet where he shaved and dispensed with the moustache which was a bit of a wrench as he'd had since he left school. Then, dressed in his new clothes he bought a single ticket to Woodbridge. With its ultimate destination in Norwich, the first of his two trains was hauled by a Class 47 diesel and was sufficiently comfortable to allow him to doze for ninety minutes before he had to change. It was the variation of the rhythmic clatter which woke him as the train ran over the steel bridge crossing the River Stour just after Manningtree station. The panorama from the carriage window was spectacular – a wide open vista over the river with a seemingly never-ending sky in a light blue-grey. It was just as well that he'd been woken since the next stop, Ipswich was where he had to change trains. The Class

47 shuddered to a stop at Platform 3. Jock crossed the line by the footbridge and waited the arrival of what the regular commuters called the *Rattler* at Platform 1. It was a further forty-five minutes before the Diesel Multiple Unit delivered him to Woodbridge. When he arrived he crossed the road to the Anchor where he hoped he could get fed, have a couple of drinks and acquire some local knowledge.

*

Ben had managed to get away from the Academy a little early under the pretext of having some urgent family business to attend to, which in truth, he did. Tina had had the day off, so Ben didn't have to worry about their usual travelling together arrangements. As he stood on Platform 9 at Liverpool Street he barely noticed the man in the red waterproof jacket and woollen hat, carrying a holdall walk passed him. He did notice him however at Ipswich on Platform 1 and again when he struggled to get the holdall from the overhead luggage rack at Woodbridge where he got off. Just another weekender Ben thought as he continued the one stop further to Melton where he too got off and collected his MGB for the drive to Orford.

When he arrived home the cottage was cosy and warm and the last thing he wanted to have to do was drive the 150 miles or so to Burton Overy. Tina had been expecting them to go to the Jolly Sailor for a meal and consequently she had nothing prepared.

'It'll be OK, I'm sure Diane will knock something up for us.'

With weekend bags packed, the cottage secured, Ben and Tina left Suffolk for Leicestershire.

Three hours later Ben, Tina and Hazel were in the Greyhound enjoying a late supper and a relaxing drink. Kate and Stuart had opted to stay in and watch a documentary about Britain's membership of the Common Market.

Chapter Forty-Six

Jock awoke in a pleasantly furnished bedroom in the Crown Hotel in Woodbridge; the hotel to which he'd been directed from the Anchor. He got up, took a bath, got dressed and barely recognised himself with a naked top lip when he looked in the mirror. He went to the dining room for breakfast. It was still early and there were not too many guests down as yet. Well it was the weekend after all. He picked up one of the complimentary newspapers and although he wasn't, he put on a show of being interested in reading the paper just in case anyone was taking an interest in him. Suddenly he straightened in his chair as he stared at the following column inches on page 5.

Reprisal Attack on Warehouseman

Billy Kelly, a warehouseman at the Williams' Shipping Company in Southampton for 10 years was found shot dead yesterday morning. The police suspect that the shooting was a reprisal carried out by the IRA after Kelly had assisted notorious fugitive Duncan McClean to steal armaments illegally imported from America for supply to the IRA by American sympathisers.

'So, notorious fugitive I am is it?' Jock chuckled to himself in his finest Sean Connery voice.

After breakfast and with his freshly acquired local knowledge he put on his new waterproof coat, the sort yachtsmen and pleasure boaters wear, and walked down to the quay to meet the man from the brokerage. The weather was clear and bright and reasonably mild for mid-January. There were a quite a few visitors on the quay, sightseers perhaps, or maybe bird-spotters. The man in the Anchor had told him all about the river's mud flats and how at low tide the various resident and migratory species of wading birds that fed there attracted visitors. According to his man the River Deben was something of a Mecca for bird-spotters. Jock didn't feel at all conspicuous. Clearly his coat was 'de rigueur' in this part of the world, even for dog-walkers. He spotted the boat immediately and waved to the man standing on the deck who he assumed to be the broker. The man waved back. They shook hands and Jock was given a guided tour of *Ironside*, formerly a Thames sailing barge, now converted to a houseboat. After an hour or so, they appeared up the companionway and onto the deck where they shook hands again, both men happily satisfied with the outcome of their meeting.

Ever since Jock had learned of Helen's release from East Sutton Park it had been his intention to get reacquainted with her and not only in order to retrieve that to which he genuinely believed was his entitlement; his share of the gold and other treasures. He and Ken his erstwhile partner, Helen's late husband, had risked life and limb to liberate this bounty from the Kaiseroda salt mine towards the end of WWII. It all made sense to Jock when he established that Helen had a cottage near Great Glen. The pub in Great Glen was the address to where the gold had been delivered all those years ago. This had been confirmed by the landlord. It had then transpired that she also had a place near Ipswich. This was also most fortuitous from Jock's perspective. In the determination of the great weapons rip-off from the IRA the plans and meticulous preparation with the Palestinian known initially to Jock as Tom Wenzl had ultimately chosen the Suffolk coast as the location for the final delivery of the arms shipment. Since collection from Southampton the roundabout trip, by road, canal, river and sea had been designed to throw the IRA off the scent. And, by a whisker, it had been successful. Now, with the play's last scenes being enacted it was obvious, to Jock at least, that he should also have a base in East Anglia. He'd done his homework as part of the strategic planning. The deal with the terrorist organisation buying the weapons had ultimately been agreed and the final point of delivery was to be on the River Deben. The houseboat in Woodbridge could not have been better from every aspect, but particularly so from the point of view of anonymity and convenience. It was a nice place too. If pressed, Jock might have shown a little compassion for some of the casualties on the way but he had absolutely not one iota of sympathy for Black September or the IRA. As far as Jock was concerned the whole exercise was a business arrangement, pure and simple. He was only in it for the money.

*

The phone on DS Armstrong's desk rang.

'Sorry to bother you sir, we met the other day when you visited Gerry Doyle in the hospital – I was on duty outside his room.'

'Ah yes, I remember. How are you – bearing up under the strain of such an arduous task?'

'Well yes sir, but I thought I'd just check something with you.'

'Sure, go on.'

'We had a Roman Catholic priest turn up this morning, Father O'Connor he said he was. Wanted to visit Doyle. I wasn't sure whether to let him in or not so I told him I'd have to get clearance from you before I could.'

'Could what?' Cartwright wasn't really concentrating.

'Let him in to see Doyle, sir.'

'Ah, right yes. With you now. Well done lad. Where is he now?'

'He's gone for a cuppa. He'll be back in 20 minutes.'

'What do you think constable… constable…?' Armstrong needed his name.

'Hazelwood, Alex Hazelwood sir. I think he's genuine. He certainly looks like a priest with the little white dog-collar, you know, not like the all-the-way-round-the-neck job the vicar at my church wears. It was just his accent made me unsure, Northern Irish.'

'You did the right thing to call me. Well done Alex. I'm sure it'll be OK. Most of the local IRA sympathisers are in custody since Thursday. Just keep an eye on him. Can you leave the door ajar and eavesdrop on the conversation – just in case?'

'I'll try sir.'

'Good lad. Keep me informed.'

'Sir!'

Since the ambush, Brian O'Connor had been back to London and met up with some pals in the Alliance in Mill Lane. He'd been given chapter and verse on the abortive stake out at Limehouse Basin. Even though he was no longer a regular member of the IRA and tried to distance himself from the majority of their activities he still had certain sympathies with their cause; enough to get involved every now and again. He hadn't been to Belfast in years and was somewhat out of touch with the current situation. But, the Republicans were still very much at war with the Unionists and the British and he was a Republican. Brian did occasionally meet up with one or two old mates connected to the Kilburn Battalion for a game of pool and a couple of jars. Gerry Doyle had been one of them. A good friend of long standing. They'd been at the Christian Brothers' School together in Belfast. They'd enlisted in the IRA together. They'd both moved to London together. They went back a long way. It was as a result of Michael Doyle having called in a favour a couple of weeks ago, and then the news of a dozen or so men being arrested that had prompted Brian to go and see Gerry in hospital.

PC Hazelwood put his *NME* on the chair as he stood up at the approaching figure of Father O'Connor as he returned from the cafeteria

'It's OK Father, you may go in.'

'Bless you son.'

Gerry was still in poor shape although his general condition had improved. Brian was quite shocked to see his old friend in bed with his leg in traction, suspended on some kind of rope and pulley arrangement.

'Ah well now, I'm pleased and relieved to see you Gerry.'

'Good to see you too Father – although I'm hoping you're not here for the last rites.' The opening dialogue was for the benefit of the policeman who was almost certainly listening at the door which he had wedged open a couple of inches. But try as he might, Hazelwood couldn't hear a single word of what followed the initial greetings. In whispered tones Gerry and Brian swapped whatever information they each had on recent events. Gerry was clearly upset as a result of his brother being arrested although he was pragmatic enough to understand that there was little could be done until the outcome of the trial when he would be tried for murder and conspiracy at least, and that wouldn't be for months. For his part, Brian confessed that he was heartily sick of the whole business. He spoke quite frankly to his friend.

'Gerry, you know I am a Republican. I always will be. But, the killing, the maiming, where is it getting us? Yes, I remember the early days when there did seem to be a point to it all; when it seemed that our generation could do something about it, where previous generations had failed. Yes, the bloody British had and still have a great deal to answer for. Yes, the Protestants and the Catholics have been at each throats even since before the Great Famine. But the Protestants are the aristocracy. Even though we Catholics make up 75% of the population, only 5% of Irish land is in Catholic ownership. I remember my grandfather telling me how Lloyd George had made half-hearted attempts to promote a peace initiative but how they were doomed to failure because he repeatedly refused to negotiate with the IRA. Was it not Lloyd George who had called Michael Collins "a murderous gangster"? What's changed Gerry? Even our own Prime Minister, Brian feckin' Faulkner – internment? – for feck's sake! We're in a war for sure but we will never win and I for one want no further part of it.'

It was an impassioned speech and as it was highly unlikely that Gerry would ever again take an active role in the IRA's resistance to the Unionists' position, he too admitted that, as much as it galled him to do so, it was perhaps time to concede. Had Guinness been available the two former comrades in arms would no doubt have been weeping into it.

'I've just one last mission,' stated Brian, 'and if it's the last thing I do, well, so be it.'

'I think I can guess, and I thank you for it.' Gerry's gratitude almost did reduce Brian to tears.

The two old soldiers hugged each other as far as was possible, with Gerry confined to bed. They shook hands and Father O'Connor left to plan his last mission, blessing PC Hazelwood on his way out.

Chapter Forty-Seven

Samson had made steady progress down the Thames and by lunchtime was off the Maplin Sands heading north-east into the West Swin channel. Sam Reynolds had lost count of the number of times he had made this passage to the extent that he barely needed to check the Admiralty chart. The only slight challenge now was with the tide. It was almost low-water meaning that he would be heading into the new flood-tide thus reducing the boat's speed to about four knots. On the plus side there should be sufficient depth of water to cross the shallows between the Maplin Bank and north-east Maplin buoys into the East Swin. By mid-afternoon *Samson* was edging across the Swin Spitway at the southern end of the Gunfleet Sand. The sea was flat, just a gentle swell. Any more than that and there would have been a real possibility of grounding in the Spitway. But Sam was experienced enough to know what he was doing. Turning to starboard at the Wallet Spitway buoy Sam looked at his watch. Although it would be dark by the time they reached there, he decided to call into Harwich, just a short distance up the River Orwell and then into the Stour. The light was already fading as Sam and his son passed the east coast resorts of Clacton and Frinton, and as the Naze Tower hove into view at Walton the crew were both looking forward to a ten hour's stopover at the Halfpenny Pier. From there next morning they would be in a prime position to get into the River Deben an hour or so before the top of the next flood tide. Sam knew the Deben well. He'd been to school in Felixstowe, messing about in boats on the coast between the Orwell and Deben rivers. Whilst it was a very pretty river, the Deben entrance had a certain notoriety. Quite frequently vessels foundered on the massive shingle banks which protected the estuary. An easterly gale during the winter could move thousands of tons of shingle, blocking a familiar channel into the river whilst opening up another. It was essential therefore for a boat the size of *Samson* to only attempt an entry into the river when the tide was high. This was one of the reasons that the Deben had been chosen as the destination for this illegal cargo. Once the tide began to ebb, it would not be possible for other vessels to cross the bar and follow them.

Sam brought *Samson* alongside the Halfpenny Pier at Harwich and the harbourmaster, Chris Jones was waiting to take his lines. With the boat secure, Sam, his son Joe and Chris made their way on to the quay and straight across the road and into the Alma; a watering hole patronised by many seafaring folk. *Samson* hadn't berthed at the Halfpenny Pier for several months and there was an amount of catching up to do with friends, acquaintances and various other old seadogs. 'Where're you bound? What're you carrying?' Many questions but few answers.

It was another early start for *Samson* but then crack-of-dawn, or even earlier starts were an occupational hazard for mariners who depended on 'catching the tide'. Joe cooked breakfast as they made the final leg of the passage from London to Methersgate Quay on the River Deben approximately one mile upriver from Waldringfield. Surrounded by agricultural land, it was from that same quay, that in years gone by Thames barges would carry hay, corn and animal fodder to London. They would then return with cargos of horse manure to be spread on the farmland. Apart from a few yachts the river was deserted and Sam laid the boat alongside the quay where Joe hopped ashore and made the lines fast through metal rings set in the stonework. Sam looked at the ship's clock. The arrangement was that they would be met by some form of road transport on to which the arms shipment would be loaded for an onward journey to a final destination which hadn't been disclosed – not to Sam anyway. If the transport was late there was every chance that *Samson* would be left high and dry by the receding water as the ebb tide set in. The prospect of this situation was not one which Sam relished in the slightest. Ten hours or so stuck on the Deben mud he could well do without. As he sat in the wheelhouse with a mug of tea pondering various contingencies, a brand-new Yamaha SS50 motorcycle pulled up on the quay. This was followed by a fairly well-used Leyland FG motorised horsebox. Dismounting from the motorcycle Jock, who for just the second time in his life had acquired a vehicle legally, removed his gauntlets and shook hands with the horsebox's driver, Yousef El Khatib. Joe was already at work in the *Samson*'s hold. The baskets and the crate were strapped up and ready to go. The Hiab took the strain and without too much bother, the cargo was transferred to the horsebox. Jock liked the idea of a horsebox. A stroke of genius. Who would suspect a horsebox, driving through rural Suffolk to who knows where, containing nothing other than a horse or two? Brilliant subterfuge. El Khatib gave the contents of the containers a cursory examination then, satisfied with what he had seen he handed an envelope to each of Jock and Sam. Throughout the entire half-an-hour the transfer had taken, Yousef El Khatib didn't utter a single word. He locked his horsebox, lit a cigarette, climbed into the cab, started the engine and disappeared back the way he came without so much as a gesture.

'I bet he smokes Camels!' Sam and Joe laughed at Jock's guess.

With the weight in the boat significantly reduced, *Samson* was riding almost two feet higher in the water and pulled away from the quay without too much difficulty although the mud had clearly been disturbed, judging by the clouds of it swirling in the boat's propeller wash. Jock waved the boat off as Sam set his course back downriver on the ebbtide. He knew only too well that by the time he got to the estuary there would be an insufficient depth of water to see him safely over the shingle bar but he was cheerfully resigned to mooring at Felixstowe Ferry where, with any luck, the ferryman would run them ashore for a meal and a few drinks in the Ferry Boat Inn. Jock was also feeling the need for refreshment and retraced his route back through Sutton and Melton to Woodbridge and the *Ironside*, his new home. He parked the Yamaha, wishing it was an Ariel 350 and walked over the road to the Anchor. Sitting with a pint of bitter he wondered how long it would be before Helen received the envelope from Belfast. His quiet pint didn't last long before his ears were again being assaulted by local knowledge and the breeding habits of pied avocets and oystercatchers.

Chapter Forty-Eight

In the Midlands, at their address in Burbage, Mabel and Albert, Ben's grandparents were surprised one morning to receive a letter from Belfast.

'Now who can that be from? We don't know anyone in Belfast, do we dear?'

'If you open it, maybe we'll find out.' Albert always had a sarcastic yet sensible suggestion to make. Mabel slit open the envelope, withdrew two sheets of paper and looked straight to the signature at the bottom of the first page

before reading the handwritten text.

'It's from someone called Thomas O'Rourke,' she said.

'Never heard of him!' responded Albert. 'What's he say, what's he want?'

Mabel read the letter to herself before answering.

'Well, it seems this here Thomas O'Rourke is the son of a Maggie O'Rourke who died in a road accident near Oxford at the beginning of December. His mum was a widow and he's been clearing her stuff from the house in Belfast and he came across a letter which his mum had written to him. He's enclosed it. I'll read it out 'cos you haven't got your glasses on. *Dear son, I'm not sure what'll become of me. I'm having an illegitimate child and I'm traveling with the child's father who has been my lodger for several years. Duncan McClean is his name. When we left Belfast, Jock (that's what we call him) said that if anything ever happened to us or to him some of his papers should be sent to Helen Blake. I don't know where she might be, but her late husband's parents are...* and she's used us and our address. Shall I carry on?' Mabel enquired.

'Of course, get on with it, intriguing, isn't it?'

I'm not sure what these papers are but I know they're important. Can you please make sure that Helen Blake gets them. (it's the big envelope in the bedside table)… and she's just signed it, *Your loving mother.'* Mabel went back to Thomas's letter and studied it for a moment.

'He says, Thomas O'Rourke that is, that he wanted to make sure he had our address right rather than just send these important papers whatever they might be. So, he's asking for us to telephone him, and he's put the number here, which is the number for the pub he's now running with his girlfriend, Ciara Doyle. Well fancy that?'

'I'm not sure about this. We know that Jock's a bad 'un. What's he want now with our Helen, sorry Hazel? He's got a lot to answer for, and I think the police are still after him.' Albert was anxiously tamping his pipe. 'I'd say let's not get involved.'

'Well, surely it can't hurt can it, a few papers, important or not. I'm going to ring him.' And she did straight away before Albert could dissuade her from doing so.

It was Ciara who answered the call. She'd heard that Maggie O'Rourke was dead. She was hoping that Jock McClean was as well. Mabel was bombarded with all manner of matters that she didn't understand; who was Gerry, her uncle, and why was he in hospital? Why had her dad Michael been arrested and where are their guns? Anyway, Mabel managed to confirm her address and asked Ciara to pass on the message to Thomas. Ciara wasn't that keen on cooperating.

'Well I guess I might although why I should do anything to help that bastard Scotsman, God only knows!' Ciara had put the receiver down, none too gently either. Mabel had recoiled at the venom in Ciara's closing line. There was more to all of this that perhaps she'd imagined. Perhaps Albert had been right. A few days later a large envelope arrived from Belfast, addressed to Helen Blake, care of Mr and Mrs A Blake. Mabel rang Ben and gave him chapter and verse of this latest development. Ben suggested that opening the envelope was something that only his mother should do, but perhaps with other people on hand should whatever the contents were give rise to her needing comforting, advice or just a friendly face.

'Why don't you deliver it here, in person at the weekend? We'll all be here, including Kate and Stuart. If Frank's still about I know for certain that Mum would be delighted to see him. He could drive you over.' And so it was arranged.

*

The daily papers that Friday were full of speculation and sensationalism.

Black September Suspect Detained at Dover

Acting on an anonymous telephone call Yousef El Khatib, a Palestinian national, travelling on a Lebanese passport was arrested at Dover last night in connection with several atrocities including the massacre of Israeli athletes at the Munich Olympic Games last year. He was detained by immigration officers when they became suspicious as he attempted to board a cross-channel ferry to Calais. Customs officers subsequently discovered that the van he was driving, a Leyland horsebox, was crammed with a comprehensive armoury of weapons, ammunition and explosives understood to have been stolen…

The piece continued putting the details of the recent arrests of IRA terrorists and the shooting of Ahmed abu Mousa into context. The piece ended as follows:

Police believe the tip-off may have come from
a member of the IRA.

Jock reread the report and reacted to the last line with scornful derision.

'Och aye, the polis dinnae know Jack Shite!'

*

Mabel was just finishing off the washing-up when Frank arrived to collect her and Albert for the ride to Burton Overy. Mabel chattered nonstop during the journey regaling Frank with her memories of Helen as a Land Army girl on his farm during the war, and how after her father died, Frank had almost been a surrogate, looking out for her and treating her in every way like his own daughter. Frank barely got a word in, but nodded and grunted in all the right places. Albert slept the whole way. When they arrived at Marsh Cottage, Kate made coffee and everyone with the exception of Hazel was in the sitting room. Mabel provided the background; the reason for their visit whilst Hazel was upstairs in her bedroom with the large envelope bearing the Belfast postmark.

The envelope lay on the bed. Hazel stared at it but couldn't even begin to imagine what the contents might be. With a nail-file from her dressing table, she carefully and hesitatingly opened the envelope and withdrew the entire contents and lay them on the bed. Picking up the first page she recognised the handwriting even after all these years. It was a letter.

Christmas Day 1965

My Dear Helen

Please forgive me and please read this confession.

Forgive me for the way I have treated you, for the way I have involved you in all manner of illegal activities. Forgive me for being the cause of you being sent to prison.

Forgive me for the sins that I have committed. Forgive me for the sins I have not yet committed but that I know I will.

I love you. I have always loved you since that day you asked me to meet you to sort out the black-market stock Ken and I had stored in your house. You didn't know it, but upstairs in that house were two dead bodies; two men I had to shoot when they became too curious. Can you ever forgive me for that? I really thought that when you abandoned your baby son after Ken had left you, we would be able to get together. Well we did in one sense but not in the way I was hoping. Still we had fun while it lasted. I had to shoot my mate Ron, he knew too much. Can you forgive me for that? I never meant to kill Ken you know. It was an accident and it wasn't until afterwards that I realised how much you still loved him. Will you ever forgive me for that?

It's not too late for us. It'll only be a few years or so now but when the business I'm in at the moment is over I should be a rich man and I'll be a changed man. I will be a reformed character I promise. I will go to church and confess all my sins before God. It shouldn't be too long now.

I know I am wanted by the police in England and in Northern Ireland but I think I can continue to escape their grasp. With you by my side I know I can. I will do everything you ask if you'll be mine. Don't try and find me, I'll find you wherever you are. I'll be in touch as soon as I can.

Please forgive me and marry me when the time comes.

All my love
Jock

As she read the letter Hazel's immediate reaction was impassive, but the pathos, the sob-stuff aroused an emotional torment and the tears cascaded from her eyes. Helen knew that the woman she had become was the person that her memories had made her. She had been fond of him it was true, but how could she possibly entertain what he was now proposing, let alone forgive him for anything? She sat on the bed weeping and regretting so many of the decisions she had made in her life. At the same time, she was painfully aware of the consequences of those decisions. Now this wretched Scotsman was attempting to tug at her heartstrings... how dare he! Hazel was going through an emotional wringer. In the past she had been sensitive yet impulsive, impressible and irrepressible. Now? Now she just felt wretched. This letter had reduced her to a state of desolation and despondency. Ben called up the stairs.

'Everything OK mum?'

'Yes,' she lied as a second wave of tears threatened to overflow her deepest slough of despair.

After a while, Hazel picked up the next document. It was the last will and testament of Duncan McClean properly prepared by a firm of solicitors in Belfast and witnessed by a Michael Doyle and a Ciara Doyle. Her flow of tears had reduced but they were falling on to the document as she skimmed through it. He was leaving absolutely everything to her, well, to Helen Blake. She didn't want any of it and for a second she was on the verge of ripping it into pieces. But her instinct prevented her from doing so. This was evidence. Together with the letter, here was enough to commit him to prison for life. A signed confession. Eight years earlier before its abolition it would have been the death sentence. With her composure regained she picked up the last sheet of paper. Perhaps it should have been attached to the letter; it was a PS.

By the time you read this I will have finished with it all and I hope we can be close. You and I have something special to share and I want my part of it. J.

Downstairs everyone was sitting silently waiting for Hazel to come down and communicate as much or as little of whatever was in the envelope from Belfast. For all that he looked relaxed as he sat smoking his pipe, the butterflies in the pit of Albert's stomach would not settle. He knew something was wrong. Similarly did Frank who, on the opposite side of the room was puffing away making his contribution to the smog which was gradually drifting throughout the whole ground floor of the cottage.

Upstairs Hazel had replaced the letter and the will into the envelope. The necessity to do what was right, what was honest and decent, was now drilling into her conscience dispelling any further introspection. She went to the bathroom and tidied herself before going down to the living room, to those who were her nearest and dearest. She stood on the bottom step of the staircase, put on a brave face and, almost by way of making an announcement gave a resume of what was in the envelope, her initial reaction to it and the mental process she had gone through to arrive at her decision.

'Jock McClean is not "Jack the Lad" nor "Jock the Lad"; the loveable rogue he would like to think he is. He is an immoral reprobate, a common criminal and a confessed mass murderer, a terrorist. He is an unspeakable monster of depravity; a villain who doesn't know right from wrong. He is nothing more or less than a conman, a liar and a thief, without one single saving grace.' The vociferous exclamation was highly charged and electrified the atmosphere as Hazel delivered her character reference.

'Well, he seems to think highly of you!' The flippant remark from Stuart immediately dispelled the gravity of Hazel's description and instantly the mood was lightened. Even Hazel managed a smile and Tina crossed to the bottom of the stairs and put her arm around Hazel's shoulders. She continued.

'If we didn't have sufficient already, we most certainly have enough evidence now, a signed confession even, to present to the police. I intend to make an appointment to see Detective Inspector Cartwright as soon as possible.' There was a round of applause. It was Albert who spoke next.

'Problem is he is such an elusive bugger. How many times have the police failed to capture him? Even with enough evidence to hang him five times over, none of it's any use if he's on the loose. What you have there in that envelope is a weapon and a shield. If he turns up you threaten to send the envelope to the police – you hide behind the threat. If he then buggers off you give the envelope to the police anyway – a weapon. Whatever happens, you've got to be vigilant. We've all got to be careful. None of us is safe until this bastard is behind bars. Sorry for the language Mabel.'

'Well said Grandad!'

'And now I think we all need a drink.' It wasn't so much as a suggestion or an assumption as an order and Hazel started passing coats back from the pegs in the small hallway. Hazel, Albert and Mabel rode with Frank in the Jaguar. The rest piled into Stuart's Maxi. The destination? The Old Greyhound!

*

Wally Whitehead had also received a letter at his cottage in Foxton. Wally never received letters, only bills. Maybe this was a bill? He opened the official looking brown manilla, studied the content and had to sit down. It was a registration document for a Porsche 111. It seemed the owner was one Walter Whitehead of Union Cottages, North Lane, Foxton. Himself! Jock had transferred ownership of his car to Wally.

'Daft sod,' thought Wally. 'Din't 'e know I don't drive and ain't got no licence? Still, I could sell it I s'pose.'

Chapter Forty-Nine

On Sunday 21ˢᵗ January, Gerry Doyle asked the very pretty nurse Bridget for the telephone trolley. Dutifully she went to fetch it and wheeled it through to his private room, pausing just briefly for a bit of flirting with PC Hazelwood who had drawn the short straw and was on guard at the door again. Gerry rang his niece at the Blackstaff Bar in Belfast. It was just a courtesy call really, to see how she was holding up with her father in prison. The conversation naturally turned to Maggie O'Rourke's letter to Helen Blake, at an address in Burbage. He made a note of the address, the same one that Ciara had scribbled down on the pad behind the bar when Mabel had rung to confirm it. After the call, Gerry set to putting two and two together. He was well aware of the relationship Jock McClean had previously had years ago with Helen, when he had been the IRA's contact at Limehouse Basin. He also knew Jock still carried a torch for her. Perhaps she was the link. If Jock was writing to Helen then perhaps someone could get to McClean through her? He made another call. This time to the Alliance in Kilburn.

*

Fred was up early. Fred was always up early. He put the kettle on and went and stood on the quay outside the office while he waited for the kettle to boil. He noticed that the *Nancy Blakemore* was back on her berth which prompted him to call in on Wally after breakfast. Later that morning he walked up the towpath on the Market Harborough Arm, and on to the lane to Wally's cottage. He was warmly invited in. Wally had a coal fire burning in the grate and the pair of them sat in front of it while Wally related the memorable moments of trip to London with Jock. Then in quite matter-of-fact manner, Wally took the manilla envelope from behind the clock on the mantle-piece.

'What do yo' mek o' this?'

Fred removed the document from the envelope and perched his spectacles on his nose.

'Blimey!' then after a minute, 'Ah, 't all meks sense now. 'S'wot I cum up to tell yo'. Keys are under t' wheel arch.'

*

Later that week Mabel was at home finishing tidying up. Albert was down the garden cleaning out the chicken shed. There was a knock at the door.

'Now who can that be?' she asked herself. She opened the door and there stood a man in a suit and tie, a very respectable man by the look of him.

'I hope he's not one of those Jehovah's blokes,' she thought out loud.

'Sorry to bother you Mrs Blake – it is Mrs Blake isn't it? I was hoping for a word with the young Mrs Blake, your daughter-in-law, I believe.'

'Oh sorry, she doesn't live here. She lives in Suffolk near Ipswich. I've never been there but it's by a river, very pretty I understand.'

'Oh I see.'

'Can I give her message?' Mabel volunteered.

'Well no, I'm afraid, I have to see her personally, I have some good news for her.'

'Ooh!' Maybe it's the man from Littlewoods? she wondered.

'She did say something about spending time with her son in Burton – she also has a place there you know. Lucky isn't it, some people with their houses by a river and another one in the country.' Mabel would have been happy exchanging small-talk with this nice man, a very nice man, for as long as he was prepared to stand there and listen.

'Could you give me the address please, it's very important that I get to see her.'

'Well, no, I can't. Thing is, my memory isn't what it was – I can't remember it. But the pub in the next village, the Old Greyhound – they'll know there. The landlord, Jamie, nice lad, he was best man at my grandson's wedding, that's Hazel's son…' Mabel hadn't noticed that the very nice man had gone.

'Well that's a bit rude!' Maybe not such a nice man after all, she thought.

*

Jamie was about to call 'last orders' for the lunchtime session at the Greyhound. There had not been many customers for a Thursday but he'd been pleased that Ben had been one of them. At least he'd had someone to talk to. The man in the suit and tie walked in.

'Sorry sir, we're just about to close.'

'That's OK, I don't want drink. I was hoping you might be able to give me directions to Helen Blake's cottage. I understand it's here about somewhere.'

Ben stood and tried to look intimidating. What was that dialect, that accent?

'Who wants to know? I'm her son and I'll take her a message.' Ben thought maybe he should offer an excuse for the lack of cooperation. He couldn't be too careful. 'She's not been very well for a few days and not up to receiving visitors.'

'Oh I see. You're her son you say, then you'll be Ben?'

'Yes that's right.' Ben was curious, Jamie was eavesdropping.

'And you'll be Jamie, you were best man at Ben's wedding?' Curiouser and curiouser thought Ben.

'You seem to know a lot about us.'

'More than you might think. Look Ben, I don't know whether to believe that Helen's unwell or not, but I understand entirely why would want to protect your mother. Either way I have a proposition which might cheer her up. We have a plan that'll be to our mutual advantage.' Ben had placed the accent and realised that he should at least listen to what the man had to say.

'She's not Helen anymore. My mother changed her name to Hazel. Go on anyway,' encouraged Ben, 'are you sure you wouldn't like a drink?'

'Oh, OK then, thanks, a pint of Guinness please.'

'Are you from Northern Ireland?' Ben asked.

'A long time ago, Belfast actually. I've been in London for years now. Can't get used to English beer though.' The conversation continued.

The man in the suit introduced himself as Danny McFaddon. Somehow, he knew all about the letter to Helen from Jock. Jamie locked the pub doors and the three of them sat down to listen what McFaddon had to say. After almost an hour, and two more pints of Guinness, Ben was comfortable with what he'd heard. He discussed the proposal with Jamie while Danny had gone to the toilet. Jamie was also happy with what they'd heard, in fact Jamie thought it was a fantastic plan, 'Like something out of the movies.' All they needed to do was get Hazel to agree.

'Leave it with me.' Ben said. 'I'm fairly certain that I can talk my mother into this. Is there a number I can call you on?' He wrote it down and the man in the suit, a very nice man, Danny McFaddon left.

Ben thought it prudent to walk back to Marsh Cottage. It would give him time to think. When he arrived, he was greeted by his mother.

'You've been a long time?' she queried.

'Yes, I know,' he admitted and gave a full explanation of the reason for him staying at the pub until mid-afternoon. His mum gave him a look that said 'seriously?'

'Yes mum, and I truly believe he was absolutely genuine. This is the right way to go now. It's the only way to go.'

'Well, if you're so certain and Jamie agrees as well, I'll go along with it. Ben was quite taken aback by his mum's willingness to assent to what he had proposed as the means to resolving their 'problem' once and for all. He kissed her on the cheek and was about to leave the room when Hazel stopped him in his tracks.

'Now, be a good boy and play to me. I haven't heard you play for ages.'

Ben went and sat at the Steinway and flexed his fingers. He thought about it for a moment and then, from memory, he played 'La Cathedral Engloutie' by Debussy, the impressionist composer – the 'Submerged Cathedral'. It always put him in mind of the village of Dunwich; the village just a few miles up the coast from Orford, the village that yielded to coastal erosion in the thirteenth century, and where it is said that, when the conditions are right, the muted bell in the church tower may still be heard ringing in the swell of the North Sea. It seemed appropriate at this time.

By the time the resonance of the final chord had faded away, Helen was on the verge of tears again. And, she wasn't the only one. Kate and Tina also had a touch of melancholia, prompted no doubt by the music. But Stuart could always be relied upon to lighten the mood.

'Come on then, none of you are cooking tonight. Let's get down the pub!'

There were no dissenting arguments. As they walked into the pub, Jamie looked over towards Ben and with a gesture that asked 'Well?' Ben nodded and put a thumb up.

'Drinks on the house!' announced Jamie. 'Diane, the special menu please, if you please!'

The rest of evening was steeped in fine-dining, wine, beer and optimism.

The next morning, Ben called Danny McFaddon on the number he had provided.

'We're on!'

'Fantastic! Don't worry about a thing!'

During the next few days, Ben and Jamie spent several hours, mostly in the pub, detailing the preliminaries of Danny McFaddon's plan. They involved Hazel, who should revert to her previous Christian name, making contact with McClean to acknowledge receipt of his letter and proposal. She would need to inform him that she required a few days to think it over and would meet with him on 31st January to give him her answer.

'Do you think he'll see it as a trap?' Ben asked.

'Well, that's a risk we have to take,' suggested Jamie. 'Your mum will have to give him her word that there'll be no police.

'But don't you think we should let the police know what we're doing?' Jamie didn't answer.

'Where are they going to meet?'

'I know the perfect place. Havergate Island. It makes sense on every front. It's only a little way from my house. Jock knows where I live, remember, from the Christmas card? And he'll assume that mum is visiting me. He won't suspect a thing. There's a ferry service from Orford Quay over the river. There'll be a few hardy bird-spotters and once they've all dispersed to go twitching or whatever they call it, Mum and Jock will be on their own. Then it's down to Danny McFaddon to do his bit.'

'OK sounds good. Just one flaw in the plan we'll need to sort out.'

'I thought we'd covered everything.'

'How do we get in touch with Jock?'

'Ah – good point!'

The two conspirators thought about this minor hiccup for a moment. Eventually Ben came up with a possible solution.

'I reckon Fred might know, but whether he'll tell us is another matter.'

'We can but ask him,' Jamie said, and then added an afterthought, 'knowing how he fancies your mum I'm sure he'll tell us.'

It was almost like they were sixteen again. Lying on the railway embankment at Newton taking down train numbers while scheming this, that and the other. But then this was altogether much more serious and potentially dangerous. The gravity of what they were planning was immense. If it all went wrong the implications didn't bear thinking about.

'You can use the phone in our living room,' Jamie offered.

Ben dialled the number for the Waterways Board office at Foxton. Fred answered and after a few minutes in which Fred took to put a face to the name, he made the connection. Ben asked the question straight out.

'How can I get in touch with Jock? Mum, Helen, has received a letter from him and wants to reply.'

'I 'ope she knows as wot she's a-doin' of.'

'Oh yes, I'm pretty sure she does,' Ben reassured him.

'Well, Jock's only gone an' given 'is Porch to Wally. I seen the registration paper din't I? The address 'e put on there, were a pub in Woodenbridge in Suffolk I think it were.'

'You mean Woodbridge?'

'Aye, lad, that were it, Woodbridge, the Anchor, Quay Street.'

'Thanks Fred, you're a treasure.'

'I know. I should be buried! Now yo' tek great care whatever it is yo' and your mam are at. 'E's dangerous, 'e's a wrong-un. Oh arh, an' summat else, if yo' knows anybody wants a Porch, Wally's got one he wants to sell!' Fred laughed.

Ben was still concerned about whether or not the police should be informed. Jamie was firmly of the opinion that having located Jock and with a watertight plan all but finalised, a plan with a guaranteed conclusion, the police would only get in the way. They'd be involved after the event anyway.

'Based on our experience so far I would say that if finding people was so difficult, you wouldn't ask the police to do it! They've cocked up every chance they've had. We'll succeed this time and we can let the police know after it's all over.' Ben wasn't totally convinced but he was prepared to reluctantly share Jamie's confidence.

'Let's hope you're right!'

So with the minor hiccup solved, they set about listing the cogent points that the letter that Helen, not Hazel, Ben's mother should send to Jock ought to contain.

Havergate Island.
Wednesday 31ˢᵗ January
Two o'clock.
Blue anorak and woolly hat
Bring a bottle

'Bring a bottle? What's that for?' Ben asked.

'It's an extra incentive,' explained Jamie. 'If he's told to bring a bottle he'll assume there'll be something to celebrate.'

'Ah, good thinking, mate!'

That evening, Ben, Jamie and Hazel were alone in the cottage. Stuart had taken Byron to dog-training class and Kate was at choir practice. The chance encounter with Danny McFaddon was explained to Hazel, and between them, Ben and Jamie provided the outline of the McFaddon proposal. Then they added the finer detail of their own deliberations, the flesh on the bones of the plan and how it would be implemented. Ben was half-expecting to encounter some resistance from his mother. Now the idea which had been floated earlier was about to be put into action he fully expected some reservation or hesitation. However, resistance, reservation, hesitation, were there none! Paper, pen and envelope were placed on the table and Hazel began to write.

Dear Jock
I was surprised to hear from you after all this time.
I've read your letter but to be honest, I'm not sure. Your
will is certainly a very generous gesture and I would like to
take this as an indication of your good faith. Even so, we

*need to talk – in private, out in the open where we're both
unknown and unlikely to be recognised.*

Ben and Jamie were very impressed with the letter thus far
and began to prompt and make suggestions on how it should
continue. Hazel continued.

*Please meet me on Wednesday 31st January on
Havergate Island at 2 pm. Take the ferry from Orford
Quay and I'll be waiting for you on the jetty wearing
my blue anorak and a woolly hat. You might like bring
a bottle – you never know we might have something
to celebrate.*

*Yours sincerely
Helen*

The letter was folded and placed in the envelope which was
addressed to the pub in Woodbridge. Ben had a stamp and
before there could be any second thoughts he took the letter
to the pillar-box outside the village shop and posted it. While
he was out, he used the public to confirm all the arrangements
with McFaddon.

When he returned, there were three champagne flutes on the
table along with a bottle of cider.

'I thought we should propose a toast to a successful
conclusion,' Hazel said as the contents of the bottle were shared
between the three glasses. She apologised for the cider and
promised some real 'fizz' on Wednesday night.

'I think we should have a big party – OK at your cottage Ben?'

*

DI Cartwright was going over the reports he had now
received from the various section leaders involved in the

abortive stakeout and fracas at Limehouse Basin. It was some consolation that a group of terrorists had been taken off the streets but to Cartwright's way of thinking it didn't compensate for the fact that the weapons hadn't been seized and even more disappointing for him at least, McClean had evaded him yet again. Perhaps, he was thinking, I'll just leave the case in the 'pending' drawer and wait for a lead. He'll make a mistake sooner or later. He decided to give DC Almey at Hinckley Road another call to ascertain whether or not his lad on Porsche surveillance had anything to report.

''Fraid not sir. Nothing at all apart from a couple of old bargees were giving it an admiring looking over. It's still here. Shouldn't wonder the pub landlord will want it out of his carpark before much longer.'

*

'Letter here for you Jock.' It was the landlord of the Anchor. 'Came this morning.' Jock took the letter and a sip of the scotch which been placed before him on the bar-counter. Since buying the houseboat and moving in, Jock had soon become a familiar figure on the Quay at Woodbridge, and even more so across the road at the pub. He opened the envelope and moved to a table to read the letter. He could hardly believe it. Helen had responded! And she wanted to meet him and talk! This was more than Jock had ever hoped for.

When he woke on Wednesday, the last day of the month, it was still dark. He'd spent most of the night wide awake anyway, thinking about his impending liaison and it wasn't until four or five-o'-clock that he'd finally dropped off. He stuck his head out of the companionway. Everything seemed to be in monochrome; every shade of grey between black and white. It wasn't actually raining but it looked as though it might at any time with the low dark clouds scurrying across the sky on the brisk, cold north-easterly wind. The tide was out and *Ironside* was settled in the mud. He had plenty of time but he didn't want to be late. He dressed and went to the café on the quay for breakfast before showering and putting on a clean shirt. He walked into the town and bought a bottle of Moët & Chandon. It slid easily into the voluminous pocket of the waterproof jacket. After several hours of walking up and down the quay, polishing *Ironside*'s brass fittings the time came for him to go. He was excited yet apprehensive. Today was to be the first day of the rest of his life; a changed life. If she said yes, the new Duncan McClean would be a transformed character. He would change his name, his identity and along with his bride to be they would become pillars of the local community. He knew that wearing his yachting jacket he became just another bird-spotting yachtie, but as an additional disguise he felt a pair of binoculars would help him blend in with the bird-watchers. He pulled the companionway hatch closed and locked the doors. He mounted his new Yamaha, kicked it into life and rode off to Orford.

For Hazel, today was going to be not only the first day of the rest of her life but the day she would be rid of the ghost from her past for ever. She was brimming with optimism in the certain knowledge that the haunting she had endured for the last ten years would finally be over. She had stayed the night at Ben and Tina's cottage in Orford and it would only take five minutes to walk to the quay and get the ferry over to the island. Ben had emphasised the importance of sticking to the plan absolutely to the letter. So, she didn't want to be late or to encounter Jock on the same ferry crossing. She spent the morning in leisurely fashion, and it wasn't until midday that got dressed into her jeans, a sweater and her walking boots. She gave Ben and Tina a hug, slipped on her anorak and went to join the few people on the quay queuing for the ferry to Havergate Island. The weather was grey with barely a break in the low cloud. The wind had eased however and although it was a little on the chilly side it wasn't especially cold.

The ferry-boat, the appropriately named *January Storm* pulled alongside the pontoon and the few returning passengers disembarked. A similar number of people descended the steps from the quay to the pontoon and stepped on to the boat. Licensed to carry twelve passengers, according to the sign mounted on the side of the wheelhouse, Helen glanced round and counted six including herself. Somewhat incongruously one of their number was carrying a golf bag. The twenty-minute trip across the river was smooth enough and the mud on the river's banks was gradually being recovered by the rising tide. The ferry glided alongside the wooden jetty on the bank of the island and one by one the passengers stepped out of the boat.

'Mind how you go now, last return ferry at four o'clock. Don't be late!' Having issued his warning, the ferryman took the empty boat back towards the mainland. It was one-twenty.'

The bird-spotters slowly walked away, in this direction and that, some following the well-worn footpaths others choosing to do their own thing. Helen, constantly reminding herself that she had assumed her former name for the purposes of this encounter, stood by the jetty awaiting the arrival of the next crossing, which, she estimated, would take about forty minutes. She gazed at her surroundings, salt marsh, vegetated shingle and mudflats. She shuddered. In her mind's ear she could hear every note of Britten's 'Sea Interludes'. If ever there was a work so evocative of a place, so descriptive, this was that place and Britten's music was that work. This was an inhospitable place to all but the birds. Her fellow passengers had completely disappeared from view. In the distance looking towards the North Sea, she walked a short distance to the east and could make out the Orford Ness lighthouse and the so-called 'pagoda' buildings which had been constructed for the Atomic Weapons Research Establishment. There was something decidedly maleficent and macabre about this place. She looked back towards Orford and could see the ferry plying its passage back towards the island. She walked back to the jetty with palpitations now fluttering through her entire being. Within a few minutes the ferry was again alongside the jetty and the four passengers were disembarking. Where was Jock? She didn't recognise any one of the four as Jock. The ferryman made his announcement and when Helen made no move to get on board he assumed she was staying and headed off. Three of the latest group of visitors, obviously friends, wandered off to the east along the designated footpath. They were soon out of sight. Helen was now shivering as she remained standing by the jetty looking a little forlorn. But then she turned with a start when a man in a red yachting jacket with a pair of binoculars slung around his neck approached her.

'Hello Helen, it's been a lang time.' She couldn't immediately recognise the face, but the stature and the voice were unmistakable.

'Hello Jock.'

Together but apart they slowly walked away from the riverbank in the direction of one of the Pagodas, both with heads bowed. Neither of them spoke. Neither of them knew quite what to say.

Without warning flocks of birds, panicked, rose into the air with a cacophony of shrieks and squawks and cries of alarm. Terns, plovers, dunlin, pintail, wigeon. The sound of the shot followed a nanosecond later.

The man in the red jacket slumped to the ground the blood already seeping from the hole in his forehead.

Even Jock would have known that life was not forever but nothing could have prepared him for its finality, its irreversibility; the final full stop.

The man on the pagoda had packed his golf bag and was walking north and across the Ness to where a man in a dinghy waited to pick him up.

'OK Brian?'
'OK Danny.'

Fifty yards offshore the *Samson* was lying to the tide waiting to collect two men from a dinghy.

The End